Cat Striking Back

ALSO BY SHIRLEY ROUSSEAU MURPHY

Cat Playing Cupid

Cat Deck the Halls

Cat Pay the Devil

Cat Breaking Free

Cat Cross Their Graves

Cat Fear No Evil

Cat Seeing Double

Cat Laughing Last

Cat Spitting Mad

Cat to the Dogs

Cat in the Dark

Cat Raise the Dead

Cat Under Fire

Cat on the Edge

The Catsworld Portal

Cat Striking Back

A Joe Grey Mystery

Shirley Rousseau Murphy

HARPER LUXE

An Imprint of HarperCollins*Publishers*

FIRST HARPERLUXE EDITION

HarperLuxe™ is a trademark of HarperCollins Publishers

Library of Congress Cataloging-in-Publication Data is available upon request.

ISBN: 978-0-06-188506-8

09 10 11 12 13 ID/OPM 10 9 8 7 6 5 4 3 2 1

To the memory of Willow
She lives on in the wild clowder

It was this unfathomable longing of the soul to vex itself—to offer violence to its own nature—to do wrong for the wrong's sake only—that urged me to . . . consummate the injury I had inflicted upon the unoffending brute . . . my wonder and my terror were extreme . . . I could not rid myself of the phantasm of the cat . . . I am not more sure that my soul lives, than I am that perverseness is one of the primitive impulses of the human heart . . . which give direction to the character of man.

—EDGAR ALLAN POE, "The Black Cat"

1

The setting moon laid its path across the sea, brightening the white sand and the little village, picking out the angles of its crowded roofs and glancing off the windows of the shops and cottages; moon glow caressed the shaggy pines and cypress trees and pooled dark shadows beneath them along the narrow streets. The only sound, at this predawn hour, was the hush of waves breaking on the shore. But inland, all was silent. Where the hills rose round and empty, the moon's path washed in bright curves. Between the moonlit hills, the narrow valleys were cast in blackness so dense that the tomcat had to make his way by sound and by whisker feel, by familiar smells, by the degree of the slope and the feel of the earth beneath his paws, rocky or soft or bristling with dry grass or smooth where sand had blown across the narrow game trail, each encounter marking more clearly his exact location in relation to home. The tomcat traveled alone, encumbered by his heavy burden.

Padding down toward the first scattered houses, he walked clumsily, not his usual bold gait but spraddle legged and awkward, stepping wide around the half dozen mice that dangled against his chest, their tails gripped tight in his sharp teeth.

He was a big cat, muscled and sleek coated, as silver-gray as burnished pewter. A narrow white strip ran down his nose, and his belly and paws were white, too—one paw spattered, now, with mouse blood. His tail was docked to a short, jaunty length, the product of a kittenhood disaster. His yellow eyes gleamed with the look of a fighter, but his eyes were alight, too, with a smile; he turned once to look back up the hills behind him, watching his tabby lady Dulcie and their younger, tortoiseshell friend Kit move away, trotting higher up across the open land. He had only just parted from his two companions, the lady cats not satisfied only with hunting, but hurrying off to follow their overly curious noses—typical females, he thought tenderly.

Take care, Joe Grey thought, watching the two cats moving swiftly away up the moon-washed hills. They looked very small and alone, careening close to the scattered boulders where they could find hurried shelter. He could hear, as could they, the yipping of coyotes far away, up the higher slopes. Though this yipping of adults and the answering yaps of their cubs meant, surely, that the group of larger predators was all together, preoccupied with their offspring and not wandering far afield to sniff out unsuspecting felines.

But still Joe thought again, *Watch your backs, you two.* And nervously he turned away, dragging his clutch of mice, hurrying down past the wooden frame that was the beginning of a new house, then past a re-model where the front garden was piled with raw earth waiting for the construction crew. He could smell, over the musty miasma of dangling mice, the fresh scent of raccoons on the trail, and of possums and coastal deer, wild creatures who had made their way down from the hills in darkness to hunt or graze or to slip in among the houses to quench their thirst at a fishpond or a leaky garden hose. As he descended, the houses began to crowd closer together. Far below him the setting moon began to dip into the sea; soon the last thin slice of gold lay reflected and then perversely drowned itself, moving on to light other lands.

Lands he had never seen, and had never longed to see. Life, for Joe Grey, was right here and right now, he didn't long to travel. His perpetual balancing act between the normal life of an ordinary feline and his more stressful role within the human world itself was all the excitement one tomcat could handle.

Now, with the moon vanished, darkness gripped the yards and houses around him and all but hid the rooftops below, as if a black cloth had been dropped down over the sleeping village. Only a few scattered lights shone, disconnected and eerie, perhaps from the bedroom of an insomniac or the kitchen of an early riser. Farther down along the main street glowed the softly lit storefronts of the village's upscale shops and restaurants. Though Molena Point was a small and close-knit little community, it was also a tourist town whose business folk offered high-end couture and accessories, valuable antiques and fine jewelry. None of which interested Joe Grey, in itself. But all of which attracted the more sophisticated and enthusiastic thief, who in turn did interest the tomcat.

A tail jerked in his mouth as one of the mice began to struggle. He clenched his teeth harder, but he didn't want to further injure the little beasts. They were a gift, a gift of love and caring, and they should remain lively to be of ultimate use. One stunned mouse came wide awake, wriggling wildly as it tried to flip up, tried to see and understand where it was and how to escape, to understand why it hung upside down, and Joe felt a shock of pity for the small creature.

It had been difficult enough for him and Dulcie and Kit to trap the mice alive between their paws without hurting them, to patiently collect the half dozen mice unharmed, and the three cats had suffered considerably at the little beasts' extended terror. One of the disadvantages of possessing human intelligence was that they had to answer to a deeper empathy for other animals than would an ordinary feline. They cared about their prey, they cared that the creatures they caught were hurt and terrified. Ordinarily they killed their catch quickly, ended the victims' distress as fast as possible, sending the little animals on to their maker with a minimum of pain. But not this morning. This gift must arrive lively and full of fight.

Hurrying along a sidewalk where flowering bushes overhung the concrete, he crossed a narrow residential street, the macadam warm beneath his paws, a pleasant holdover from yesterday's bright sun and the mild night that had followed. Cutting through the overgrown yard of a house that, with the declining real estate market, had stood empty for far too long, he glanced up at its stark black windows. No curtain, not even a crooked shade broke the reflection of receding night. Joe wondered at such human foolishness, to let a valuable property stand empty month after month. Even a run-down, derelict house, in this village, could command an easy million.

Yet he knew that the sale of this neglected home was delayed not only by the economy but by a marital dispute, a battle over dividing up the spoils. No one but humans could so royally complicate life. A pair of cats would fight it out tooth and claw, winner take all, loser to slink away defeated, and that would be the end of it. But not humans. Human lives were far more complicated—nuanced, some folks called it. Joe Grey called it indecisive.

The neglected property with its overgrown garden did, however, provide fine hunting for the neighborhood cats. More than a dozen cats lived on the few blocks of this short street, and for that reason, Joe and Dulcie and Kit seldom hunted here, leaving the local game, the mice and moles and gophers, to the feline residents. Though they did have one human friend in this neighborhood, a bright, kind woman to whom they felt drawn, and who was always happy to see them. It was to her home that he was delivering the captive mice.

Pushing through a forest of stickery holly bushes into the overgrown side yard, trying to keep his dangling charges from catching on the protruding thorns, he was just approaching the empty swimming pool when a smell stopped him, a smell that made his fur bristle.

When the divorcing couple vacated the house, the pool had been drained. Why they hadn't covered it, why the city hadn't made them cover it, the tomcat didn't know. The concrete and tile chasm was cracked and stained. Silt and debris had collected in its bottom into a sour-smelling mire. But now, another kind of stink drew him up short, a scent far stronger than the rancid mud or the sweet, musty smell of the mice he carried.

The stink of death, of blood and human death.

As many murders as the tomcat had witnessed in his busy life, he knew that smell intimately, but he still found human death unsettling, not at all like the death of the simpler animals who were his normal prey.

Sniffing again, he told himself this might be animal blood, but he knew it wasn't. He stood looking around him, listening. He'd like to drop the mice so he could get a clearer scent message. But he'd hauled them this far, partly at Dulcie's insistence, had nearly put his neck out of joint, and he wasn't dropping them now— it would take the little beasts only a second to realize their opportunity, come fully alive, flick away from his reach, and run like hell, scattering in every direc-tion. In Joe's opinion, the intended recipients were far more needful of his gift than were the dull little rodents of their time on earth—let them scamper on into mouse heaven where they could live in mousy glee with no more cats to chomp on them. As he approached the abandoned pool, the grass growing up through the cracks in the coping tickled his paws. Standing at the edge, he looked over.

In the first weak light of dawn, the mud and slime on the bottom still held the blackness of night; the view was murky even to a cat's sharp vision. He could see that one area had been disturbed, the mud and moss so churned up that surely something much larger than himself had squirmed around, or had been moved around, and then had been dragged across the pool to its far side; the drag marks were accompanied by a line of shoe prints embossed sharply in the mud. A man's shoes, and the indentations had been there long enough to have filled with seeping, muddy water. The double trail led to the tile steps which, if the pool had been full, would be underwater. The tile was covered with slime that would be slippery, but the wide track led upward and over the coping to the tile apron. Moving around to stand above the steps, he studied the disturbed surfaces.

From this angle, he could see dark spatters of what looked like blood. Letting the mice rest for a moment on the tile while still firmly gripping their tails in his teeth, he took a good whiff.

Yes, blood. Human blood, nearly dry now despite the damp surround. He could tell, by other scents, that it was a woman who had died here.

The footprints and the slithery smear headed across the patio to the concrete drive and straight up toward the street. He followed, taking care to leave no paw prints on the pale cement. Halfway up, the trail stopped. From that point on, the drive was unmarked. Someone had dragged the body from the bottom of the pool to this juncture. And then, what? Studying the concrete, he found several small marks where the tire of a car had picked up mud and deposited it. Sniffing along the concrete, dragging his mice, he caught the faint scent of the man, too, though it was so mixed with the smell of human blood and of sour mud, that he wasn't sure he would be able to identify it if he should smell it again later. There were no other tire marks, no other footprints. The tomcat, standing alone on the empty drive dangling his mice, studied the surrounding yards and looked up and down the street.

It was such a peaceful Sunday morning, the sky just beginning to lighten above a tangle of pale clouds and above darker and more serious clouds that smelled of showers. The sea wind was clean and fresh, blowing from the south. There was no other sound, even the birds were quiet, no doves crooning, no scream of a nervy crow. There was no sound of a door closing somewhere, no distant car starting up.

But suddenly he did hear a car turning off from the next block. He bristled as it made its way down the street, moving slowly as if scanning the neighborhood—he relaxed as the driver began tossing out Sunday papers, *thunk, thunk,* one by one, into the neighbors' yards. The tomcat dodged away as a paper sailed to the gutter in front of him.

Other than the paper man, he could not see another human soul on the empty street; he stood looking around him, filled with a sudden chill. A woman had died here and been hauled off. And Joe Grey wondered, not for the first time, why he had been the one to happen on the scene. Was there something in his nature that drew him to such events? Some hidden sense that pointed his inner compass toward human violence and suffering, some weird feline perception, some impossible or poorly understood magnetism?

But the tomcat huffed at that idea. That was Dulcie's kind of thought, that was the fanciful conjecture of females. Joe was a down-to-earth tomcat. What happened, happened. There was nothing mysterious about it.

And yet even Joe's human housemate, who did not believe in things occult any more than Joe did, would accuse him of being drawn to murders, of being attracted to human death as surely as a nail is attracted to a magnet. He could just hear Clyde scolding, over the dinner table or at breakfast.

"Why is it, Joe, that you are always the one to find the body? Or to stumble on a burglary?" That wasn't true, and Clyde knew it. Sometimes the case was well under way before he got involved. But still Clyde would grouse at him: "Why is it you *have* to have your paws in police business? Why are you always there, right in the middle of a case?"

It did no good to point out that Dulcie and Kit were just as involved in the details of human crime, in what went on at Molena Point Police Department. In Clyde's view, the cats' preoccupation was all Joe's fault, and he could already hear Clyde's comments about this discovery. But whatever his housemate might imagine, the fact was that a woman was dead, apparently only Joe had happened on the evidence, and the tomcat was burning with questions.

Dangling his mice, he padded on up the drive to the street, studying the concrete, seeking further tire marks.

He found no more, only the few small hints down the drive behind him, hardly visible. And when it rained, he thought uneasily, those would be washed away. The smell of rain was strong, the clouds and wind shifting in an unsettling manner.

Pausing at the curb, he studied the parked cars. All were cars he recognized, all belonged in this neighborhood, all were fogged with the night's damp breath as if they had been sitting here for many hours.

Even so, he made the rounds along the one block, sniffing tires and walking close to engines to see if he felt any warmth. There were only five cars parked on the street, and four in driveways, all of them familiar, all tires and hoods cold, and not a whiff of lingering exhaust. As he returned to the empty house and made his way back to the swimming pool, the sun was rising, the tops of the hills to the east catching its glow, the dawn beginning to brighten around him.

Along the steps that descended into the empty pool, the blood was drying, as were the muddy shoe prints, as if several hours had passed. Whatever had occurred had taken place, he'd guess, maybe late yesterday afternoon. Any earlier and the hot sun would have dried all the marks to a powdery consistency that would easily flake. Very much later and the prints would still be wet. Studying the scene, he was startled when the rising light of morning dimmed suddenly, as if someone had appeared from nowhere, stepping up behind him.

But it was only cloud shadows, the mass of darker clouds moving in below the white ones, gray and dense and smelling more heavily of rain, serious clouds descending over the village—only some twelve hours later than the weatherman had predicted. That guru of scientific data had said it would rain last night.

With the primitive methods humans used, such predictions couldn't be easy. Joe and Dulcie and Kit had known it wouldn't rain until morning, they'd known they had the night to hunt. Though the month of June *was* temperamental, scorching one minute, dark with rain or fog the next.

But now, for sure, the rain was coming, and if it got here before the law did, the cops would find little left of blood, of drag marks or of footprints, the evidence would all be washed away. That mustn't happen. The cops needed to see this, he needed to get them here before the rain hit.

Before hastily departing the scene, he took one last look for additional evidence, circling the house, investigating beneath the overgrown bushes—and making doubly sure that he, himself, had left no paw prints. His jaws were aching with the weight of the mice. Prowling, he found nothing more of significance until, beneath the yellow flowers of a euryops bush beside the drive, he spotted a pair of dark glasses. They smelled of suntan oil. He studied them, but left the silver-rimmed shades untouched, lying among the dead leaves, and hurried away from the scene. Pushing through between several overgrown mock orange bushes, he scorched up an oak tree to the neighbors' roof and headed across the peaks to deliver his gift, and then to alert the law, though with some small misgivings.

If that was a murder scene, he'd be glad he made the call. If it wasn't, if the seeming evidence led to some other scenario that he had not imagined, he would be deeply embarrassed. In all the time he'd been secretly passing tips to Molena Point PD, he had never once given the cops a false lead, to do so would tarnish the perfect record of the department's most reliable snitch.

But no fear, he'd smelled human death. And though he didn't rejoice in knowing that some innocent human had died, he knew, in every perceptive cell of his silver-gray tomcat body, that the evidence would prove him right.

2

Hurrying over the rooftops the two blocks to the Chapman house, Joe was careful to carry his gift of mice high enough so he wouldn't trip on them; at his every leap, his mousy burden dragged him down, thudding against his chest and against the roof shingles. Below him along the street, folks had begun to awaken. He glimpsed a man out walking in the cool early dawn. Two women in jogging clothes strolled along gossiping and exchanging giggles. As he jumped clumsily from tree to tree and over a narrow alleyway, above him the sky darkened even more, and he broke into a gallop, praying the rain would hold off until the cops had a look at the bloody swimming pool.

He had no question that as soon as he called the department, a squad car would head up there, that a uniform or maybe one of the detectives would take a look at the pool, and get a blood sample. Once forensics had established that that was human blood, which shouldn't take long, Detective Garza or Davis would cordon off the scene and get to work. He wondered if any missing-person's report had come in that could be tied to the dead body. He thought the dark glasses lying beneath the bushes were a woman's, but with the smell of suntan oil on them, he couldn't be sure.

Leaping from an oak limb down onto the Chapmans' roof, Joe backed down a bottlebrush tree and into the heavily layered miasma of crowded bushes, flowers, and small trees that was Theresa Chapman's garden—a tangle that might be criticized by the neighbors as an unkempt mess but which, to the neighborhood felines, was a jungle of delight in which to hide for a nap or for amusement, to hunt small rodents, and just to play.

Sheltered among the overgrown flowers and shrubs, Joe headed for the laundry-room window. Leaping to the sill, he clawed open the glass slider, releasing onto the morning air the sharp scent of female cat, the stink of used sandbox, and then the sweet smell of kittens. Apparently the latch was broken. The window was secured by a lock that allowed the pane to open four inches, just enough for Mango to come and go; when

Theresa was home, she left the slider open. Quickly Joe slid on through.

The Chapman house was a remodel that had once, early in the last century, been a poky little summer cabin. Now, with the living room and kitchen enlarged and the addition of deep bay windows throughout the sunny rooms, and new sliding glass doors onto the back deck, the house was a charmer. Even Joe, with a tomcat's disdain for architectural niceties, found the home appealing. The interior was, in fact, so commanding in its bold lines that the tangles of homey clutter in which the Chapmans liked to live did not detract from its imposing presence. Cluttered house, cluttered garden, but handsome and sturdy home. The mix seemed to suit exactly Theresa Chapman's two-sided temperament.

She was a thin young woman with a perpetually delighted smile, as if all the world had been made new for her. Dark brown hair, brown eyes, prominent cheeks that she tried to erase by constant dieting, but which in truth only added to her charm. Her friends and neighbors said she should leave the dieting alone, but Theresa wouldn't listen. Thin as a rail, still she dieted, seemed almost to starve herself, striving to thin those round, smooth, and appealing cheeks.

Theresa was a loving friend to every animal she met; she cried easily over lost or hurt animals, and she was giving and loving with her human friends. Only when she took offense at real or imagined wrongdoings did her emotions flare with sudden hurt and rage. Yet Joe and Dulcie and Kit, who overheard a lot of village gossip, some by accident and more on purpose, had never heard anyone say a bad word about her.

Dropping down onto the counter that held the laundry sink, Joe leaped to the floor and diffidently approached the big cardboard box in the corner where the kittens were nestled with their mama.

Theresa had left the yellow tabby shut in the house with her nursing babies for the duration of the Chapmans' three-week vacation, wanting to keep the little family safe. She had left ample food and water, which the housekeeping service would replace regularly. Of course she hadn't counted on anyone else, on any strangers, gaining access. But last night, surely after Theresa and her husband had left, Joe and Dulcie found the female locked out of the house, separated from her bawling kits, and with no way to get back inside. They had come upon her yowling and clawing at the back door, frantic to get in, and they couldn't imagine that the Chapmans had accidentally let her out as they were loading up to leave. Carl Chapman might do that, but not Theresa, not with her responsible and loving care of every cat she knew. They were certain

Theresa would have checked on Mango the last thing before leaving. Had Mango slipped out past her at the last minute? That didn't seem likely, not as careful as Theresa was. Or had someone from Charlie Harper's cleaning service come in right after they left and accidentally let her out?

But why would they come in to clean so late in the day? And Charlie's employees would never be so careless—nor, of course, would Charlie.

"Those kittens can't last very long without milk," Dulcie had said worriedly. "We have to get her back inside." She had looked frantically at Joe, her green eyes wide, all her maternal instincts on full alert. "Did someone go in there after they left, maybe planning to rob the house?"

Softly she'd padded up the back steps, approaching the yellow cat, who had backed against the door snarling defensively, guarding her children. The cries of the kittens was heartbreaking, and one of them was clawing determinedly at the door, his mewls loud and demanding.

Rearing up, Joe had peered between the door and the molding. The dead bolt gleamed back at him, solidly engaged.

Leaving the frantic female, they had circled the house looking for a way in. If they could gain access, they could open the door from inside—no trick at all for clever paws.

They had tried all the windows, leaping up, balancing on the sills and clawing at the sliders, but all were solidly locked. They clawed at the knobs of the front and back doors, and at the garage pedestrian door, with no luck, the dead bolts holding them tight. It was when they leaped to the back deck to try the glass sliders there that they'd found the deep, fresh pry marks along the slider's edges, as if the door had been jimmied.

If it had been pried open, it was locked again when they tried it. Even with both of them clawing and straining, they couldn't force it open. Had someone come in this way, burglarized the house, and then carefully locked the door as he left?

Or had a thief locked it behind him when he entered, the cats had wondered, and was still in there?

Maybe he had gone into the laundry, frightening Mango so that she fled to another room as she tried to lead him away from her kittens. Maybe then, confused, she'd fled out the open slider. Moving on around the house to the far side, they had found the laundry window unlatched, but closed. The scent of the mama cat was strong around it, and when Joe leaped to the sill, he was able to slide it open four inches. There it stopped, against the auxiliary lock.

Dulcie leaped up beside him, nosing at the yellow cat hairs caught in the window frame and molding. "An entrance that would be too high for the kittens to reach." They kept their voices low, always wary of being overheard. "But," Dulcie said, "if Theresa left it open for Mango, who closed it?"

"Theresa wouldn't leave it open while they're gone," Joe whispered. "She wouldn't invite raccoons or possums inside, to get at the kittens. No," he'd said with certainty, "Theresa left it closed, with Mango and the kits safe inside. Someone else was here, someone let her out. Or drove her out."

Frowning, Dulcie had peered down into the laundry room. "We have to tell Charlie—once we've let Mango in."

Charlie's Fix-it, Clean-it service took care of all the houses on this street when the owners were on vacation. One of their specialties was their responsible care of their clients' pets—and the cats trusted Charlie; she was their close and reliable friend.

Squeezing in through the window's four-inch opening, Joe dropped down onto the counter beside the laundry sink, Dulcie directly behind him—before they could open the back door and let Mango in, there was a thud behind them, then a thud on the floor as the yellow female dove past them, streaking to the cardboard box.

Her frantic kittens squalled even louder at the cry and smell of their mother. A fifth kitten was still at the back door, yowling and clawing. When he saw his mama, he fled to her, scrambled into the box, and began frantically nursing before she even laid down.

Hastily the female settled in among her little ones, all the time scowling at Joe and Dulcie, her ears back, her slitted eyes never leaving them. To a queen with kittens, the presence of a tomcat wasn't comforting; many tomcats would kill those little babies. All five kittens piled onto her, greedily sucking and pushing as if surely they were starving.

A big bowl of kibble stood at the end of the laundry counter, and there was a large bowl of water in the sink, high off the floor where the kittens couldn't climb in and drown. Theresa had left the tap dripping into the bowl, and the sink drain open to avoid an overflow. It was Theresa who would have done this, no one thought Carl Chapman cared that much about Theresa's cats. Joe didn't think he cared about much of anything, even including the delightful Theresa.

"She made it as safe and comfortable for them as she could," Dulcie said softly. "She even unplugged the washer and dryer so the kittens wouldn't chew on live cords. *She* wouldn't leave the window open, *Theresa* would never leave the mama outside."

"And why," Joe had muttered warily, "would she leave the door open from the laundry room to the rest of the house? Leave the kittens to roam where the electric cords *are* still plugged in?" Standing on his hind paws, he had peered from the laundry room through the kitchen to the living room. "I can see two lamps plugged in. No, someone's been in here. And maybe still is?"

Dropping from the counter to the linoleum, the cats headed through the kitchen to inspect the rest of the house. Behind them, the female growled, but she didn't follow. They had searched the three-bedroom house from one end to the other but could see nothing obviously missing. The plasma televisions were in place, the nearly new DVD and CD players. There was a plasma computer monitor in the little home office, a checkbook on the desk, items that surely any thief would take. It was hard to know, in the comfortable clutter of the Chapman home, whether anything else might be unaccounted for. When at last they returned to the laundry room, they managed to pull the kitchen door closed with their paws beneath the crack. Again the yellow cat hissed and yowled and this time she left her box, stalking them, stiff legged and threatening. To avoid a confrontation, Joe leaped to the counter and directly out the open window. Dulcie had followed and, balancing on the sill, they'd slid the glass closed behind them, leaving the mama cat safely confined. It would be a long three weeks for her before Theresa would be home to love and comfort her.

"Charlie will give her plenty of attention," Dulcie had said, dropping down into Theresa's tangled garden. "She'll find out what happened, she'll know if anything's missing."

That had been last night. When Joe got home, pushing in through his cat door, when he told Clyde and Ryan where he and Dulcie had been and what they'd found, Ryan had risen at once to call Charlie, but Clyde stopped her, his hand gently on her arm. They'd been sitting in the living room reading after supper, Clyde in an ancient pair of jeans and a faded T-shirt, his dark hair rumpled. "What's she going to tell Max? Who's she going to say was in her clients' empty house this time of night, to find a break-in?"

While Charlie knew that the cats could speak and were quite capable of using the phone, Max certainly didn't. If Charlie suddenly went charging out at night to check on a burglary, he'd start asking awkward questions, and one didn't brush off Max Harper's probing.

"Maybe he isn't home," Ryan said hopefully. "Maybe he's still at the station."

The hours of a police chief could be long, and Max was no exception. "She'll think of something," Ryan said confidently, gave Clyde a green-eyed grin, and punched the single button for the Harpers' number.

The upshot was that Max was indeed working late. Charlie had left the two big dogs guarding the ranch house and barn, and had come down the hills to have a look. She'd called back afterward, once she left the Chapman house. She said she'd found nothing more amiss besides the pry marks on the sliding door, that the mama and kittens were fine, and that she'd check again in the morning. Of course she hadn't reported the problem. That was the one glitch in Charlie and Max Harper's marriage, that Charlie was forced to keep information from him. This upset her considerably, but it would distress her a lot more if Max learned the truth. If he were forced to believe the vital role that three unnatural felines played in the workings of Molena Point PD—and Joe was mighty glad Charlie was fully committed to keeping their secret.

3

Now as Joe carried his gift across the rooftops, the sun had slipped away again and the smell of rain filled the morning. Leaping to the sill of the Chapmans' laundry-room window, clinging with sharp claws to the ledge, Joe slid the glass back with one armored paw. Moving inside, he clawed the window closed again behind him, dropped to the counter and then to the floor, the mice swinging. When he looked up at the female in the box, among her kittens, expecting her to be charmed by his mousy present, she laid back her ears and glared and hissed at him.

Before approaching, to drop the mice at her feet, he turned to the closed door that led to the kitchen. Pawing at the throw rug that lay before it, he pushed it into the crack, hoping to keep the mice from escaping into the rest of the house.

There was little he could do about the washer and dryer. Nothing was as frustrating as having a mouse escape beneath a washing machine, where you could see its beady little eyes peering out but it was safe from your reaching paw.

He scanned the room, and with a stroke of genius he leaped to the counter, knocked the plastic dishpan off, pushed it across the room with his shoulder, depositing his little gifts in the deep receptacle. The whole time, the yellow cat growled and hissed. Pausing beyond the reach of her claws, he stood for a moment staring down into the dishpan where the mice crouched, confused and dazed. He hoped the little beasts would remain sufficiently stunned not to jump out before Mango could snatch them up.

He expected her to eat most of them—Dulcie said she needed more than kibble when she was nursing kits. But he hoped she'd save a couple, to start training the kittens. Dulcie had laughed at that, had said those kits were too young to train, that to give them a mouse would be like buying a tricycle for a human baby. But Joe wasn't so sure. That one tom kitten, who had clawed so boldly at the back door, seemed plenty aggressive despite his tender age.

Joe thought about his own kittenhood. He could hardly remember his mama, she had died or run off shortly after he was weaned, long before she was able to teach him much of anything. Certainly she hadn't taught him to hunt. He'd had to figure that out for himself, had to teach himself how to catch a mouse in San Francisco's mean alleys, how to avoid the bigger stray cats, how to avoid the city's wharf rats that would kill and eat a kitten—had had to figure out, alone, how to stay safe and keep from starving.

With these matters sharply in mind, he felt strongly that kittens should be introduced early to the basic skills of life. The hunting and survival skills, mastered when one was young, would never be forgotten. Without those talents, life was twice as hard and one might never grow into a strong and self-sufficient adult— might never grow up at all.

Watching the yellow female, Joe backed away from the dishpan hoping she would approach. She twitched her nose at the mousy scent but didn't move, she was too wary of a tomcat near her kittens. Only when he turned away, to press against the door that led to the kitchen, did she step out of the box and approach the dishpan to peer in—as the mice scurried around the dishpan scrabbling at the slick plastic walls, her ears came up and her eyes widened. Staying between Joe and the kittens, she reached a paw in with keen interest. Smiling, Joe left her to them. Pushing open the door to the kitchen, he slid through fast and shut it behind him, leaving the bunched rug in place and leaving mama to her feast. Hopefully, inviting a first session of training for the little tomcat.

Now, with access to the rest of the house, what he wanted was a phone so he could reach the dispatcher before the rains began, washing clean the swimming pool. The kitchen was done all in white, white cabinets, a white tile floor, a small oak breakfast table with white pads on the chairs, and a deep bay window above the sink. When he reared up to scan the tops of the counters, he spotted the wall phone hanging just to the right of the window—hanging in plain sight of anyone walking up the drive.

Warily he leaped up and looked out, making sure he didn't have an audience. Knocking the receiver off, he eased its fall with a quick paw and punched in 911. He was crouched low, his nose to the speaker, when the window brightened above him and he looked up to see the clouds blowing more swiftly, revealing a widening hole of blue sky—maybe the rain would hold off. Sniffing the air, he was unable to make out much in the closed room. He flinched, startled, when the dispatcher picked up.

"Police," the rookie said crisply, the young man obviously prepared for any manner of disastrous emergency call.

"Detective Garza or Davis," Joe said, wishing his favorite dispatcher had been on duty. "There's been a murder," he said quickly. "Evidence of a murder." Mabel Farthy would have put him straight through without wasting time with needless questions.

But the sensible rookie did the same, he switched Joe straight to Davis. Joe could tell by the hollow sound that he'd left the line open so he could jot down names and locations—though he would be aware of this address if the Chapmans' phone didn't block caller ID.

Detective Davis came on the line. As Joe relayed his message to her, he pictured the middle-aged, squarely built woman sitting at her desk, severe in her dark uniform, her dark Latin eyes unreadable, photographs of her two sons in police uniforms tucked away on the bookshelves behind her among stacks of notebooks and files. He told Davis about the drag marks and the footprints in the pool and up the drive, about the splatters of blood, and the dark glasses lying in the tall grass, silver-framed glasses that he thought were a woman's.

Davis didn't ask his name, she didn't ask who he was or where he was now. Juana Davis knew his voice, and she knew her questions wouldn't be answered. Like Detective Garza and the chief and most of the other officers, she had moved on beyond questioning the identity of this particular snitch.

She said, "Did you see anyone on the street or in the neighborhood?"

"No one," he said. "And no strange cars, only those that belong in the neighborhood. All of them cold, cold engines, cold tires."

"Anything unusual about the empty house? Anyone at the windows?"

"Nothing that I saw," Joe said. "The footprints end halfway up the drive. If the rain gets here before you do, it'll all be washed away." Wanting her to hurry, he reared up and pressed the disconnect button. As he clumsily took the cord of the phone in his teeth and lifted and pushed it back into place, he hoped Davis was already heading for her squad car. Beyond the window, dark and light sky alternated as a high, fast wind played hopscotch with the water-filled clouds, scudding them to hide the lifting sun and then allowing brightness to bathe the village in a skirmish of shadow and light.

Dropping down to the floor, he slipped back into the laundry room, shutting the door behind him. Mango was still in the dishpan. The little yellow tom kitten had left his nest and was standing up with his paws on the edge of the pan, trying to look in, his blue eyes bright and one small paw lifted.

Springing to the laundry-room window, Joe slid it open, hurried through, and closed it again behind him;

he headed across the rooftops toward the empty house, his pace faster now that he was relieved of the heavy mice—and though he endured another stab of pity for the poor little beasts, he enjoyed far more the bold and predatory wildness so evident in that tiny kitten.

Now as he raced over the rooftops, the air smelled heavier with rain and the sky grew darker again above him. *Come on, Davis. Be there. Hurry up, before it starts to pour.* He glimpsed a man two blocks over, looked like the same energetic runner he'd seen before, walking now but still moving swiftly, swinging his arms. The gossiping women were not in sight. Probably they'd finished their walk and were cozied up at home, in one kitchen or the other, enjoying coffee and fattening sweet rolls, effectively undoing whatever weight-loss program they might be pursuing.

He expected Juana to be there already, but when he came down a pine tree and onto the roof of the house next door, there was no cop car, nor was Juana's Honda in sight. He smelled water below him, and felt its cool breath though it wasn't raining yet. When he looked down at the side yard, he froze.

The lower half of the driveway was glistening wet, while the upper half was dry—as if rain had already come pelting down, but only in that one place. From the center of the drive, back to the pool, the concrete was soaking wet, the bushes still dripping. The coping around the pool glistened with water, as did the portion of the pool's tiled walls that he could see from that angle. Backing swiftly down the pine tree, he raced to the pool to look over.

The muddy concrete bottom was all changed. The drag marks and footprints were gone. A skin of fresh water lay over the mud, still settling into new indentations where the mud had been reconfigured into long, fan-shaped trenches, the sort that would be made by the force of a hose sluicing across it. Swinging around, Joe looked for a hose.

There, just beyond the edge of the pool, beside the house. A hose wound on a caddy, its nozzle still dripping, the neat rubber coil shining wet, with grass stems sticking to it where it had been dragged across the lawn. He studied the rest of the yard.

Nothing else looked different except, near the street, where the driveway was dry, the tall grass at the edge was matted down in a narrow path where someone had not wanted to leave footprints on the concrete.

Trotting up for a look, Joe found blades of grass still springing back into place; and now he could smell the vague scent of a man mixed with the smells of mud, bruised grass, and another sharp, medicinal smell that, try as he might, he couldn't place. He was still sniffing, trying to sort out that one elusive smell, when he heard a car coming. Jerking to alert, he headed fast up the pine and onto the neighbors' roof again, where he crouched low on the rough, curling shingles.

Davis's blue Honda parked across the street but the detective didn't get out, she sat behind the wheel studying the parked cars, scanning the neighborhood and the neatly kept houses and observing the empty house, watching its curtainless windows. How many times had Joe watched Juana Davis work a scene, always careful, always patient, never missing a detail. How many times had he and Dulcie and Kit worried that she'd find cat hairs at the scene?

But there were never cat hairs in the detective's carefully detailed reports. *Thanks to the great cat god,* Joe thought. Or maybe thanks to some benign quirk in Juana Davis's own subconscious that, as far as Joe was concerned, didn't bear close examination.

When at last the detective swung out of the car, she carried a small satchel, a black leather bag that Joe knew contained basic crime scene equipment. And, the tomcat thought, smiling, wasn't that a vote of confidence for the department's unknown snitch.

Juana crossed the empty street, still studying the Parker house and its blank windows. She saw no movement there. Scanning the overgrown bushes, the tall grass, and the piles of leaves that had blown onto the porch and heaped against the front door, she thought what a pity it was to let this place go to ruin. The neighboring houses were well kept, the front gardens neat, some of them really beautiful. Divorce or not, the Parkers were foolish to let their investment go to hell. This house was worth enough to greatly ease the life of both members of the dissolving marriage, particularly to ease the life of Emily Parker. Juana knew, from gossip and from information picked up by the officer who patroled this neighborhood, that the Parkers had had several violent arguments, and that Emily wasn't in an enviable position. As much as Juana disliked the idea of prenup agreements, which surely indicated a lack of trust and true love, this was one time that the woman would have benefited. Maybe, she thought, prenups indicated not only a lack of trust, but of judgment. Or a lack of faith in one's judgment. Ever since the word "judgmental" had become politically incorrect, clear and logical thinking seemed to have gone out the window with it.

The Parker house had been empty for nearly a year. James had left Emily without warning after placing the house in someone else's name and, without Emily's knowledge, filing for bankruptcy. What he meant to do with the valuable property depended largely, Juana thought, on the outcome of the divorce proceedings, and she hoped Emily Parker had a good lawyer.

Walking up along the side of the drive, watching for footprints, she carried just the small evidence bag that held some basic equipment and a couple of cameras. Anything else she'd need was in the trunk of her car. Halfway down the drive, she stopped, puzzled.

Though the cement drive beneath her feet was quite dry, that in front of her glistened with water, her first thought was that it had rained just in this one spot, as it did in the tropics—but Molena Point wasn't the tropics. She studied the tracks near her where the dry grass had been matted down and was wet. Looked at the grassy hose farther on, wound neatly on its reel, and it, too, was wet.

She photographed the area, then made her way carefully along the edge of the drive, watching the concrete for footprints and scanning the ground under the bushes. She circled the house looking for any sign of a break-in, but halfway back to the pool, she paused.

She took another photograph, then pulled on a latex glove and picked up the pair of silver-rimmed dark glasses lying in the tall grass. Dropping them into a paper evidence bag, she put that in her pocket. Then, pulling cotton booties over her regulation shoes, she approached the pool along the far side, where the apron was still dry save for a first few scattered raindrops.

The bottom of the pool had been hosed, and not long ago. Water was still settling in the long ripples of mud, like those a concentrated stream of water would leave in its wake. There were no drag marks such as the snitch had described, no footprints leading across to the steps. Standing at the edge of the coping, she suddenly felt watched, felt as if the perp was still nearby or that someone was, concealed in the yard or perhaps in the empty house. The feeling unnerved her. She didn't often experience this sharp and sudden unease—when she did, she had reason. What had she seen and not consciously registered to prompt that instinct?

Looking around her, she assessed the area even more carefully. If she could believe what the snitch had told her, then someone had been here just moments earlier, between the time he observed the scene and when she arrived, someone who had watched the snitch leave and then had immediately washed away the evidence.

She wouldn't want to think the snitch was lying. She knew his voice, and over the years she'd learned to trust him, as had the rest of the department. How many times had he helped them, and never once given them cause to doubt his word. Whoever the guy was, he and the woman who sometimes called, their tips, and sometimes the delivery of evidence, had always resulted in information that led to arrest, to indictment, and, most often, to a conviction. The department's snitches were would-be cops, she thought, smiling. And more power to them, they were good at what they did.

She considered the house, wishing she had a search warrant in hand, then moved on and, in a workman-like manner, searched around the pool for blood, kneeling to take samples then photographing the area despite the lack of any remaining shoe prints or drag marks. On the pool's bottom a bird's feather floated, along with bits of dry grass, as the fresh water eased into the sour mud. She shot a long video of the settling water, then went through a roll of still shots of the pool bottom, the walls, and the surround. Then she moved around the pool to where the paving was dry except for the gathering raindrops. Looking along the pool's stained sides she considered individual chips and flecks of dirt in the old, cracked tile. Kneeling, she lifted some samples of a stain that had been missed by the hose, placing them on glass slides. Four looked and smelled like blood. She paused in her work long enough to call in, to ask the dispatcher if she'd come up with any missing-person's reports from the surrounding area. But as she worked, she couldn't shake the sense of being watched.

She had no idea that the snitch sat on the roof above her, ready to melt away out of sight if she turned to look up.

The gray tomcat smiled with satisfaction each time Juana scraped up a bit of what he knew was human blood. She worked fast but carefully until the rain started. When it began coming down in earnest, she pulled off her booties and packed up her slides and equipment. Joe watched her circle the house again before she headed for her car, and only then did the tomcat decide to abandon the scene himself and head home. He wasn't partial to a drenching rain, and he felt hollow with hunger. This was Sunday morning, and Ryan, in her new mode as a blushing bride—which probably wouldn't last too long—would very likely be cooking up a fine breakfast.

But then, hurrying over the roofs, shaking raindrops off his ears, he felt the rain stop again as suddenly as it had started. He watched the last clouds part above him and begin to move away, allowing shafts of sun to stream through onto the wet shingles. Just a harmless summer rain, a passing shower—but that harmless little rain, together with a judicious hosing down, had sure screwed up the crime scene. Joe wondered where that would leave the department, wondered what Juana would make of what little evidence she'd been able to retrieve. Would she decide that, without a body, she didn't have enough to run with? That her morning's work had been for nothing? She had, after all, only his anonymous description of the original scene.

And where was the perp hiding, that he could return and hose down the place and vanish again so quickly? *Was* he in the empty house? Was the *body* in there? Earlier, circling the house, he had found no hint of fresh scent. He wondered if Juana would take the little remaining evidence seriously enough to come back with a search warrant. Wondered if she had enough evidence so the judge would be willing to issue a warrant. His head filled with questions, but with his stomach alarmingly empty, the tomcat headed for home—no cat can think productively on an empty belly.

One thing for sure, he thought as he raced over the rooftops, he was keeping this morning's events to himself. Though Ryan would listen with interest, he didn't need Clyde's acerbic remarks. He didn't need to be told that he was only imagining a murder and that if he had any sense, he'd learn to stay out of police business. Though Clyde's harassment was half joking, though Joe knew Clyde respected the results of his past investigations, he didn't feel, this morning, like being hassled by his teasing housemate.

4

Having parted from Joe Grey before dawn, the two lady cats had followed the elusive scent of the band of feral cats that they'd detected during their hunt, had followed their trail and then followed the faint sound of the cats' voices softly laughing and talking, these cats who were like themselves.

This was the clowder in which Kit had grown up, the band whose leaders had so tormented her. The band she had left the moment she was big enough and brave enough to go out on her own—and the moment she discovered a pair of true friends among some very special humans. Oh, that had been a change in her life, to come to live with humans she soon learned to love, to live in a warm house with wonderful food, and music, and with all the joys of the human world.

Kit did love her life, and surely she loved her house-mates. But still, sometimes, she missed the clowder. Sometimes, despite all her domestic pleasures, she felt strongly drawn back to that wild life. When, this morning, high up in the hills near the ruins of the old Pamillon mansion, she and Dulcie saw five wild, speaking cats slip up over a nearby crest and pause to look down at them, Kit had felt a thrill clear down to her paws. Watching those members of her old clowder, she'd reared up, staring at them—and staring straight at the tomcat who had once been her love, and from whom she had parted.

It had been only a few months ago that Sage, badly wounded, had been brought into the village where Kit's human friends cared for him—and where he asked Kit to be his mate. She had refused him, had realized that she loved him more like a brother. But now, watching Sage, whom she had so painfully rejected, she considered intently the small, buff-colored female who crouched beside him.

Was this Sage's new love? This scrawny, bleached-out, nondescript young cat as thin as a sick rabbit? Kit stood tall on her hind paws, looking. Did she even remember this waif of a young cat from among the clowder? For a moment, despite the fact that she *had* jilted Sage, Kit was riven with jealousy.

But then she thought, startled, had she seen that scrawny cat in the village? Had she seen that little cat among humans? Oh, but that wasn't likely. The clowder cats never went there unless in a terrible emergency. And then it was only brave Willow who would come seeking human help. Certainly that scrawny, nervous young cat would never come down into the human world.

As she watched, the pale cat reared up, too, and opened her pink mouth, staring down at them, intently interested in Kit and Dulcie, her thin little face filled with excitement—until Sage nuzzled her and pushed her away.

But even as Sage bossed the little buff-colored cat and demanded her attention, she ignored him and continued to stare—and Kit could see clearly the younger cat's wild yearning. She seemed to know at once that cat's dreams.

She's like me! Kit thought with surprise. *Not just that she can speak, we're all alike in that. She feels the same hungers that I do, she wants to understand the whole world the way I always did, she wants to know everything. She isn't content in the clowder, she wants to see and smell and taste everything in the world, she wants to know more than she'll ever learn running with the clowder, she wants to know human ways . . .*

The words of an old English tale filled Kit's mind. ". . . A pretty little dear her was, but her wanted to know too much . . ." And Kit's heart had gone out to the young cat. *She's like me when I was her age, she wants to know what it's like to live among humans and hear music and ride in cars and have more wonderful adventures than a clowder cat can ever know.* And Kit yearned for the young cat as she would yearn for the ghost of her own younger self.

Beside her, tabby Dulcie watched the silent exchange, saw Kit's jealousy but then, far stronger, Kit's fascination with the buff-colored cat. Dulcie had been a grown cat when she and Joe found Kit up on Hellhag Hill. Kit had been just as thin and scrawny and half starved as this little waif—and as full of dreams. Kit was grown now, but that spirit still burned in her, that often irrepressible kindling of curiosity and joy, so much joy that sometimes Dulcie thought the little cat would explode.

As Kit and the pale cat silently regarded each other, Sage's look made Dulcie uneasy. Clearly he didn't want Kit's flighty and irresponsible ways to infect his sweet new lady, he didn't want his chosen mate to be a dreamer. He wanted her to be an obedient wife, he wanted a family, he wanted a steady female cat who could give him kittens, a stolid, matronly cat, a cat he could understand and who would understand him. How sad, Dulcie thought, that he had chosen this cat who seemed not like that at all, who seemed so like Kit. Another dreamer, another impetuous rebel he might never be able to make happy? Sage had tried to change Kit, and had failed. Did he think, now, that he could force this little scruff to his wishes?

Dulcie didn't think so.

As the buff-colored cat reared up to look at Kit, as the two stood staring at each other across the blowing grass, Sage fluffed himself up to twice his size and lashed his tail, his ears back, his eyes narrow, and growled fiercely at his lady.

Kit looked startled, then turned away so as not to make matters worse, and headed down the hill, her glance at Dulcie hurt, and very sad.

The pale cat remained where she was, looking after Kit longingly. But at last, at Sage's prodding, the bony little waif turned away and obediently followed the bleached calico tomcat back up the hill toward the fallen walls and crumbling mansion of the old and ruined estate.

Dulcie, hurrying home beside Kit, down the hills through the rising dawn, had no idea where this meeting of the two young females would lead, but she knew a friendship had been formed—and, she thought uneasily, knowing Kit, she wouldn't be surprised to see this meeting turn to trouble. To *some* kind of trouble, as the tortoiseshell's enthusiasms so often led.

They were halfway down the hills, were just passing a newly framed house, skirting its skeleton of raw timbers, stepping carefully to avoid dropped nails, when Kit said, "I've seen her before. When Lucinda and Pedric and I walk up here, sometimes I see a pale little shadow slipping away among the broken walls. Once, for a second, she stood atop a wall looking down at me, but then she turned and ran." Ever since the weather had turned warmer, and the tourists were returning to crowd the shore on nice mornings and late afternoons, Kit's two housemates had abandoned walking the beaches and sea cliffs and taken to tramping the hills. Tall, slim, eighty-something Lucinda Greenlaw had always been a walker. She had, during a long and abusive first marriage, escaped from her pain at the hands of a philandering husband by indulging in solitary rambles over the Molena Point hills. Now she was wed again, this time happily, and Lucinda and Pedric were both enjoying the world anew, including their long and pleasant rambles accompanied by their tortoiseshell companion.

But Joe and Dulcie, too, sometimes glimpsed the clowder cats as they hunted, saw them like swift shadows flicking away among the hills or into the ruins. Because of the dry weather, the clowder had moved back within the walls of the old estate, wanting the water that ran in springs there and wanting to be safe in its shelter from the coyotes that had drawn closer to the village to quench their thirst—ever since the weather turned hot, Dulcie and Wilma, her human housemate, tucked up in bed at night, could hear coyotes on the hills, ever closer to the village, yipping and yodeling.

Some people called their noise singing. Dulcie and Wilma, knowing how dangerous the beasts were, called those cries bloodcurdling. When the yipping was near, neither of them slept well. The three cats, until just this past week, had kept their hunting to the daylight hours. When sporadic rains had begun, leaving puddles for the wild creatures among the far woods, and the coyotes had moved away once more, the cats began their night hunting again, though they stayed near the scattered houses or near boulders where they could race for shelter.

Now, descending the hills, suddenly Kit broke into a run, wildly circling Dulcie then skidding to a stop inches from the older cat's nose, Kit's yellow eyes blazing with laughter. "Free," she mewled. "I'm free!"

Dulcie puzzled over this, as she so often did over Kit's behavior. Had Sage, taking a new cat for his mate, cut the last painful thread that bound Kit to him? Did she no longer feel responsible for having hurt him, having spoiled his life as she had once thought?

But then, just as suddenly, Kit sat down in the tall grass, looking so sad that Dulcie thought she might weep.

"She's not the one," Kit said, looking forlornly at Dulcie. "She feels as trapped as I did. She wants . . . Didn't you see? She wants . . . Before she settles down to raising tangles of kittens, she wants to see what the rest of the world is like. Oh, I feel so bad for her. Didn't you see . . . ?"

"No," Dulcie said crossly. "I didn't see anything! Leave it, Kit! Leave it alone. It isn't any of your business."

"But—"

Dulcie faced Kit, her ears back, her teeth bared. This would never do. Kit's concern screamed of trouble. "Leave it alone, Kit. You will not entice her away. They're happy, Sage is happy."

"*She's* not happy, she—"

Dulcie raised an armored paw to slap Kit. "You will not ruin Sage's life again! Why would you do that?"

"Because . . .," Kit said miserably, "because . . ." She glared at Dulcie, and turned and trotted away, tears running down her tortoiseshell nose. Dulcie shouldered her to a stop, her teeth gently in the nape of Kit's neck.

For a long moment they stood looking at each other, Kit so upset that if Dulcie let go, she thought Kit would fly at her with all claws bared.

But at last Kit backed away. "She won't be happy," she said grimly, "thinking about all the wonders she's never seen. And so, Sage won't be happy."

Dulcie said nothing. She moved away, heading on down the hill. They were quiet for a long time, padding toward the village, Kit's sadness like a weight that pressed on Dulcie, too. But then suddenly, Kit came to life again.

"I know what to do," she said, leaping away. "I know exactly!" And she raced like a mad thing through the gardens of the first scattered houses, skidding to a stop beneath a porch, looking back at Dulcie.

Padding under the porch beside her, Dulcie said not a word. She didn't want to hear Kit's harebrained idea, she didn't want to contemplate what kind of trouble this would stir to life.

Seeing Dulcie's look, Kit didn't offer an explanation. She licked her fur and her dusty paws, and they went on at last, in a tense silence. The rising morning smelled of rain, the clouds overhead throwing changing shadows across the crowded cottages and shops.

Coming down into the village, the two cats took to the rooftops. Below them, early cars were on the street as locals and tourists set out to attend church and then

Sunday brunch or, despite the threat of rain, to play golf or to hike along the coastal cliffs. Soon they parted, both cats, having hunted all night and feasted on rodents, heading for their own homes and housemates, longing, now, for "people" food, for a little something to settle a cat's digestion. Dulcie's Wilma had promised a rich quiche, and Kit looked forward to Pedric's paper-thin Swedish pancakes with Lucinda's mango syrup, which was, in Kit's opinion, the best breakfast that a cat ever licked from her whiskers; and for the moment, the plight of the pale little feral was set aside, at least in Dulcie's mind. Whatever Kit was thinking, she kept to herself.

5

Joe arrived home, over the rooftops, to the welcome smell of pancakes and sausages, the heady scent rising up to him as he leaped from the neighbors' shingles to his own. Landing on the wet, slippery shakes, he could hear Clyde's and Ryan's voices from the back patio. The rain had been short and light, only a few showers and then one serious effort, and even that didn't last long. Now the sky was clearing, the June sun brightening and warming his damp fur. Pausing beside the second-floor skeleton of the new construction that would be Ryan's office, he crossed to the edge of the roof to look over.

Below, in the big, walled patio, the two lovebirds were kissing and Joe backed away, unsure how much of this newlywed mush he could take. Ryan had put the big umbrella up over the patio table to keep their breakfast dry, a nicety that Clyde wouldn't have bothered with. Ryan Flannery was, Joe thought smugly, the best thing that had happened to Clyde since Joe himself had come on the scene to brighten his life.

Looking over the edge, his paws soaking from the wet shingles, he watched Clyde move back inside the house, presumably to flip the sausages that he could hear sizzling in the pan. He could see, beneath the umbrella, a corner of the patio table carefully set with clean place mats, fresh napkins, and a centerpiece of flowers. Clyde's bride might say she wasn't domestic, that she was more used to a hammer and saw than a mixing spoon, but she had a nice touch around the house. In the four months they'd been married, life had taken a real change from his and Clyde's rough bachelor ways. No more breakfasts with their two plates slapped down carelessly on sections of the morning paper. Now the household reeked of domesticity, sometimes as cloying as a rerun from the fifties, but, more often, just as comforting.

Leaping from the roof down onto the high garden wall and again to the top of the cold barbecue grill, he dropped to the paving beside Ryan's big silver Weimaraner. The sleek, handsome dog lay stretched out on the rain-damp bricks, soaking up the brightening sun. Lying down beside Rock, Joe rolled over, presenting his own belly to the warm glow. Rock huffed at him in greeting, and with an inquisitive nose began to smell Joe's four extended paws, sniffing the mouse smells, the rat and rabbit smells, maybe a hint of kitten smell, and the heady scents of the wild hills. The big dog gave Joe a look that said, Why can't I run free like you? Sighing, he rolled over and drifted into a light sleep—with one ear cocked for the first sound of plates being set on the table. Joe watched Ryan as she crossed the patio to finish planting a flat of begonias, gently tucking the little, delicate nursery flowers into the rich earth of a raised container, an occupation that, again, seemed out of character for the dark-haired, green-eyed beauty. He was far more used to seeing her running a heavy Skilsaw or dipping her trowel into a bucket of plaster, wearing jeans and muddy boots instead of a flowered housecoat.

Rock woke the minute Clyde began dishing up. Casting Joe a look of urgency, he trotted across the bricks to stand expectantly beside the redwood table, his chin on its corner, his eyes never leaving the kitchen window. They watched Clyde push through the screen door backward, letting it slam. Turning, he descended the steps bearing a huge tray laden with plates piled with pancakes, eggs, sausages, and all the fixings. As Clyde laid out their breakfast, Ryan moved to the barbecue sink to wash the dark earth from her hands. As she and Clyde took their places at the table, Joe leaped to the end of Ryan's bench where, now, he and Rock stood shoulder to shoulder sniffing the good smells and drooling with equal greed—he watched Ryan turn away, hiding a grin.

It amused Ryan greatly that Joe Grey and Rock looked like mismatched twins, their sleek gray coats exactly the same color, their eyes the same pale yellow. And, a source of gentle humor, Joe Grey's tail was docked to the same jaunty length as Rock's, both tails sticking straight up when the animals were happy.

In Rock's case, the short tail was the correct style for a Weimaraner. Joe's shortened appendage, however, had been the result of a kittenhood accident when a drunk had stepped on his tail and broken it. Clyde had found the sick and feverish kitten in a San Francisco gutter, had rushed him to the vet where the infected part of the tail was amputated, and then had taken Joe home to nurse him back to health with antibiotics, love, and plenty of rare filet. The two hadn't been parted since.

But what tickled Ryan the most about the similarity between the two was that dog and cat were so very alike in spirit. Rock's wild, defiant, adventuresome view of the world had enchanted her from the moment she first encountered the valuable but abandoned stray. And then when she'd met Joe, his attitude, even before she discovered that the cat could speak to her, had been just as bold and brash. The big difference, of course, was that only the tomcat had use of the English language.

When she'd first suspected Joe's ability to speak, when she'd finally convinced herself that this impossibility had to be true, and then when they'd had their first conversation, that had been a time of spine-tingling amazement, an experience from which she was sure she would never quite recover. And surely she'd never be the same after her first conversation with Joe and Dulcie and Kit all together, an impossible communication between their two species that had left her with permanent goose bumps.

But, while Rock didn't speak, while her good dog knew only command words and hand signals, knew the names of the humans he loved, and the names of everyday items that she and Clyde had taught him or that he had absorbed on his own, the Weimaraner was so clever and such a quick study that he didn't need to talk to her. Body language was enough; they understood each other very well. The trouble with Rock was, he was often too clever. He knew how to climb a six-foot chain-link fence as skillfully as any cat. And with only one afternoon's training, he had learned to track a scent trail on command. For most dogs, reliable and unfaltering tracking skills took many months of training.

The fact that Joe Grey himself had taught Rock, that Rock had not learned from her own slow teaching but under the skilled tutelage of the gray tomcat, had impressed her considerably. She didn't know whether she was more proud of Rock for his quick mastering of the valuable tracking skills, or of Joe for the clever patience with which he'd tutored the big Weimaraner.

Serving the animals' plates, she set them on the bench, side by side. Dog and cat exchanged a glance of understanding that neither would steal from the other, and dived into their breakfasts. The issue of gourmet rights had been settled some time back, Joe laying down the rules with teeth and claws, and Rock with a gentle but insistent growl. Rock didn't seem to mind that his breakfast was mostly kibble, with sausage and egg crumbled in for flavor, while Joe was treated to exactly the same fare as the humans.

On the other side of Ryan, the white cat hopped up silently, her gentle eyes on Ryan as she lifted one soft paw. Crowded onto the bench, against Ryan's leg, she looked up trustingly, knowing that her own small bite of the human's breakfast was forthcoming. It saddened Ryan that the other two Damen cats, who had been far up in years, had succumbed to separate illnesses not a month apart, shortly after she and Clyde were married—saddened her, and stirred her, that the two lifelong friends had gone within weeks of each other. As if somehow deciding, with their mysterious feline connection, that their closeness in life would not be broken by death, that they would move on into the next world together.

She glanced across the patio to the high back wall, its white-plaster surface still shaded from the rising sun. In the shadow at its base marched the little row of graves: two markers for the cats, two markers for their two departed canine friends, each marble plaque attesting to an urn of ashes buried beneath. Scrappy. Fluffy. Barney. Rube.

Barney, the golden retriever, had died before Ryan and Clyde met. Rube, the black Lab, had died just this last year. Ryan had suffered with Clyde over Rube's illness, had tried to comfort Clyde and Joe when the vet put Rube to sleep. Afterward, she had tried to comfort the little white cat. She had held Snowball for hours, talking to her, trying to soothe her over the loss of her doggy companion. With Rube gone, Ryan herself seemed to take Rube's place in nurturing

Snowball; the white cat came to her far more often even than she sought out Clyde or Joe for tenderness and reassurance.

As they all tucked into breakfast, there was near silence at the picnic table. Only the scrape of a fork on a plate, Rock's eager slurping, the occasional car passing out front on the street and, from half a mile away, the rhythmic pounding of the sea against the cliffs and sandy shore. When the animals had licked their plates clean, Clyde looked across the table at Joe.

"I have an announcement."

Joe looked back warily, his claws involuntarily stiffening at the implication of some portentous, and probably unwelcome, decision. Whatever was coming, he wasn't sure he wanted to hear it.

Ryan, watching the two of them, was both uneasy and amused by the tomcat's possibly well-founded suspicions. She was still wondering herself if Clyde's decision had been a wise one. This particular resolution would be life changing for Clyde. Another big adjustment even after bringing a wife into the household—and that meant one more upset in the tomcat's life. Ordinary cats didn't like change. In that respect, she thought that speaking cats weren't so different.

The moment she'd moved into the house, when they returned from their honeymoon, the household had morphed from a casual bachelor pad to the more complicated involvements presented by an added resident, particularly a female partner. Now, if she and Clyde pursued this new endeavor, their newly established routines would change yet again, and that would change Joe's routine.

How would that affect the tomcat? Would further disruption of Joe's comfortable home life complicate his other, secret life? That mustn't happen, she thought, watching the gray tomcat. Joe Grey's undercover investigations were far too unique and valuable to let this new venture get in his way.

6

Joe watched Clyde warily, waiting for the bomb to drop. Whatever Clyde meant to tell him, obviously Ryan already knew; her green eyes hid a smile but also a hint of worry. Certainly any statement coming from Clyde and begun in this serious vein portended nothing good, such serious pronouncements could easily end in disaster. One case in point would be Clyde's purchase of a derelict apartment building, which he'd intended to remodel for rental income. A project that had ended in a tangle of embezzlement, identity theft, and murder, to say nothing of the complications resulting from Clyde's inept carpentry skills.

Another example would be the time Clyde decided that Joe should visit the old folks' home on a regular basis in order to cheer up the needy elderly. That seemingly charitable endeavor had not only put Joe and Dulcie in considerable danger, but had resulted in the discovery of a large number of anonymous dead, buried and forgotten in a garden of hidden graves.

So what was this new insanity? Joe looked at Ryan. She said nothing, just sat quietly waiting for Clyde to drop this one on him.

"What?" Joe said coldly.

Beside Joe, Rock eyed the last bite of Joe's breakfast. Joe glared a friendly warning at the silver Weimaraner and lifted a daggered paw, for which he received a doggy laugh and doggy breath in his face.

"What announcement?" he repeated.

"I'm selling the cars," Clyde said.

"You're what?"

To some, such a comment might seem of minor importance. People sold cars every day and bought new ones, the world was based on obsolescence. But this statement coming from Clyde was a shocker. He might as well have said he was giving away all his worldly possessions and joining a nudist colony. At last count Clyde had owned eighteen antique and classic automobiles, collectors' items all, and he loved those cars like his own children. In restoring them, he labored over every detail, as a sculptor labors over every inch of clay in preparing his bronze castings.

"You're going to do what?" Joe repeated quietly.

Clyde took another bite of pancake and sausage, another sip of coffee. "Sell the cars. Except the roadster," he said, referring to the vintage yellow convertible that sat, pristine and shining and completely restored, in their attached garage.

"I'm going to sell the cars," Clyde repeated slowly, as if Joe was, regrettably, growing deaf.

"You're selling the cars." Joe looked at Ryan. Her green eyes, turned to him, were wide and innocent.

This transaction would include cars both domestic and foreign, ranging in age from eighty years to more recent and overblown fishtail models, and in value from a few thousand into the high six figures, each car either already painstakingly restored, lavished with love, from its wheels and pistons to its new leather upholstery—with love and skill and plenty of cash—or cars in the process of being restored, to a few wrecks still patiently awaiting their turn at Clyde's skilled automotive rejuvenation, rather as an aging actress awaits her appointment to go under the knife of a highly paid plastic surgeon.

Ever since Joe had first met Clyde, when Clyde hauled him out of that San Francisco gutter, Clyde's one huge passion in life, besides charming women, and his dogs and cats, had been old cars and the rebuilding thereof. When they lived in San Francisco, he had collected cars, renting an old garage over in Marin County where he'd worked on them, on weekends and his days off, taking Joe with him. That was where Joe learned to hunt, stalking mice along the bare stud walls and loose building paper of that decrepit old garage.

When they'd moved down the coast to Molena Point, Clyde had sold his two beautifully restored convertibles, but when he opened his upscale automotive repair shop, he began to collect old models again, ferreting them out by newspaper ad and word of mouth, driving halfway across the state to haul them home on a flatbed trailer. The garages at the back of the space he rented from the foreign-car agency had been largely reserved for his own growing collection of wrecks destined to become collectors' items. In short, a nice share of their income had been generated by those restorations, besides which, they had had Clyde's complete involvement. Joe didn't think his housemate could exist without those old cars.

"You mean you're selling all the restored cars and getting a new batch to work on," the tomcat said reasonably.

"No. Selling them all. Finished. Not buying any more cars," Clyde said.

"This is some kind of midlife crisis?" Joe said. "A man doesn't have a midlife crisis while he's still on his honeymoon, just four months after the wedding." He looked suspiciously at Ryan. Was she responsible for this sea change? "Are you two having problems?" He prayed that wasn't so.

Ryan laughed. "Midlife crises happen to disenchanted, bored men with no positive philosophy, no positive take on life—no burning reason for living their lives."

In Joe's opinion, Ryan Flannery Damen was the world's best reason for living. Anyway, nothing about that description fit Clyde. The tomcat had never observed any of the bored, flat, jaundiced, arrogant, or dully disinterested symptoms associated with the emotional demise of a human creature. In some ways, Clyde Damen was still twelve years old, enthusiastic about life to the point of sorely trying a cat's patience.

"You need the money?" Joe asked, though he could hardly believe that. Clyde had a comfortable savings account, and Ryan was even better off. She had a nice inheritance from her first husband, and her construction firm did very well indeed. Joe turned to look at her. Did she not approve of the cars? Had she talked Clyde into selling them? Joe couldn't believe she'd be so selfish and unfeeling. He studied her, then eyed his housemate again, waiting.

Ryan started to grin, her green eyes dancing.

Clyde said, "We're going to buy a couple of houses. Go into—"

"We're not moving!" Joe yowled, going cold right down to his claws. The thought of changing houses, of losing his happy home as he knew it, hadn't entered his mind. Talk about life changes. It was bad enough for a human family to move their children around, haul them across the country to a new house, painful enough for the children to have to survive in a new school. To a cat, moving seemed far worse. Territory meant everything, its smells and hiding places and hunting grounds were a large and vital portion of a cat's life. To be removed from home and domain, deposited without introduction onto foreign soil could, without understanding treatment, disorient and nearly destroy a little cat.

"We're leaving our home?" Joe said, unable to control his dismay. He loved his home, he loved the new upstairs that Ryan had built, he loved his own private cat tower, on top of the second-floor roof, that Ryan had built just for him. The thought of moving to another house made his breakfast want to come up, mice and all.

"We're not moving," Ryan said hastily, reaching to take him in her arms. "We're not going anywhere, we're buying a house as an investment." She smiled as Joe relaxed, leaning his head on her shoulder. "If this works out," she said, "we're going into business remodeling houses." She lifted his chin, smiling down at him. "Houses instead of cars. That make sense to you?"

"Into business?" he said dumbly. "You're selling your construction firm?"

"I'm not selling, and we're not moving. I wouldn't give up the company! This is just a side venture," she said, her green eyes searching Joe's. "We thought it would be fun, working at our own pace—just a few remodeling projects that can pick up the slack for my crews between jobs or when things get slow."

"When is the construction business ever slow?" In Molena Point, people waited months, years, for a contractor. "You mean because of the economic downturn?"

"Exactly," Ryan said. "We're hedging our bets. Does this sound okay? You approve of this?"

Joe grinned. Even with that small hint of joking sarcasm, how many humans would ask their cat about family financial matters?

"There is something troubling about it," Joe said, glancing at Clyde then back at Ryan. "Clyde's a wizard with cars, he can turn any old heap into new. But you *do* know he can't drive a nail? That it's an all-day project to change a leaky washer in the kitchen sink?"

Ryan ignored that. Maybe she thought she could teach Clyde. "We're going up to look at the Parker house today, it's just up above the senior ladies' place. We—"

Joe stiffened at mention of the Parker house. "You can't renovate that place, you can't look at that house, it's a crime scene."

They stared at him.

"There's blood in the pool, and—"

Clyde slammed down his fork. "Don't start, Joe! The Parker house is not a crime scene. Where did you get that? We talked to the Realtor early this morning, she said we could look at it. Where do you get this stuff!"

Joe said, "Someone died there. Detective Davis—"

"Leave Juana Davis out of this! What the hell did you tell Davis? You think every—"

Ryan stopped Clyde with a hand on his arm. "What, Joe? What are you saying?"

"Davis ran the scene this morning," he said, licking a smear of syrup from his shoulder.

"Tell us," she said, again hushing Clyde.

Scowling at Clyde, Joe gave them a blow-by-blow of the morning's events, from the time he entered the overgrown yard of the Parker house, dragging his mice, until, crouching on the roof in the first hesitant drops of rain, he had watched Juana Davis carefully remove and bag small samples of what looked and smelled like human blood.

When he'd finished, Ryan was quiet. Clyde was scowling, shaking his head, as if the tomcat had conjured blood and drag marks from thin air, as if Joe had made up this nutty, twisted scenario to bedevil him and, worse, to torment the officers at Molena Point PD.

Ryan reached across the table, taking Clyde's hand and squeezing it hard. She looked at Joe with an admiration that warmed the tomcat clear to the tips of his claws. "You want to come with us?" she said. "Maybe Davis will let us in if she's already worked the house. If I hide you in my tote bag and if *we* put on shoe protectors, maybe we can have a look." And as Joe's beautiful housemate rose to pick up their breakfast dishes, he gave her a smile that warmed *her,* in turn, clear down to her pretty toes.

7

Well, *he* hadn't killed her, the woman killed herself, falling like that. She could be so damned clumsy, flinging herself away from him, stumbling or hitting something and then blaming him. Every damn time blaming him, and now she'd sure as hell done it, she'd really put him on the spot. He hadn't slept all night, playing it over, seeing her lying there in the mud at the bottom of the empty swimming pool, going down there and realizing she was dead, and then later having to haul her out of there, drag her the whole length of the pool through the stinking mud and up the steps and nearly falling. Wondering what the hell he was going to do with her, trying to figure how he was going to get rid of the body. Why the hell did she have to be so clumsy, why did she have to do that!

It'd happened so fast, he still couldn't believe she'd just swung away from him and fallen. Still couldn't believe she was dead. She'd been a pain in the ass, but they'd had a good thing going, too. And then after it happened, after trying to revive her and finally knowing she was dead, the way the damned woman had timed it, he'd had to wait hours before it was dark enough to get her out of there. Couldn't bring her up out of the empty pool in the daylight and haul her to the car, he'd had to wait at home worrying that someone would come along and find her.

Right at first, when he realized she was dead, he'd thought of calling the medics or the cops, but what would he say? *They'd* say he killed her, that he'd pushed her. They'd look at that big bruise on the side of her head and they'd think the worst. No, you get cops nosing around, who knew what else they'd find? You bring the cops into it, everything would hit the fan.

She'd start to stiffen up soon, he didn't know how long that would take. Would she be harder to move then? And all the time he waited he was thinking, *Why the hell did she do that? Why the hell did she have to go and screw things up?*

He often worked Saturday but had come home early, around five, his last day before vacation. Had been all ready to head out and she knew she was supposed to be waiting, she knew it was important to leave before dark. *She'd* told him that! Had made him promise to be home early, before the neighbors all went in to supper, that the neighbors had to see them pull away. *She* was the one who said it was important for the neighbors to see them putting their suitcases in the car and heading out—and then she'd gone off like that.

She'd left her suitcase by the front door, beside his, had left her purse, too, but no sign of her. With her purse right there, he knew where she'd gone. And didn't that put him in a rage. He'd stood there for a minute swearing, calling her everything he could think of, then he'd left the house, going out through the back, hoping the neighbors wouldn't see him. Had shut the door real quiet, had slipped through the backyards to the next street, had walked the two blocks and turned back onto his own street, to the empty Parker house. If someone had seen him, if it came up later, he'd say it was a last-minute errand while she was getting dressed to leave.

They'd told everyone they planned to leave early, drive a few hours, pick up a burger, pull in somewhere around midnight. Their story was, drive up the coast then over to Reno for a few days to see her sister, then fly out of Reno for Miami and the Bahamas. So why the hell did she take the chance of going out at the last minute and screwing things up?

Well, she always did as she pleased, whatever spur-of-the-moment notion took her. It had been real hot the last few days, hot for the central coast in June. She liked that, liked lying naked in the hot sun. She couldn't sun-bathe naked in their own yard, the neighbors in three houses could see right down on her. She'd tried a few times to do that, and he'd really given her hell. Why the hell did she place such value on an all-over suntan? He'd told her a hundred times not to take her clothes off in public. Now look what she'd done, look where it had gotten her.

Approaching the Parker house, he knew she'd be back by the empty pool, hidden by the overgrown bushes where she thought no one would see her. Walking up the cracked driveway he'd smelled the coconut stink of her suntan oil long before he saw her—but as he passed the empty house he jerked to a stop: an explosion from the bushes and a white cat burst out from right under his feet, stared at him, and bolted away. Some neighborhood cat scaring him nearly to death. He'd stood, chilled, his hands shaking, trying to collect himself. He never could abide cats—and he couldn't let her see how upset he was, she had no notion how sick cats made him. The look in its eyes before it ran, the way it glared at him, wouldn't leave him.

He'd moved on at last, had found her back there, lying there naked as a jaybird, lying on that blue beach towel, her clothes folded up in the tote bag she carried, a bottle of suntan lotion and a bottle of water beside her. She'd looked up guiltily, and then yawned. Said she fell asleep, hadn't meant to be gone so long. When he lit into her, she sassed him back. Said her tan was fading, and didn't he like her to have an all-over tan? Didn't he like her to look nice?

"Nice for who?" he'd said, thinking about the neighborhood couples they hung out with, the guys he played golf with—the guys he sometimes wondered about.

"Nice for you," she'd said sharply. "Who else would I want to look nice for, baby?" And she'd reached up to him.

"Get up and get dressed, I'm not rolling around in the dirt with you." But then he'd laughed. "I'll give you a roll later, in some fancy hotel with a good bottle of Scotch and maybe a mirror on the ceiling." That made her laugh. But when he'd pointed out that the sun was going to set soon, that it sure as hell couldn't tan her much, she'd snapped at him again, seemed like she was always snapping at him.

"I told you I fell asleep. The cool evening air's good for my skin." Half the time, the woman made no sense. Except for the one thing she was good at. Then her head was clear, then she was all business.

"Get dressed," he'd told her. "Get up now and get dressed."

"It isn't even close to dark yet." Instead of pulling on her clothes, she'd just lain there looking up at him, and didn't that make him mad. He'd jerked her up, madder every minute. "Get dressed and get home! I'm ready to leave *now*!"

That's when she'd started mouthing off at him. "I'm not your slave. This whole thing was my idea, my planning. I'll get dressed when I'm ready. As for the neighbors, I'll make sure they see us." When she started getting shrill—that made him nervous because someone might hear her—that was when he smacked her, just a light back of his hand to shut her up, and the dumb broad had swung around and slapped at him. He'd hit her lightly to knock some sense into her, a little whack usually settled her right down. But when he whacked her, that was when she lost her balance or maybe slipped—all of a sudden she was gone, falling backward into the pool, trying to catch herself but there was nothing to grab, and he couldn't grab her, it all happened in a split second. He'd heard her hit the concrete with a hard *thunk*, and then she didn't move. He kept telling her to get up. She didn't move, just lay there facedown, sprawled naked in the mud, her long hair hiding her face.

Swearing, he went around the pool and down the mud-slick steps, nearly falling, crossed the stinking mud, slipping twice, knelt down, and shook her. Her body was limp, and that was when he started getting scared. He tried to turn her over. When he lifted her head, blood started running out from beneath her hair.

Sickened, he'd pushed her hair away to look. There was blood all over, underneath her hair, her hair soaked with it, a pool of blood that curdled into the sour mud and mixed with the mud on her face. A hell of a lot of blood, some of it running out of her ear. Behind her ear, the base of her head was already swelling and turning black and blue.

But then, even as he knelt there, the blood had stopped running. He kept telling her to get up, he couldn't believe she was dead. He'd thought of trying that breathing thing but it was too late. He looked up to the top of the pool, terrified someone would be standing there, but there was no one. He had to get her out of there before someone saw her, before some neighbor who might have heard them did come nosing around. He couldn't move her until dark—it was the middle of June, it wouldn't be dark until late.

Now, at five thirty, folks would be getting home from tennis or golf or shopping, and the two neighborhood families with kids home from some outing, and kids racing out in the street playing catch or riding their bikes, people going out to stand in their yards talking and gossiping. And *they* were supposed to make a big show of heading out on vacation.

Well, she'd sure as hell screwed it up, and what the hell was *he* supposed to do now? He felt trapped, and his fear began to build. Standing in the empty pool looking down at her, bloodied and dead, he'd wondered if anyone had seen her going down the street earlier, seen her heading for the Parker place, or seen him slip down there later? Anyone seeing them would wonder why they weren't leaving. She'd told everyone when they'd take off. Had bragged to everyone about the fancy vacation, the fancy Miami and Bahamas hotels where they'd be staying. She knew all the details, flight time, connecting flight, room prices, she'd made it all sound so great. She might be inept and maddening in some ways, but she handled those kinds of details like the pro she was.

He kept coming back to what he was going to do, now that their careful plans were shot to hell. His nerves were shattered, thanks to her. He wasn't sure he could pull this job off alone.

Leaving her lying in the mud, he'd walked home as nonchalantly as he could, as if he was out for a stroll before he got in the car for a long trip. Up ahead three women had stood in a yard talking, but then they'd gone inside. He could hear kids yelling in a backyard, and that had made him sweat, afraid they'd come racing out to the street and see him, and that one of them would remember, later. The yards of the houses on his left were wooded, dropping steeply down to the street below. The street he was on, his own street, ran on up the hill for half a mile, where it ended at a narrow, precipitous drive along the side of the hill, a view of the roofs below. Walking casually past his neighbors' houses, he couldn't stop seeing her dead.

He'd managed to avoid meeting anyone. Slipping into his own house, he'd tried to figure out how to handle this. He'd never thought too much about how to get rid of a body, how hard that would be. One minute he was glad she was dead, with her bitchy ways, the next minute he was scared as hell, angry that she'd done that to him. In the empty house, he'd stood looking at her purse and suitcase, feeling a stab of loss, and for the first time since it happened, he found it hard to breathe.

It always took a while to catch up with him. He went into the bathroom, got the prescription asthma spray he used. *She* said his inability to breathe was more in his head than in his respiratory system. That was another thing that maddened him, her know-it-all attitude.

He'd *told* her he had a mild case of asthma and that it was easily controlled. When they were first married she'd tried to baby him over it, but he'd shrugged that off. She never knew the real cause; he'd tried to hide the severity of those attacks from her.

Usually he could ease the breathing, but he couldn't stop the tightness in his chest that made him feel like he was being crushed, as if he was sealed inside a wall. In the bathroom, inhaling the spray, that dark memory from his childhood filled him.

He'd had the vision for so many years that sometimes he was no longer sure if that horror had really happened. Not sure if he'd *seen* that victim when he was a child, or even if *he'd* been the victim, himself. Or if the vision had come only from Poe's dark tale that he'd read over and over, the story of the man sealed in a cellar wall. Only, this time when he couldn't breathe and that scene hit him, it was *her* he saw, it was *her* sealed, dead, inside the cellar wall.

He'd sat shakily at the kitchen table until the breathing came easier, then he'd gotten up, poured a glass of milk, and found some crackers. And soon, with some food in him, he started wondering if he *could* move her now, if he dared get the car out before dark and go back, if he dared take a chance. The notion ate at him until he headed for the garage, unloaded the car's toolbox and blanket from the trunk to make room, and stuffed them in the backseat. He found the shovel and put that in, too.

He'd checked the street several times, looking out the living room windows. At last he had backed the car out, shut the garage door, and headed down the street—just as three kids careened around the corner on their skateboards.

Losing his nerve, he'd turned around and headed back home. The neighbors, glimpsing the car, might not know for sure he was alone, with the tinted side windows, would maybe think they'd forgotten something. Damn neighbors minded way too much of other people's business—but he needed them. If he went ahead with the plan, he sure as hell needed them.

He had put the car back in the garage, had spent hours pacing the house waiting for it to get dark, sweating and trying to breathe slowly and deeply. At dusk he'd wanted to try again, but when he looked out the front window, two couples were walking their dogs. Puffy little mutts that looked more like wind-up toys than something alive, and their owners strutting along after them like they were some kind of big deal. That was another thing about pets, they were not only dirty and of no practical use, they wasted a person's time, to say nothing of wasting money. And right now those dogs, bringing the neighbors out on the street, were sure as hell hindering him in what he had to do. She'd never known how he felt about useless animals, he was way too good at making people believe what he wanted them to believe.

He'd left the house lights off. In the dark he'd poured himself a small bourbon, knowing he daren't drink much, that he had to keep his head clear. He'd kept looking out the window, but had ended up having to wait until full dark before the street was empty. This time, going into the garage, he'd disconnected the motor for the garage door by pulling the cord, had pushed the door up manually so it was quieter. Had gotten in the car and backed out hoping no one saw, had closed the door again by hand and headed down to the Parker house.

Turning into the cracked drive, he'd pulled down to where it turned to enter the garage, where the overgrown bushes should hide the car. Getting out, he'd walked back up the drive and stood among the dark bushes looking up and down the street.

He could see no one on the street or in the yards. Studying the lighted windows, he could see no shadow standing behind the curtains or shades as if looking out. He could smell roast beef cooking, and fish frying. Taking the flashlight from the glove compartment, he'd walked between the bushes and through the long grass on down to the pool. Insane to let a house go like this, with the prices of real estate in this town.

It was dark as hell in the back, and he was afraid of a misstep, of falling into the empty pool himself. Wouldn't that be ironic, if he, too, died down there. He had a flash of her making him fall, reaching up from the pool and dragging him down, and that constricted his breathing, so he had to slow until he got his breath. All his life he'd had to deal with constricted breathing. All his life he'd known that wasn't fair.

He didn't want to shine the light until he was down inside the pool, and twice he slipped going down the slimy steps. He was down inside the concrete hole at last. Crossing the muddy tile, he shielded the light in his cupped hand, wondering how much would reflect up out of the pool.

She was there lying in the dark, as he'd left her, but the shock of seeing her sprawled, of his light playing over the blood and bruise, made his stomach twist.

At last, kneeling, he got his arms under her, to lift her. Her arms were stiff, her head and neck stiff. Her torso was limp, difficult to handle, stiff arms and legs sticking out. Sickened, he lifted her as best he could, carried and dragged her across the pool and up the steps, slipping and silently cursing—and leaving a drag trail of mud and blood along with the track of his tennis shoes, a mess he would have to clean up once he got her out of there.

She was even harder to handle loading in the trunk. He got her in at last, got the dark wool lap blanket out of the backseat and pulled it over her, covering her face. He didn't want to look at her face; he still had a sense of her watching him. The blood had mostly dried, but some of it was sticky. He shut the lid as quietly as he could. Getting in the car, making sure he'd slid the shovel onto the floor of the backseat, he headed up toward the hills.

He drove for a long time, back and forth among the dark and empty hills, trying to find a place to bury her. His headlights picked out very little beyond the road. He tried to scan the night-black hills by memory, tried to identify the few dim lights of the scattered houses as he looked for a stretch of empty land where freshly dug earth wouldn't be noticed. And as the car nosed along the dark roads, fear rode with him, chill and black.

8

He stopped several times to look out at an empty field, but in every case one house or another was too close. He wanted a place where he wouldn't have to carry her for miles across rough fields in the dark, but isolated enough so no one would hear him digging. The night was so still. Even from inside a house someone might hear the sound of the shovel, or a dog would hear and start barking. Though the night was cool, some hardy soul might be sitting on his front porch, his ears tuned to every small bucolic sound. To such a listener, the clink of a shovel would echo like thunder. And he'd have to do it all in the dark. If he used the flashlight, he'd sure as hell be seen. She'd really screwed things up, had really made it hard for him.

He'd headed home after midnight, discouraged with her still in the trunk. He was exhausted and his nerves were shot. He'd put the car in the garage, put on clean tennis shoes, and in the dark neighborhood he'd headed on foot back to the Parker house. Hoping somehow, even in the dark, to clean up the tracks he'd left. He carried the flashlight in his pocket, but when he got there he was afraid someone would see a light moving around the yard or reflecting up from the pool. Consequently, he couldn't see what to clean up; if he tried, he'd only make a mess of it. He'd have to come back in the morning, the minute it started to get light.

Before leaving the Parkers' yard he removed the tennis shoes so as not to leave a muddy trail, dropped them in the plastic bag he'd stuffed in his pocket. He walked home in his stocking feet, bruising his heel on a pebble, thinking about the people on his block, about their routines on Sunday mornings.

Two couples slept in, late. Two men he knew casually would probably play an early round of golf. But what did their wives do? He'd never thought to ask, never paid attention. Did those women garden on Sunday mornings? Leave the house to go to church? Or sit idly drinking coffee, looking out the windows? *She'd* know what they did, that was part of her job, to know about the neighbors. And now she could tell him nothing.

Walking home, he saw no one. He heard two cats yowling somewhere down the street, sending chills up his spine. Everyone on the damned block seemed to have cats. If he'd known that when they bought the place, he might have thought better of moving where it wasn't easy to conceal his disgust—but he had no choice, he needed to be liked and to be accepted, that was part of their program.

At home, he cleaned up the tennis shoes in the kitchen sink, left them drying by the back door. He sat in the kitchen for over an hour drinking cold coffee from the morning and wishing he still smoked, to calm his nerves. He thought about going over to the all-night grocery east of the village and getting a pack, take the other car, but he didn't feel like going anywhere. Around three in the morning he went into the bedroom, lay down on the bed, and pulled the spread up over himself—but then he could smell her sweet scent, and he ended up moving into the guest room, jerking the comforter up over his legs.

He woke, startled, 5:45 by the red numbers on the clock. It was light out. Rising quickly, he splashed water on his face, pulled on the same jeans he'd worn the night before, found some dry shoes, and an old pair of gloves. Walking back to the Parker house, he eyed each quiet, sleeping home he passed. The sun would soon be up, and his neighbors would be waking.

He didn't think, until he was walking up the drive, that the water might have been cut off, considering that the house had been empty for nearly six months. Hurrying back to the reeled hose at the edge of the bushes near the pool, he tried the faucet and breathed easier. The water was on and had good pressure. Unreeling the hose, dragging its length to the far end of the pool, he looked down to where she'd died.

Even in the early light, the drag marks were sharp and clear, broken by the line of his footprints. Ducking down to the height of the bushes so as not to be noticed from next door or from the street, he crouched at the edge of the coping, hosing down the pool, sluicing the sides and bottom with a strong, condensed stream, sending the mud into new configurations until he was sure he'd destroyed every drag mark and footprint.

When he was satisfied with the looks of the pool and steps, he hosed the drive up to where he'd loaded her body, where the muddy trail stopped. As he worked, he kept seeing her body stuffed into the trunk of the car. The morning brightened but then dimmed again as a spread of clouds began to creep across the rising sun. He didn't hose clear to the street. The next-door neighbors' drapes were still closed but he worried that someone would come out later to get the paper, would glance over and see the driveway wet. He stopped well back, where the water might not be noticed.

If those clouds did mean rain, that would solve the problem just fine, it wouldn't take much to wet the rest of the drive. This time of year the weather was erratic, so maybe, for once, luck was with him. Winding the hose back on the reel, his hands were cold in the soaked gloves. The wet tennis shoes had turned his feet cold, too. He had brought some rags, with which he wiped the shoes down, pressing the threadbare towels against the wet canvas to soak up water, to keep from leaving footprints on the way home. Departing the Parker house, on the back street, he decided maybe a real walk would help his breathing and clear his head—give him time to decide on a story if some neighbor saw that they were still here. He did maybe a mile along the side streets, a swinging walk that let him breathe easier and that set his heart beating with more strength.

Circling back at last to his own street, he knew he had to eat, though he didn't feel like it. He went in the house through the side door, tied the wet shoes and gloves and wet jeans in a plastic bag and got dry ones. He was frying a couple of eggs when, glancing out the kitchen window, he saw a car pass, heading slowly downhill toward the Parker place, and he did a double take.

He thought he knew the driver. A square-faced woman with dark, short hair, wearing a dark jacket. She slowed as a kid on a bike passed her, then moved on, but he got a good enough look to be sure.

Molena Point PD had only a few women, and this one was a detective. What the hell would she be doing here, and at this time in the morning? He flipped his scorched eggs onto the plate, feeling cold. This had to be a coincidence, she was just passing. But, turning off the burner, he went out the back and headed for the Parker house.

A block before he reached it he crossed to the opposite side of the street, and three doors above the Parker place, at a neat white Cape Cod, he moved deep into shelter behind a toyon tree covered with red berries. Behind him, the Cape Cod's windows were shuttered, and there was no sound from within.

Had some busy neighbor seen him in the Parkers' yard, and called the police? The detective parked across the street, just beyond where he was concealed. She got out, stood looking up and down the street at each house, at each yard. She was squarely built, probably in her fifties, her dark uniform severe. Black stockings, regulation black shoes. She crossed to the Parker yard, again stood looking. When she headed on back, toward the swimming pool, his stomach lurched. When she stopped, staring down at the wet drive—wet only half the way—he felt sick.

She stood looking down at his wet tracks, then moved away to examine the neatly wound, wet hose. He watched her take a camera from the bag she carried and photograph the wet drive. What the hell *was* this, what had brought her here? He looked around at the neighbors' houses, but no one had appeared, no one stepped out on a porch as if to come and speak to her.

When she moved down the drive to the pool, he could hardly breathe. He had to shift position in order to see her where she'd paused on the coping, then he backed away, sweating—that was when he saw a cat on the roof of the next house. A big gray cat stood at the edge of the shingles, staring down as if it, too, was watching the woman. The appearance of another cat, after the one that ran across his path, generated a wave of fear almost like a premonition.

When the detective turned, as if to head back to her car, he didn't wait. He slid away out of sight between the two houses, kept moving between houses down to the lower street where he hurried back toward home.

Entering his street two blocks above the Parker place, he heard a power mower start, and he saw the guy up at the corner, at the blue house, beginning to mow his lawn. Pretty damn early to be mowing the lawn on Sunday. When he looked back down the hill to the Parker place, the cop's car was still there. From this angle he couldn't see the detective, didn't know what she was doing, but the cat was still there on the roof. He knew it was silly and childish but he didn't like the sight of that cat peering down at the place where all his troubles had begun. It was not a good sign to see a cat there.

He'd finally gotten used to *her* succession of cats, so he didn't act so shaky around them. She'd had several dogs but he never paid them any attention. It was when he was near the cats that he had to be careful and act natural.

When he was a boy, he hadn't played much with other kids, he'd been a loner, a reader. He read everything, but he liked science fiction best. He thought about his mother's old black cat that he'd hated, the way it would stare and stare at him while he wanted to be left alone to read, and the two things were related in his mind: Poe's story "The Black Cat" and his mother's cat. The more her cat watched him, the more he read Poe, read it over and over, sickly drawn to the story; and the more the fictional cat and the live cat ran together in his mind.

His mother never knew what happened to that cat. She said it got old, that it must have gotten sick and gone away to die. She said animals did that. Lucky for him that she'd come up with her own explanation about why it had vanished.

He'd thought she'd get no more cats, but then she came home with that pale kitten, that she'd loved and tended like a baby. Loved it more than she'd ever loved him. It was after he got rid of the kitten that his fear and disgust of cats began to get out of hand. It was then that his breathing got bad.

And then years later, when he got married, when they'd been married only a few months, *she* came home with a cat. She'd had a dog then, and he'd never imagined she'd get a cat, too. When she came in carrying it, he thought she was going to shove the soft, furry thing right at him. When he backed away from the cat crouched in her cuddling hands, its yellow eyes had blazed like fire, straight up into his eyes.

How could she love such a thing?

She'd looked at him, shocked. He'd said she startled him, coming in with a cat. He'd said he was allergic to them, that he'd never told her. She'd looked so dismayed that he said he'd always been allergic, but only if he got close, only if he petted them, that otherwise they didn't bother him at all.

She'd kept the cat away from him, and he'd never let on how he hated it. He was good at that, that was what made them such a good team: He could be whatever the situation called for—on the outside.

Later he was glad he'd accepted the cat, the animal seemed to settle her down, to keep her from her nervous times. She'd had a succession of cats, and all these years he'd tolerated them, had grown skilled at acting natural around them, had never let her see how he detested them. But the cats always knew, her cats wouldn't go near him.

Now when he looked down the street again, the cat on the roof had disappeared. He went on around his house to the back, slipped in through the side door, and locked it. He threw the cold cooked eggs in the sink, ran the garbage disposal, put the dirty skillet in the dishwasher so as not to leave anything for the housekeeping people to wonder about. Snatching up her purse and bag from the front entry, he went through the house to the garage, shoved them in the backseat of the car. At the last minute he went back to the kitchen, got the bag of wet shoes and clothes, dropped it on the floor of the backseat.

He had to reconnect the automatic door opener so the housekeeping service wouldn't wonder about that either. That Harper woman ran a hands-on business, she was in and out of all the houses her people maintained, the nosy bitch. It would be just like her to try to open up the garage for some reason, maybe to vacuum out the cobwebs, and he sure didn't want the police chief's wife to start asking questions.

Hitting the remote, he winced as the door rumbled up then rumbled down again behind him. By now, some neighbor was sure to be up. What if they heard the door, and remembered it later? Well, it couldn't be helped, he thought nervously.

He meant to head up into the hills again where, in full daylight, it would be easier to find a place to bury her. But then, changing his mind, he went on up his street to the dead end, pulled off into the woods, and walked back down the lower road to see if the detective was still there, nosing around. He'd rest easier when she left, when he was sure she'd found nothing, then he'd head for the hills, find the right place. Lay low until it got dark and he could bury her. Then he could get on with their plan.

9

It was nearly noon when Charlie Harper locked her small SUV and let herself in the front door of the Chapman house. Pausing on the threshold, the tall redhead brushed a scattering of straw from her faded jeans, a remnant from some last-minute stable chores at home. She stood for a moment looking around the big, square living room, trying to see, in daylight, anything strange that she might have missed last night, among the Chapmans' usual clutter. The bright room was inviting, with its creamy crown molding and cheerful, flowered couch and chairs arranged around the pale stone fireplace. Deep bay windows flanked the front door, and at the back, long glass sliders faced the deck—complete with pry marks, now, on the outside molding. Of all the houses that Charlie's Fix-it, Clean-it cared for, the

homes on this street seemed to her particularly wel-
coming. Maybe, she thought, amused, that was because
they all had resident cats to greet a friend or visitor.

She didn't do the cleaning for her company any
longer, but she still saw to her clients' special needs and
she always enjoyed caring for their pets while they were
gone on business or vacation. Shrugging off her jacket,
she wanted to head straight through to the laundry
to make sure that Mango was inside and that she and
her kittens were all right. Instead she stood listening,
alert for the tiniest sound from the kitchen or from the
rooms down the hall. The fact that Mango had gotten
out continued to worry her. She knew that her crew
hadn't been in the house since the Chapmans left last
night, and even if they had, they were all totally reliable. Most of her fifteen crew members weren't just
employees, they were her friends whom she trusted to
be responsible.

The silence in the house was complete, not as if
someone waited unseen, but with a sense of emptiness
that convinced her she was alone. But still, as she turned
from the entry to walk through the bright rooms, she
carried a small canister of pepper spray concealed in
her palm.

She saw nothing out of place. Theresa's clutter looked
pretty much as it had last night, rumpled bedspread

dragging on the floor at one corner and the pillows scattered across it, clothes piled on a chair, spilling to the floor. She checked the guest room, which looked a little better, checked the window locks, found them all secure.

But the cat had gotten out somehow. Mango herself hadn't closed the laundry window behind her as she made her escape, sweet Mango was just an ordinary cat, not like Joe and Dulcie and Kit, who could have managed such a feat.

She had inspected the house carefully last night after the phone call that brought her down the hills to the village. Before entering she'd put on gloves in case something did come up missing and she'd need to call the department, though she didn't want to do that. She'd examined the scars on the glass door sliding mechanism, examined the closed laundry-room window, noted the crumbs and glass rings on the kitchen table. There was always plenty at the Chapmans' for her girls to clean up, she'd thought, smiling. After she'd been through the house last night, she'd called her crew, had told them not to clean there until she notified them.

In case there *had* been a break-in, with items missing that she didn't realize among the clutter, her reputation, but more important, Max's reputation and that of Molena Point PD, were at stake. If one of her residential charges was burglarized, the few anticop types among the citizens of Molena Point would be thrilled, would be busy at once using the newspaper and word of mouth to smear the department, to put the law in as bad a light as their creative zeal could invent.

She wouldn't let that happen, she thought stubbornly. But she'd be glad when she sold the business and put an end to the worry—she'd built her cleaning and repair business from nothing and she was proud of what she'd made, but not proud enough to keep on with it at Max's expense.

She'd started with just enough money to buy an ancient RV, some used tools, and the bare essentials of cleaning equipment. Now, three years later, the service was so busy that often, when she couldn't get additional, reliable employees, she had to turn away prospective new customers. After a couple of failed jobs earlier in her life, the experience of building the business had made her feel strong and independent for the first time, had assured her that, even after the false starts, she was capable of constructing a solid venue with which to support herself. So it wasn't easy, now, to put her successful baby on the market.

But the stress was getting to her. She always felt on guard, she was always aware of something possibly going awry that could put Max and the department in a bad light—and, too, now that she was finally doing the kind of artwork she'd always longed to do, and had discovered the joy of writing and illustrating her own books, as well, she hungered for more unbroken time.

She had just signed a new book contract, she needed time for that work, and Charlie's Fix-it, Clean-it had morphed from a milestone of personal triumph to what she had begun to think of as a millstone weighing her down.

Never happy, she thought wryly. *But we do change, that's what life's about, to grow and learn. That's what we're here for.*

Moving through the kitchen to the laundry, she breathed easier when she saw Mango snuggled down in the box with her kittens. Kneeling to pet the little family, she puzzled again over why anyone would jimmy the glass door and apparently break in and yet, as far as she could see, would take nothing.

She looked around the laundry half expecting to have to clean up mouse blood or whatever might remain after Joe Grey had brought his promised gift to Mango. Scraping up mouse guts wasn't a job she relished, but she didn't see a sign of any leftovers. She didn't remember the dishpan being on the floor by the cat box. She picked it up and set it back on the counter, then fetched a flashlight from the laundry shelf and, kneeling again, sent a beam of light under the washer and dryer, hoping not to see a small dead body where an injured mouse had escaped. She'd at least prefer little beady eyes peering out.

Happily, the space beneath the machines was empty. If indeed Joe had brought a gift, Mango had cleaned it up nicely. She'd brought Mango an apricot this morning, which Theresa had told her the funny little cat loved. Theresa doted on her cats.

Charlie was fond of Theresa. Despite her tendency to make up harmless stories, to change facts on the spur of the moment—Charlie didn't like to call it lying— she was a gentle, sweet-tempered young woman most of the time. Unless something sent her into one of her upsets, which could put her almost out of control. In some ways, dark-haired Theresa Chapman had plenty of self-confidence; she did as she pleased and didn't let Carl run her. Yet in other ways, at other times, she showed no confidence at all; she would back off submissively from Carl and allow him to bully her.

Mango, as she left her box to eat the apricot, glanced uneasily at the closed kitchen door. Charlie watched her, petting the kittens and listening again to the house. She knew it was empty—but Mango would be nervous if someone had gotten in last night; she wouldn't know they weren't still there. Charlie was just glad that she and her kits were all right, that no one had harmed them. Two of the kits were yellow, two brown tabby, and one a deep rust as red as Charlie's own hair. Leaning over, she laid a lock of her long hair down across the kitten, who happily snatched at it. The reds matched perfectly, and she thought that would amuse Theresa.

Last night when she'd examined the pry marks on the outside molding, she'd tried to call the Chapmans, thinking that maybe Theresa had locked herself out at some point, and had had to get in that way, that that would explain the damage.

There'd been no answer, and she'd tried again this morning. The trouble with vacationers, they left their cell phones in their hotel rooms, didn't want to be bothered. They figured they'd return their messages later, and then forgot or didn't want the interruption from their carefree days. Maybe they'd gotten her messages and thought the scratched door wasn't serious enough to bother about, as long as the cats were all right. In her message, she had assured them of that. She had no other number to try, no name of any hotel. Theresa said she wasn't sure, herself, which little towns they would be staying in, that they meant to head up the coast for a few days, that after that Carl had grand plans. All pretty vague, Charlie thought, smiling. Theresa had confided in her that the two had had their troubles, so maybe an unstructured vacation was intended to be low key and healing.

Because Charlie had found Mango safe inside again, thanks to Joe and Dulcie, she hadn't included that near disaster in her messages to the Chapmans; that would make Theresa frantic. She didn't like keeping things from her clients but in this case she'd thought it best. Of the four families who were presently on vacation, all four owned cats, but Theresa was by far the most obsessive about her pets' welfare.

When Charlie had first inspected the damaged door, she'd been concerned about Theresa's collection of lovely miniature paintings, but they all seemed accounted for. They were all in place this morning, the miniatures, mostly landscapes with a few figure studies, hung close together in multiple rows, covering two dining room walls, light from the big bay window washing over their jewel-like colors. There were no spaces where paintings were missing, and she'd found no change in spacing, where they might have been rearranged. Certainly the most valuable ones were there, the two dozen best-known artists whose work was distinctive. The paintings were dear to Theresa, she would immerse herself in them, as one would get lost in a piece of music, and Charlie understood that.

Charlie tried not to have favorites among her clients, but was that really possible? Theresa was a favorite of the whole neighborhood because of her sunny disposition and, in part, because she was so vulnerable. A slim, tanned, willowy young woman in her midthirties, Theresa had no notion of how beautiful she was. Her dark brown hair, brown eyes, her long face with her rosy, prominent cheeks made a striking combination—though Theresa wouldn't hear of it. She said her "chubby" cheeks made her look like a chipmunk, and no one could tell her any different. She was not only lovely, but bright and cheerful—except that with any small disaster, particularly one that involved an animal, she would weep. Theresa's tears came easily, as did her sense of betrayal, and her resulting temper. If Theresa thought a friend had crossed her, her bitterness was cold and complete.

The four families, because of their schedules, were vacationing at about the same time of year. Eleen Longley of course went on vacation the minute school was out, the minute her students vanished from her life for a few serene months. She and Earl usually took a two- or three-week driving trip. He, being an architect, could pretty much plan his trips around hers. Eleen was a small, dark-haired young woman, bright and lively, with a natural charm that drew people to her—

more lively and determined perhaps than Earl could easily handle. Charlie had seen her stubborn moods, and some would call her hardheaded. But Charlie liked her; she'd seen the gentle side of Eleen, with her cats and with the neighbors' small children.

The Watermans' vacation trip was usually on their anniversary. That was the one cruise a year where blond, willowy Rita Waterman didn't work as a tour guide. This year, though, they hadn't booked a cruise. The last time Charlie had seen Rita, they were thinking of spending their first week in San Francisco, and were debating whether to book a last-minute flight to Greece or to the Antilles. Wherever they were, Charlie could reach them by cell phone if the need arose. She imagined Rita on the white beaches of some exotic island, showing off her tan, swimming in the warm Caribbean waters or that of the Greek islands. For a moment, she let herself imagine living that glamorous life, she and Max being waited on by stewards bearing exotic drinks and delicious tidbits—even if for only a few weeks. To see Max have a rest would be worth a lot. And the chance to see new parts of the world attracted her, the beautiful blue waters, a chance to touch a bit of the past among Greece's crumbling ruins.

But the downside of a cruise, the busy social milieu, too many people and too much meaningless conversation, didn't appeal to her, and would drive Max crazy. If she were offered the trade, she'd turn that down in a New York minute and stick to their own quiet joys, with their friends, with the horses and their other animals, in their small village.

But that glamorous life suited Rita Waterman very well; she seemed truly to enjoy the busy life. Rita was a jewelry buff; she dressed in simple, well-cut clothes that showed off various pieces of her striking collection of antique costume jewelry that came from all over the world. With her statuesque beauty and cool manners, Rita seemed always reined in, always in charge of herself. But underneath, Charlie knew, she was as vulnerable as anyone else. Charlie, when she'd first started cleaning their house and had still done much of the physical work, overheard some of their arguments, some real explosions of temper and tears from Rita.

She was certain those digressions didn't occur in public. Rita's husband, Ben, had some medical problems, which he seemed to manage well. Maybe that was why he didn't join her on her tours. He stayed home, "batching" and, apparently reluctantly, feeding whatever cats Rita had at the moment. The couple was a ripe source of neighborhood gossip, as their friends wondered about Rita's glamorous journeys alone, far from home and husband. Though certainly when she was home they had a busy social life, season tickets to concerts and plays, and they were involved in various charity functions, as well as casual dinners with their neighbors.

Charlie was amused by her own sudden interest in her clients' personal lives. A year ago, she couldn't have cared less. Only since she'd developed an interest in writing fiction had other people's lives begun to fascinate her. With one illustrated "book for all ages" in the stores and another in the works, she'd suddenly found the intricacies of other people's lives piquing her curiosity to the point where she was considering an adult novel. Turning gossip to gold, she thought, amused.

Though most of the gossip on this street was about Ed Becker, who was the handsomest man among the four couples, strikingly tall and lean with well-styled black hair and laughing brown eyes. It was hard not to like Ed, he was so boyishly charming and made such an effort to get you to like him. Max said he was a charming sociopath, and usually Max was right. But this time? She wondered idly if the stories about Ed were true. And if they were, did Frances suspect his deceptions? Or was she as innocent as she appeared?

What a waste, if Ed was a womanizer, when he had such an appealing wife. And if Frances knew about his affairs, why did she stay with him? She was just as attractive as Ed, though far quieter, seeming almost shy. They made a striking couple, Francis nearly as tall as Ed, slim and tanned, with long, dark hair and brown eyes. She was an accountant, so they took their vacation when she'd finished tax season and filed her extensions. Strange, Charlie thought, that if Ed had been intimate with any of the other three women, the four couples were still friends, having dinner together, going on outings that they all seemed to enjoy with one another.

Charlie's crews had been scheduled to come in today to clean the Chapmans' refrigerator, to empty the dishwasher, change the linens, do the laundry and the regular cleaning and attend to the list of small repairs that Theresa had given them. Mavity had started working in the other three houses a day or two ago, once the other couples had left. And that, too, was strange.

Little wizened Mavity Flowers, who had worked for Charlie since she began the service, had told her that in all three houses, a number of small items seemed to be missing, an extra camera, a laptop, a tape recorder. Things they thought the householders had probably taken with them. Mavity hadn't found any indication of a break-in, and everything else was in order: Frances Becker's lovely antiques all in place, the Longleys' first editions and paperweight collection on their shelves behind locked doors, and Rita Waterman's jewelry cabinet securely locked.

Giving Mango a last ear rub, Charlie left the laundry room, closing the kitchen door behind her. Letting herself out the front door, she hurried up the street. The neighborhood was quiet. A couple of Sunday papers still lay in the front yards. She could smell bacon frying, as if for a late Sunday breakfast. The pine and cypress trees among the houses on the downhill side cast short, sharp shadows among the scattered rhododendron bushes. The sun was warm on her back, the rain vanished.

The moment she let herself into the Waterman house, the three Waterman cats came in from outside through their cat door, to rub against her ankles as if feeling ignored or neglected.

"You already lonely?" She knelt and spent some time petting and talking to them, then she went through the house. Entering Rita's closet, knowing where Rita kept her jewelry cabinet key, she pulled on the cotton gloves to retrieve it, wanting to make sure that, though it was locked, the pieces were safe inside.

The key wasn't where it should be. She fished around until she found it where Rita had apparently moved it, and she opened the wall case.

All was in place, the ornate pendants and chokers with their faux jewels as rich and brilliant as any collection of multimillion-dollar pieces. It was interesting to Charlie that in the seventeenth and eighteenth centuries, paste gems were often used in the most intricate gold and silver settings. That once the technique for making faux gems was developed, a whole new market was created for beautiful but affordable jewelry. Now, the settings themselves were collectors' items though they were of more modest value than if they had contained real gems. These were the pieces that Rita collected, and among them were some that Charlie had specially admired, particularly one coral hair clip and an emerald pendant. She was tempted to try them on, but she didn't take that liberty. If she wanted to spend royalty money on such a piece, fine, but she wasn't messing with Rita's treasures. Locking the cabinet, she replaced the key where she'd found it.

She found nothing amiss in the other rooms, or in the other two houses. The Longley book cabinets were locked, and at the Beckers', Frances's antique furniture was all in place. She was thinking hungrily of lunch as she let herself out of the Becker house and locked the door. She was heading for her car when Clyde's yellow roadster came up the street and pulled to the curb beside her. The top was down, Clyde and Ryan in the front seat, Joe Grey in the back. She did a double take at all three: Clyde looked angry and distraught, Ryan was trying to hide her amusement, and in the backseat, Joe Grey looked wide eyed and innocent—a sure sign of trouble.

10

Stepping closer to the open roadster, Charlie was afraid to ask what was wrong. Clyde's frown was of the helpless variety, which told her that whatever it was, Joe Grey was the cause. She studied Joe. In the backseat, the tomcat sat with his white paws together, his silver coat catching the sunlight, his yellow eyes as guileless as those of a kitten.

She looked at Ryan, whose eyes, complemented by her green sweatshirt, seemed greener than ever. Ryan shrugged, her expression both amazed and amused as she watched some unspoken conflict between Clyde and the tomcat.

Charlie could understand how she felt, this was all new to Ryan. She hadn't known for very long about Joe's unusual talents. Only shortly before Christmas had she learned that the tomcat could speak to her; that revelation had unfolded on a memorable Christmas morning that neither Ryan nor Clyde nor Joe Grey would forget. Clyde's subsequent marriage proposal had added to the general giddiness of their Yule celebration, and even now, after four months in the Damen household, Ryan still hadn't settled in completely to this strange new lifestyle that was so often dominated by the smart-mouthed tomcat.

Charlie searched the couple's faces. "What's wrong, what's happened?"

Both were silent.

When she looked again at Joe Grey, the tomcat yawned.

"You haven't been by the Parker house?" Clyde said.

"No, I came up the lower street."

"Max didn't say anything about it this morning before he left? But maybe he didn't know." Clyde turned to stare pointedly at Joe. "This time, we have a disappearing body. We have a supposed murder, but there's no corpse."

They all three looked at Joe. The tomcat said nothing, his yellow eyes wide and innocent.

Ryan said, "Davis worked the scene this morning, she and Dallas are still there, stringing crime tape.

We'd wanted to take a look at the house, I'd hoped it might be for sale, it's been empty so long. I thought maybe, depending on what they found, they'd let us take a peek—but you know those two. They weren't letting us in with it cordoned off."

"Then you *are* looking for a fixer-upper," Charlie said. She daren't look at Joe, the tomcat shared fully her amusement at Clyde's pitiful carpentry skills. She knew that Ryan was convinced Clyde could convert his magic touch with cars into an equally impressive skill with houses. Ryan had said they'd make a great team, but Charlie wondered if that was just the dream of a new bride.

"We've looked at five open houses already today," Ryan said, "and we have a late appointment with Helen Thurwell to show us some others. Right now, we're on our way up to look at the Baldwin Ranch. It's been vacant nearly a year, and it *is* listed. And I want to swing by the remodel, see how the men are coming on the drain."

"They're working on Sunday?"

Ryan nodded. "It's like a circus on the weekend. The neighbors keep coming around asking what we're doing. Digging a bomb shelter? Putting a swimming pool in the garage? We lock the garage at night to keep kids and animals from getting down in there."

The four-bedroom house Ryan was renovating was charming, but the client, who had owned it less than a year, had discovered during last winter's rains that the finished downstairs rooms had, in fact, turned into a swimming pool, the house having major water problems left undisclosed in the "as is" sales contract.

Checking the drainage system, Ryan had found heavy leaks under the garage and into the basement, generated by a hidden spring uphill from the house, a flow that she didn't think even the usual French drains could fully handle. She'd decided to put in a bold new drainage system under the garage. As they couldn't get a backhoe under the roof, her men were digging by hand, working on Sunday by special permission of the building department.

Ryan said, "Did you check on the kittens? Who let the mama out?"

"Not a clue," Charlie said. "Joe and Dulcie . . ." She paused, watching the tomcat. "What? What is it?"

In the backseat, Joe Grey had reared up, his paws on the open window sill as he stared down the hill into the neighbors' wooded yards. Glancing quickly at Charlie, he shook his head almost imperceptibly, his voice silenced, the look in his yellow eyes wary. They all looked where Joe was looking but saw nothing unusual.

Dropping down onto the seat again, the tomcat spoke softly. "Someone was standing halfway down the hill under that big cypress tree, looking up at us. He's gone now but I'll just have a look . . ." Before Clyde could reach over and grab him he'd leaped out, was across the yard and up the nearest pine. Scrambling toward the top, he appeared and disappeared among the dark branches, then vanished into the highest, thickest foliage.

Joe peered down from the top of the tree, clinging to a frail and precarious branch, his paws sticky with pine sap, the prickly limbs tickling his ears. Scanning the yards below, he could see no one now standing among the bushes, and not the faintest movement of shadows. Off beyond the village, a stretch of sea danced with reflections of light like tiny signal fires.

The lower street was empty, too, and when he looked back along their own street, scanning the two blocks to the Parker house, he could see no car there; Detectives Davis and Garza must have left. He felt gratified that Davis had put enough credence in his anonymous call to not only work the scene herself but to bring Dallas Garza back for an even more thorough look. Along the sidewalk and around the ragged bushes ran a line of bright yellow crime scene tape. It circled the house and pool in an enticing invitation to nosy neighbors and small children. Just below him, all three were scanning the lower yards. Ryan had taken a pair of binoculars from the glove compartment. Joe thought she'd search with those, but instead she looked straight up the pine tree, fixing her sights on him.

To Ryan, even with the binoculars the gray tomcat was just a shadow among the concealing branches. Only the white smears of his belly and nose and paws were clear, where he hung over a branch peering down to the lower street. When she turned the glasses downward to look where he was looking, she still could see no one. She glanced at Charlie, but Charlie shrugged and shook her head. Beside her, Clyde started the car. She reached over, turned off the engine. "You weren't going to wait for him?"

Clyde sighed, and settled down to wait for the tomcat, watching the wooded yards below. Nothing stirred below, no movement but the shiver of breeze through the trees and bushes. No car was visible on either street. High above them the tomcat shifted position. What had he seen? *Had* there been someone watching, or only a passing neighbor?

"He saw something he didn't like," Charlie said. "I've never known him to be wrong."

"You don't live with him twenty-four seven," Clyde told her.

"He isn't stuck up there?" Ryan said. "You sure he can get down?"

Clyde laughed. "Wouldn't that be a trip, if Joe panicked, forgot how to back down a tree and started yowling like a scared kitten. If we don't get a move on, we'll miss our appointment. Helen Thurwell doesn't—"

"Wait," Ryan said. "Listen."

A car had started on the lower street, a quiet engine. In a moment they saw a flash of white go by. Clyde reached to turn the key, but Ryan was quicker. "You won't get far, tailing a guy in a bright yellow car!" She was out of the car before he could stop her, running downhill, racing away, cutting through the woods as the white car was slowed by the sharp curves. As Charlie ran for her Blazer, Clyde started the roadster's smooth-purring engine and moved uphill to the next cross street where he could turn back onto the lower road. Charlie watched him, then peered up at Joe Grey, some forty feet above. She didn't intend to leave him. It was Joe who'd spotted the eavesdropper; it was Joe who'd uncovered what could be a murder scene. It would be cruel to leave him behind—to say nothing of the tongue-lashing they'd receive later. "Come on," she hissed, digging her keys from her pocket. "Hurry up!"

11

A slab of bark flipped off the tree as Joe backed down. He nearly lost his grip and went slithering down as clumsy as a drunken squirrel. He hit the ground running, leaped into Charlie's SUV through the open driver's door, jumped across her, and landed on the seat. He looked up at her smugly, as if he'd planned that acrobatic descent. She hid a grin, gunned the engine, and took off.

From the top of the tree he had watched Ryan running down the lower road, chasing the white car, had glimpsed flashes of white among the foliage as it slipped away to disappear beyond the pines. Ryan was making good time. Straining to see, he'd glimpsed the car turning left at Ocean, up toward Highway 1. By then, he could no longer see Ryan but he could hear the faint echo of her racing footsteps. A startled crow screamed, a harsh and affronted cry as she passed beneath him. Behind her, Clyde's yellow roadster flashed into view, racing to catch up with her and stay on the guy's tail.

Now, Charlie made the same U-turn, heading down the hill. "Did you see him turn? Did you see which way?"

"Left, toward the freeway," Joe said. "I hope it was the same white car." He looked over at her, frowning. "What good is this? A red SUV and a bright yellow roadster. About as subtle a tail as a dozen black-and-whites with their sirens blasting." He tried to recall what he'd seen of the man, to bring back the hastily glimpsed details of that dark-clad figure standing in the bushes halfway down the hill. He'd seen him for only an instant before the guy turned suddenly and moved away, to vanish like a shadow among the lower houses. A thin man in a dark green windbreaker and dark jeans. And a hat? Yes, a brown slouch hat pulled low over his face, hiding it from Joe's high vantage point among the branches.

He'd appeared again for an instant, just above the lower street, slipping fast through a side yard. He hadn't seen the man's face, and from that height, he'd caught no scent of him. If that guy was the killer, he wouldn't know him from Adam, he'd recognize only the clothes. So what kind of undercover cat was he?

He thought the car was a four-door. It was fairly new, he had the impression of smooth, expensive curves. He'd gotten only a glimpse before the trees hid it. A few flashes of white and an occasional flash of red taillights as it braked at the curves and then as it turned, and it was gone.

Could the guy have followed Clyde's roadster up the hill from the Parker house? But why? Unless he was the killer and had been down there spying on the two detectives? Who but the killer of the vanished body would have reason to be watching Dallas and Juana?

And how had he been clever enough to spy on a pair of cops and not be seen? If those two had seen him down there, they'd have collared him, questioned him, gotten his name, run his driver's license if he had one. And why would he follow Clyde and Ryan after they'd stopped to talk with the detectives?

Joe recast the conversation at the Parker house, as he'd crouched in the backseat of the roadster trying to look sleepy and clueless. Davis had mentioned the samples she'd sent to the lab to see if they were human blood. The two detectives and Ryan and Clyde had talked about the neighborhood, about who lived on that street. Dallas said there was only one guy he knew of with an arrest sheet, and that was for a white-collar crime, a sleazy embezzlement.

Any of that might be of interest to the killer. But what, exactly, had made him slip up the hill to stand among the bushes where, in the silent neighborhood, he must have heard every word they said. Joe tried to remember if, at the Parker house before Dallas and Juana came over to the car, *he* had spoken. Could the guy have heard *him* talking? The thought made the skin along his back twitch and his fur bristle.

He couldn't remember saying a word. And later, up the hill, when Charlie, Clyde, and Ryan had talked about house hunting, about looking at an empty ranch and about checking Ryan's current remodel to see if the drain had been dug, Joe was sure he hadn't spoken.

Except . . . Clyde had said, *You haven't been by the Parker house?* And he had turned to stare at Joe. *This time, we have a disappearing body. We have a supposed murder. But there's no corpse.* And his look at Joe had been so pointed and angry that Charlie had looked into the backseat, too, fixing an intent gaze on one gray tomcat.

Well, hell, Joe thought. To the eavesdropper that would be no more than idle conversation. What could possibly lead him to imagine that they were talking to a cat, or that the cat understood them?

Still, the incident made him nervous, made him wish his human friends would be more careful. His paws on the dashboard, he looked ahead as Charlie caught up with the roadster at the intersection of Ocean where Clyde had stopped for a tangle of slow-moving pedestrians.

As Charlie pulled over behind him, Ryan caught up with the Blazer, and stood talking through the passenger window. "I lost him, way back. I think it was a Lexus. There was mud smeared on the plate." She glanced up toward the highway. "He turned left into half a dozen cars, four of them white, all heading up the hill. A UPS truck pulled in behind them, blocking my view, but three white cars turned left onto the freeway."

"You want to try to follow him?" Charlie asked. "With no more of a description than—"

"Green windbreaker," Joe interrupted. "Dark jeans. Brown slouch hat. I couldn't see his face."

"We'll take the north route," Ryan said and headed for the roadster.

Charlie followed them uphill toward the freeway, armed with enough information that, with luck and a prayer, they might be able to spot the guy. They turned left and she turned right, heading south.

Moving slowly in the heavy noon traffic, Charlie and Joe couldn't pass on the two-lane highway, the lane in the other direction being wall-to-wall cars. Couldn't catch up with the three white cars they could glimpse far ahead of them down the steep hill. At the turn-off to the little shopping plaza, two of the cars made the left and one kept moving south. Charlie glanced at Joe.

"Go for the plaza," Joe said, watching both cars turn into the shopping area. He lifted a paw nervously, willing the truck ahead of the Blazer to turn before the light changed to red again.

They didn't make it, the truck turned as the signal went red. By the time Charlie pulled into the parking lot, both white cars had vanished. She paused, scanning the rows of vehicles.

"Put your windows down," Joe said as he slipped up onto the dash.

She hit the buttons to lower the windows, and began to drive slowly up and down the rows. Crouched on the dash, Joe examined each white car they passed, sniffing the air for fresh exhaust. There were white cars in every row. He sniffed each and peered inside, studying the few drivers who were getting in or out, or who sat listening to music or talk radio, waiting for some more energetic partner to return loaded with parcels and grocery bags. A white-haired woman dozed in a white Buick. A long-haired blonde in a Ford coupe glanced around at them, and turned out to be a man. Watching for a guy in a green windbreaker, Joe thought about Ryan and Clyde heading north on the four-lane, wondering if they'd have better luck.

They covered the parking lot at a tedious crawl, then Charlie pulled into an empty slot in front of the drugstore. Cuddling Joe under her arm like a little lapdog, she headed inside to walk the aisles.

They saw no man even close to Joe's description, and their search didn't last long once people noticed him. "Oh, look at the kitty!" "Mama, that woman has a cat!" "You take your cat shopping with you? How cute." Soon Joe's claws were out, ready to bloody the next reaching hand that tried to stroke him. He could feel Charlie shaking with laughter as they returned to the parking lot.

"Let's walk it once," Joe said. "Behind the cars." She did that, and Joe sniffed at each trunk seeking the scent of swimming-pool mud or the stink of a dead body. He smelled dust; dirty clothes, as from someone's laundry on the way to the Laundromat; and bananas and various other food items from recently stashed grocery bags. But no residue of a ripening body.

"Wild-goose chase," Charlie said as she stepped back into the Blazer and dropped Joe on the seat. As she started the engine, a stout woman in the next car looked in and smiled, as if pleased to see someone talking to her cat. She pulled away, still smiling.

Joe said, "Why would he follow Clyde and Ryan from the Parker house? What was so interesting?"

"Maybe he drove up there to watch me while I checked the empty houses."

Joe raised his ears. "You think that was your prowler? The guy who let Mango out? Then he had nothing to do with the murder at the Parker house."

"The cleaning crew found a few little things missing in the vacationers' houses. Or maybe they were only out of place. Not enough to be a burglary, but enough to make me wonder."

"Dulcie and Kit and I could have a look. There was a strange smell around the Parker house—besides the body. Almost like catnip, or catmint. If he's been in those houses . . ."

"Did you smell that in the Chapman house?"

He frowned. "No. But the smell of kittens and cat box, and cat food, can cover a lot of smells. That, and Theresa Chapman's lemon room freshener. Who knows what we'd find in the other houses."

She glanced over at him, wishing she hadn't brought it up, hadn't put the idea in his head. She wanted to tell him to be careful, but he hated that, hated to be coddled. "You want to call Ryan and Clyde, see if they had any luck on the freeway?"

CAT STRIKING BACK • 125

Joe punched in Clyde's number. The phone rang once, then went directly to voice mail.

"Doesn't have it on," he growled. Clyde made him crazy when he did that. He tried Ryan's cell.

"Flannery," she said on the first ring.

"We're headed back," Joe said. "Nothing."

"Ditto," Ryan said. "I called Dallas, gave him a description, told him the guy was watching us and maybe watching him and Juana. Anything else you remember, anything you want to add?"

"Nothing," Joe said, wishing he'd seen the guy's face.

"We're going on up to look at that vacant ranch," Ryan said, "then check the remodel, then meet Helen Thurwell to look at the other houses. She wasn't happy that we had to reschedule. You want to join us?" she said brightly. He could just see her smart-assed grin, knowing how he hated looking at houses.

"I'll pass on this one," he said. All those smells of strange humans and strange animals, of sour clothes and toxic cleaning solutions. Someone else's empty house wasn't *his* territory. If it had no connection to a crime scene, he wasn't interested in exploring.

"See you at home," she said, laughing at him. "Lupe's Playa for dinner, if we get back early?"

Joe licked his whiskers at the thought of a Mexican supper. As she rang off, he imagined the yellow roadster turning off the freeway, going through an underpass or over a bridge and taking an on-ramp south again, heading up in the hills above the village to resume their maniacal new obsession of house hunting.

What good was it, he thought, if Clyde stopped collecting old cars and grew equally involved with old decrepit houses? Both pursuits were, in Joe's opinion, the human's mindless and futile attempt to revive and save the known world.

As Charlie turned down Ocean toward the village, he started thinking again about Juana and Dallas, wondering why they hadn't made that guy when he'd been spying on them.

"What?" Charlie said, looking over at him as she slowed at a stop sign.

"How could they miss him? Down at the Parker place? And if they did see him, why didn't they arrest him or at least question him?" The more he thought about that, the more irritated he became. It was the first time he'd ever felt anger at a cop, certainly at either of those two.

"You don't have much faith in our detectives," she said, pulling away from the stop sign. "Maybe they didn't see him, with all the overgrown bushes and tall fences. Even the best officer might miss someone completely hidden, Joe. Maybe he slipped inside a house.

Maybe . . ." She was silent a moment, turning onto her aunt Wilma's street, then she reached to stroke his back. "Don't be cranky. That guy might have been just some nosy neighbor, we might have gotten all excited for nothing." She pulled to the curb in front of Wilma's cottage. "If that guy was the housebreaker—or was your killer—dispatch has his description. Maybe one of the units will pick him up."

Wilma Getz's stone cottage stood beneath spreading oaks, with not a bit of lawn in front. A deep, richly flowered garden spread away to the house. The roof was dark slate, slippery to the paws when wet with rain, warm as a stovetop beneath the summer sun. In the window of Wilma's living room, they could see Dulcie looking out, lashing her striped tail, and Joe brightened at the sight of his tabby lady. Her paw was lifted, her green eyes intent on him. Charlie watched them, and smiled. In spite of the human scum one encountered, one could always find honesty and truth among the animals—and find wonder. The world was an exciting place when you knew its secrets, when you could share in a feline miracle as real and amazing as a little speaking cat lifting her paw in greeting.

Stroking Joe and picking him up, Charlie got out of the Blazer and headed inside. In her arms, Joe wriggled with impatience, then leaped down, racing ahead to the cat door.

12

He sat in his car above the deserted ranch feeling shaky. Why had those people followed him? What did they know? What had they seen? But maybe they didn't know anything. How could they? Maybe they just hadn't liked him standing down there in the bushes watching them. Though it would take someone really paranoid to get mad about such a little thing, get mad enough to follow him. He might have just been down there pruning bushes or gardening. That was *his* neighborhood, what he did there was none of *their* business.

They couldn't have seen him earlier when they stopped to talk to those two detectives, he'd been too well hidden in the dense bushes between the houses, and with the corner of the house hiding him. But the house had blocked the cops' voices, too, so he hadn't heard much of what they'd said.

The cops had been doing *something* back by the pool, but hell, they couldn't know anything.

Unless someone had seen him, early this morning? He daren't think that someone saw him last night as he loaded her into the trunk. Maybe some neighbor *thought* they saw something, a shadow moving around, maybe glimpsed his car pulling in or out of the drive, but they couldn't have *seen* anything, really. It was too dark.

Sure as hell, some crazy suspicion wouldn't be enough to bring the cops. If someone *had* seen him and recognized him—everyone knew him in this neighborhood—the cops would have come straight to his house. Maybe someone saw a shadow or heard some little sound last night, maybe thought it was some homeless guy fooling around at the empty house, trying to get in. And this morning they'd woken up thinking about it and decided to call the law. Maybe that's what this was about, maybe he was worrying for nothing.

Except for the hose, he thought nervously. Except for the water halfway up the drive. That had drawn that detectives' attention.

But what could they make of that? It was just a hosed-down driveway.

No, whatever they might imagine, he'd done too good a job of cleaning up for them to find anything to worry him; he was just having an attack of nerves. Most likely the cops were out on some crank call, just looking around. Small, quiet village like this, maybe they had nothing better to do and he didn't need to fret.

But those people in the yellow roadster. Lucky he'd overheard them talking about looking at houses, heard where they were heading. They might help him out, big time, and never be aware of it.

Could you believe that damn woman *chased* him, on foot? Running down the road like a crazy? And then their car tailing him right onto the freeway? That kind of nosiness put him in a rage. He didn't deserve that kind of treatment.

But what did it matter? He'd heard enough, and he was still laughing because he'd been able to follow them so slickly. On the freeway he'd slipped away from the yellow roadster into a tangle of trucks, had cut over two lanes between trucks, cut back into the right lane again, and gone down the next off-ramp. And had swung around onto the rise above the freeway where he'd waited until he saw them pass below, moving fast in the middle lane. That roadster was the only yellow car on the road, top down, with the dark-haired woman. What a laugh, trying to tail him in that. When he saw them, he'd swung back down to the on-ramp and pulled onto the freeway behind them as they headed back south.

He'd followed them off the freeway, staying behind a delivery van. Had stuck with them as their car wound back among the Molena Point hills, sure that if he followed them long enough they'd lead him to exactly what he was looking for. Maybe the empty ranch they'd talked about, isolated and unoccupied. A barn, a hay barn, outbuildings . . . What more could he want? He could dig the grave in privacy, completely unobserved.

Following them along the narrow roads, he'd stayed well back, and then had taken a higher road that ran parallel, where he could look down on them. He'd watched with growing interest as they reached the empty ranch and pulled in. Not a soul in sight, no vehicle or farm animal, not even a stray chicken. He'd slowed, pulled the car behind some trees, thinking that once he was rid of the body, he'd take care of the original job the way they'd planned it. Maybe do it that very night. Change vehicles, follow the same routine just the way she would, and he'd be out of there and on his way.

Below him, the couple sat in their car looking down the steep hills as if assessing the nearby properties and small acreages. He could have waited and found this place himself from the way they'd described it, but that would have taken time. He'd have to go into the village,

get a copy of the local paper, check the real estate sec-
tion. That could take hours, and then he'd have to
drive these hills for hours more, scanning the roads
looking for the rural address of the deserted property.
He didn't have the patience, he wanted to get it over
with, and he was beginning to feel pushed. The sense
of her back there under the blanket was like she was
still alive, lying there watching him. And then the picture changed abruptly. Suddenly he saw not *her* back
there, he saw the cat crouched in her place, the pale cat
watching him, the cat his mother'd brought home when
he was a boy, the pale cat, its eyes ablaze with rage.

She'd brought home a half-grown kitten, all snuggled down in its blanket in a cardboard box, a kitten
she said would be his. He hadn't feared cats then, when
he was small, and he'd liked the kitten fine. It was soon
tagging around after him and begging at the table, and
it liked to sleep on his schoolbooks. It would come up
on his bed, too, to sleep with him at night, snuggling
up to him, purring.

But then it started sleeping with its face in his face,
pressing its nose against his nose. Snuggling up to his
face and to his warm breath. He hadn't liked that, he'd
push it away but it would come right back—come back
at him real fast, pressing against his face and nose, its
body shaking with purrs. That had frightened him,

that frenzied purring. He'd knock it off, knock it to the floor, but it would be right back again. If he shut it out of the room, it would claw at the door and yowl. His mother said to be nice to it, it was only a kitten and it loved him.

It might have loved him, but even after he shoved it off the bed over and over, it came back pressing against his nose, its body rocking with frantic purrs, demented, insane kind of purrs. He had no idea what was wrong with it and he didn't care, he just wanted to be rid of it. He didn't think or care that maybe it had been taken from its mother too soon or maybe was only trying to get warm. He just wanted it gone. He began to avoid it during the day. It was always there watching him but, because he'd knocked it away so many times, it wouldn't come near, would just back away, watching him. And still, no matter how angry he got and how he shoved it, every night it came onto his bed and pressed its nose to his nose, so he couldn't sleep. It was impossible to keep it out. His mother wouldn't put it outside the house at night. She said he was being silly, that the poor little cat loved him, and that it was dangerous to leave a cat out at night.

He grew more and more desperate and angry until, one cold night when the young cat was pressing hard at him, breathing from his face, he'd grabbed it off him, held it out away from him so it wouldn't scratch, and flung it as hard as he could at the bedroom wall.

It hit the wall hard and fell and lay still. He'd gotten out of bed and knelt there, immediately sorry for what he'd done. Its eyes were open, staring at him. He'd tried to feel it breathing but he couldn't. He couldn't feel its heart beating. It was still as stone. He'd crawled back in bed and lain there, cold and shivering.

When he woke in the morning the cat was still there, lying in the same position and growing stiff. He'd shoved it under the bed behind some boxes, and crept away to school. That afternoon when he came home, he told his mother he'd found it like that, that it must have died in the night, maybe died from some kind of seizure.

Long after his mother had buried the cat, he kept seeing it; he would see its eyes watching him. It was about that time that he began to read Edgar Allan Poe, and he became obsessed with "The Black Cat." It was that story, combined with what he'd done, that shaped for all time his sick disgust of the creatures.

After he married, he'd hidden his dark obsession from her for all their seventeen years. She liked cats, she brought cats home, and he, with hard resolve, had managed to tolerate them. Because he loved her. Because he wanted her to stay with him. Because he thought secretly that if he forced her to choose, if she knew the truth, she would turn away from him. That she would choose the cats.

In every other way, they were well suited. When they planned their jobs, they turned out to always be successful. When they celebrated afterward, she was bright and happy and loving, and life was perfect. Because of her cleverness and attention to detail, they always got away smoothly. In this, they were the perfect couple. It was only her preoccupation with the cats that unsettled him. Even her penchant for sunbathing was nothing, at first, was only an annoyance.

Who would imagine that was how it would end? With her stupid need to take off her clothes in public, to sunbathe in the raw.

Down the hill below him, the couple got out of the roadster and went off among the buildings. He was well hidden up here, he'd parked high above the place under a bushy eucalyptus tree where he'd never be seen. Taking a pair of binoculars from the glove compartment, he sat studying the empty barn and outbuildings, the empty corrals. The day was warming up. He thought sickly that the body would be ripening, and he felt a cold sweat start, across his chest and forehead.

He tried to take himself in hand, tried to breathe deeply, but he had to use the inhaler. When his breathing eased, he concentrated on the empty barn, thought about burying her in there, deep under the dirt floor. This old place could stand empty for years, the way the real estate market had fallen off. Might be decades before she was found, and maybe never. He wanted to get on with this, get it over with. The recurrent fear in his chest and belly made him hunch over the steering wheel. He told himself that her death wasn't his fault, that maybe it wasn't all her fault, that maybe it *was* an accident. Only an accident. And yet something within him knew that it was more than an accident that had made her fall.

What would have happened if he'd called the cops right away? *Told* them it was an accident? But when he imagined telling that to a cop, fear shook him. What cop would believe that, would believe she'd accidentally fallen, that he hadn't shoved her?

Anyway, it was too late now, he'd run away, and he'd moved the body.

Down the hill, the couple appeared from the out-buildings and walked around the outside of the empty house looking up at the windows, then standing still as if studying the structure. They knelt down to inspect the foundation, and the dark-haired woman dug into it with a screwdriver, then lay a level up against the sides of the house almost like she knew what she was doing. She was a good-looking broad, maybe thirty-something, dark brown bouncy hair, nice shape in those tight jeans.

He thought about the women he'd had while *she* was alive and she'd never guessed, never had a clue. She'd been good friends with some of them, and no hint of her knowing. And what harm? The others were simply challenges, the value in the taking and then moving on.

He saw that the couple had a key to the house. The front door creaked as the man pulled it open, and they disappeared inside. He sat studying the barn, wanting to look inside and see if there was a good place to dig. Thinking about moving the body, putting it down in the earth, her corpse seemed to loom larger as if she was pressing up at the lid wanting out, reaching out to him. *Had* he meant to push her? *Had* something inside him meant all along to kill her? Again her eyes seemed to be the cat's eyes, the eyes of that long-ago kitten watching him.

Below him the couple stood at the living room window, looking out and talking. They couldn't see him, way up at the top of the hill the eucalyptus branches hung nearly to the ground and his car was pulled in behind some discarded machine parts, too, and a tumble of slatted wooden crates that looked like they'd been rotting there for years. Soon they left the window, disappeared from his view.

They were gone maybe twenty minutes. Not knowing where they were, he began to grow edgy. He felt not only watched uncannily from the trunk but watched from the house. He wanted to get away from there, he didn't like the sense of being observed.

But if he pulled out now and drove off, they'd be sure to see him. And even driving away, he couldn't escape *her* presence.

They came out at last, locked the front door, walked around the outbuildings again, and then went back in the barn. A laugh behind him made him jump, scared him nearly to death. He swung around in the seat, looking.

At the crest of the hill he saw two boys on bikes, heard the crunch of gravel and more laughter. Shrinking lower in the seat, he turned the key, wanting to start up and peel out. But he stopped himself from doing that. It was just two kids pedaling along a narrow dirt path that ran beyond the eucalyptus tree and on up the hill. There was more crunching of gravel, a guffaw of laughter as one lightly shoved the other. He waited, hunched low, until they'd gone.

When he looked down again at the ranch yard, the couple was headed for their car. He watched them swing in and drive on up the hill, past him. Neither looked in his direction. He sat for only a minute deciding whether to follow them or wait to look the place over. They took off across the hills, the woman's dark, gleaming hair blowing enticingly in the wind. He started the engine and slowly followed them. Staying maybe a quarter mile behind the yellow car, he wished his own car wasn't white and so easy to see. They made a sharp turn, and another, and he lost them among a stand of pines.

But then there they were again, a moving yellow spot beyond the trees. It slowed and became a car again, and as he rounded the next curve, they were pulling up in front of a driveway that was blocked by two pickups and a tall pile of dirt. He pulled over behind the first trees he came to, a stand of shaggy cypress with dense, low branches.

Was all that dirt from the drain the couple had been talking about? They'd joked about digging an indoor swimming pool, but no drain was ever that big. Still, that was a hell of a dirt pile. Maybe luck was with him. Maybe, whatever kind of drain this was, it would be better, even, than the barn, would be exactly what he wanted.

13

Wilma Getz's flowering front garden was in fact Dulcie's garden, where the tabby liked to hunt gophers and moles, and she would challenge with tooth and claw any neighborhood cat who coveted her tangled territory. The tabby might exhibit all the subtle intelligence of the rare, speaking cat, but she was a primitive little fighter when it came to her hunting ground. The feline passion for independence, just like the human passion for liberty, she believed included a right to one's own place, inviolate against all intruders.

The one-story stone house she considered hers and Wilma's together, it was just the right size for Dulcie and her silver-haired housemate. When Wilma retired from her job as a U.S. probation officer, she had moved from San Francisco directly to her dream home in Molena Point. That was before she ever met Dulcie; she had been well settled when she brought the small tabby kitten home to live with her. The slim, energetic woman hadn't known, then, what kind of cat this was with whom she would share her life. She didn't discover until Dulcie was grown the extent of the young cat's talents. That first conversation between woman and cat had been a milestone that cat lovers everywhere would envy but few would ever experience.

Charlie and Joe Grey arrived at Wilma's house, coming straight from tailing the man in the white car. They watched Dulcie leave the living room window, and then saw Wilma at the kitchen window, waving to them. They hurried across the garden, surrounded by the rich scent of apricots cooking, Joe racing ahead to disappear through Dulcie's cat door.

Because of the steep hill that rose close behind the house, both the front and back doors faced the street, one at either end of the cottage. Charlie and Joe preferred the back door, which led through the laundry room and into Wilma's blue-and-white kitchen.

Wilma stood at the kitchen counter crimping a pie crust, her long gray hair tied back crookedly with a silver clasp, her pale blue T-shirt protected by a faded apron. Dulcie had already leaped to her chair at the kitchen table, waiting for them, her tail switching, her eyes alight to see Joe. As the tomcat jumped up to join her, Wilma set a saucer of milk before them and half a dozen cookies, and stood looking at Joe. "You found a body this morning? You found where a body was?"

Joe looked up at her questioningly.

"Ryan called. They were to look at some houses, and she told me. I gather Clyde wasn't enchanted." The older woman turned away to finish crimping the crust, then set the pie in the oven. She poured two cups of coffee and sat down at the table across from Charlie.

"Makes me shiver," she said. "A body in that empty swimming pool. I'm surprised the city hadn't made the Parkers cover that hole so a child wouldn't fall in."

"This was no child," Joe said. "From the scent, I'd say a grown woman. Her blood was barely dry."

Dulcie shifted impatiently. "Tell us from the beginning."

Joe, and then Charlie, filled them in from the time Joe had first approached the empty pool in the predawn dusk until he and Charlie, and Ryan and Clyde, tried to follow the eavesdropper.

"If Kit and I had known what you were going to find this morning," Dulcie said, "we'd have come back with you from the hills."

"I didn't plan to find it. You didn't have to go off chasing the wild clowder. What gets into Kit?"

"She saw a little cream-colored cat," Dulcie said. "It was so strange, Kit felt an instant rapport with her, an instant friendship. She seems totally possessed by the little waif."

"Kit *gets* possessed," Joe said. "Some wild idea takes hold of her and she can think of nothing else."

Charlie and Wilma exchanged a look. There was no turning Kit aside when she got her claws into a new passion.

Dulcie said, "She got as excited as if she'd discovered a long-lost sister. And the young cat seemed just as fascinated."

Wilma said, "Maybe no one will ever understand Kit—and isn't that half her charm?" She looked at Joe. "This meeting between Kit and the little waif happened at the same time you came on the murder scene?"

"It did," the tomcat said. "So?" He scowled up at Wilma, his white-tipped paws kneading irritably at the chair cushion. "You're not saying there's some connection!" Wilma was no more given to flighty imaginings than was he.

Charlie watched her aunt. "What are you saying?"

Wilma looked back at them blankly. "I don't know. The thought just popped into my mind." She shook her head, frowning. "I don't know what I meant. It just flashed into my thoughts that, somewhere down the line, you'll find there's some kind of connection between the two events."

Dulcie looked at Wilma uneasily, and nudged the subject back to Kit and the cream-colored waif. "Since the weather warmed, Kit and Lucinda and Pedric have been walking in the hills, and they've glimpsed this cat more than once. Every time she sees them she stands up on her hind legs, staring yearningly at them." Dulcie laughed. "Until Sage hazes her away, forces her to turn back up the hills to the clowder, away from Kit." Dulcie licked milk from her whiskers. "Looks like Sage has chosen another female who's just as wild and willful as Kit. Why can't he find a nice, docile, matronly young cat who will be content to do as he says, and who will be happy to give him lots of kittens? Poor Sage. Where will it end? He's so . . . He's so . . . "

"He and Kit weren't well suited," Charlie said. She didn't say that Sage was a wuss, that he wasn't the macho tomcat who *should* be destined to love and cherish Kit. But then she looked embarrassed. Who was she to criticize, even in her thoughts, anything about these rare creatures? Finishing her coffee, she rose and picked up her car keys. "I need to stop by the station. I've put off telling Max that my clients may have had a break-in. Now, with what may be a murder just two blocks away, I'll have to tell him." Leaning down to give her aunt a hug, she headed for the back door. "You cats want to come?"

"To the PD with you?" Joe said. "We stroll into the station escorted by the chief's wife? Oh, right."

"I'd let you off down the street," Charlie said, laughing. "But I guess, with the noon traffic, you'd make better time over the roofs."

"I guess we would," Joe said, "and create a lot less interest." But the tomcat was eager to sneak a look at Juana Davis's report, and as Charlie headed for her Blazer, he and Dulcie lapped up the last of their milk, shared the remaining cookie, galloped out Dulcie's cat door and across the garden, headed for the rooftops.

The detectives wouldn't have much, yet, on the scene at the Parker house, not until they got some kind of match on any prints they'd been able to lift. But all the same, Joe wanted to see what was happening. Without some kind of official departmental input, he felt at sea about the case, felt left out of the loop. It was this contact with the officers of MPPD and his snooping access to the department's investigative tools and information sources that served the cats as essential backup for whatever information they were able to discover. Without that supporting data and interdepartmental communication, a cat could work his paws off for nothing. Side by side, Joe and Dulcie leaped to the roof of Molena Point PD, their ever hopeful thoughts fixed on Detectives Dallas Garza and Juana Davis who might, with luck, already have information available for their covert attention.

14

Police dispatcher Mabel Farthy had brought fried chicken for her lunch, with extra servings in case any of the cats wandered in. The plump, blond, middle-aged officer loved to spoil the three freeloaders; she'd be happy to bring fried chicken for the whole department except that, the way these guys ate, she'd have to file for bankruptcy before the end of the week. She was sorting the mail when Joe and Dulcie appeared beyond the glass door. She looked up, smiling. Before she could step out from behind her counter to let them in, Officer Brennan came up the sidewalk and the cats slipped in behind him, crowding so close on his heels that they surely left cat hairs clinging to the dark trousers of his uniform.

Leaping to the counter, they peered over, sniffing at the shelf beneath where they knew she kept her lunch. The chicken smelled heavenly. When she reached for the bag, Brennan paused, giving her a woeful look. She grinned and shook her head and the portly officer moved on. The cats watched him turn into the conference room where there was always a box of doughnuts beside the coffeemaker, maybe fresh, maybe dried out, but sweet and filling. As Mabel unwrapped their own bite-size treats of fried chicken, down the hall Detective Juana Davis stepped out of her office carrying a CD and headed for Dallas Garza's office.

"Take a look at these," they heard her say as she entered. "We sure did have company this morning."

The cats looked at each other, wolfed down their chicken, made a show of stretching and yawning, then dropped off the counter and trotted lazily down the hall as if wanting a noonday nap. It wasn't easy to want to hurry like hell, yet move as slowly as a basset hound on downers. Envisioning Dallas inserting the disc into his computer, they slipped into his office and out of sight beneath his credenza. They couldn't see the computer screen from where they crouched—it stood on the detective's desk with its back to them—but at least they could listen.

"I'll be damned," Dallas said sharply, staring at the screen.

Juana had pulled up a straight chair next to Dallas's desk. "Turn that one back," she said, frowning at the screen. "There, zoom it up. There, the jawline and ear, just beside that bush. Print it out. Can you make it lighter?" As the cats listened to the soft whir of the printer, Juana said, "There, by the window, behind the camellia bush. Print that one, too."

Again the whisper of the printer, and the cats watched it spit out another sheet. When they had seven sheets and Juana was shuffling through them, Joe Grey strolled out from beneath the credenza. Staring sweetly up at her, he leaped to the desk beside her. She was so used to the cats in and out of the offices that she hardly looked at him; she stroked him absently as she fanned out the photos.

"Try enlarging this one," she said.

Another click of computer keys and the printer whirred again.

"Is that a shadow?" Dallas said, picking up the picture. "Or is he wearing some kind of cap?" In all the shots, even the enlargement, the figure was only barely visible, a shadow among shadows within the tangled bushes.

"Looks like a cap," Juana said. "He *must* have seen me pointing the camera his way when I shot the suntan oil bottle. Did he think he was completely hidden? Or that he'd be out of focus?" She smiled. "But what could he do? He couldn't move, he was trapped there."

And Joe Grey thought, *Like a rabbit frozen in place trying to blend in with its surroundings, trying not to be noticed.*

Dallas ran off one more enlargement and took the sheet from the printer. It was as murky as the rest. "Are we looking at the killer?" he said. "Provided there is a body. Why the hell can't we have a nice simple murder, with a body on the scene?"

"Plus the murder weapon, prints, excellent witnesses, the works?" Juana said, laughing. "And what fun would that be?" Laying the pictures down, she rose. "I'll get the film over to George, see what he can get with some high-tech enhancement."

"I'll get the blood off to the lab," Dallas said. "And the prints we lifted. I don't—"

They both looked up when Charlie appeared in the doorway. Joe had been so interested he hadn't heard her voice up at the front, though she and Mabel usually talked for a while. She stood in the doorway, wisps of her red hair bright as flames in the overhead lights.

"I just stopped in to see Max for a minute. And to—" She glanced at the pictures. "Are those from the Parker house? May I see?"

"Come sit," Dallas said. "Have a look."

She sat down on the couch. Dallas handed her the pictures and said, "Someone was watching us while we ran the scene this morning—what appears to be a crime scene."

Charlie was quiet for a minute, tilting the pictures this way and that for a clearer view, then she looked up at the detectives. "This could be the same man."

They waited. Joe dropped off the desk and slipped up on the couch beside her. She glanced down at him and their eyes met for a moment, then she looked up again at the two detectives.

"When Ryan and Clyde left you this morning, they stopped up the hill where I was checking my clients' houses. We were on the street, talking, when Clyde saw a man down the hill standing hidden among the trees as if he was watching us."

She looked again at the pictures. "He was wearing a dark hat, a slouchy kind of hat. Jeans. A dark green windbreaker." Her hand, petting Joe, felt reassuring. They were in this together and that thought pleased the tomcat.

"None of us got a look at his face," she said, "with the hat pulled down. He ran down the hill and disappeared, and in a minute a white car took off. Maybe he was interested in my vacationing houses, too. A glass slider looks like someone tried to jimmy it. I didn't report it, nothing seems to be missing."

She looked embarrassed. "I guess it wasn't a very smart way to tail someone, Clyde in a yellow car, me in a red SUV. When we lost him at Ocean, we split up. They went north, I went south as far as the shops, looked all over the parking lot, then gave up."

"And you didn't call about the attempted break-in," Dallas said, frowning.

"It was so . . . I had nothing to report. Even the guy down the hill, watching. Might have been only a neighbor. If he was watching you, wouldn't he *know* he'd show up in the pictures you were shooting?"

"He might have thought I didn't have a very wide field," Juana said. "I was shooting small details, a pair of dark glasses, close-ups."

"And what was he going to do?" Dallas said. "If he'd moved and we'd seen him, we'd have brought him in for questioning. Maybe we'll have better luck when the video is developed."

"Could this be our snitch?" Juana said. "I took the call, and it was the snitch's voice, I'm sure. Was *he* hanging around to see if we'd run the scene even, when there was no body?"

"That doesn't tell us how he happened on the scene in the first place," Dallas said. "The odds of him stumbling on that particular pool... How many people spend their time prowling around vacant houses and looking in empty swimming pools?"

Juana said, "Unless they saw the murder in progress, or saw the body before it was moved. But why the snitch's continued secrecy? What's that about? And how has he known any of the information he's given us over the years? I'm beginning to think he's some kind of psychic. If I believed in such things."

"Sometimes," Charlie said, "it seems there's no other way to explain what he comes up with." Her hand had tightened only slightly on the gray tomcat. He pressed nervously against her, eased by her steady touch. Sometimes that kind of conversation, hearing the detectives talk about their unknown informant and make guesses about the snitch's identity while looking straight at Joe himself, tended to make a cat nervous.

"I'd say he was a member of the department," Juana said, rising and heading for the door. "Except, not even someone in the department would know this kind of stuff. For any one person to have gathered all the information we've received over the years from this guy—and from the woman—that just isn't possible." Brushing a gray cat hair from the skirt of her dark uniform, the detective left them to return to her own office. Dallas sat looking after her, then looked across at Charlie.

Charlie said, "I sure don't know the answer. I guess you and Max are right. If you like the help of the snitches, then run with it and don't ask questions."

Across the room beneath the credenza where Dulcie crouched hidden, the tabby's green eyes looked out at Joe and Charlie, wildly amused. Beside her, Kit was silently laughing.

Charlie said, "Were you able to lift any prints?"

Dallas nodded. "Fingerprints. Blood. Shoe prints. And with spray, we got some tire marks."

Charlie rose to leave. Joe, feeling uncomfortable suddenly, dropped off the couch and followed her. Dulcie followed Joe, the two cats trailing Charlie as far as the dispatcher's cubicle, where they made a detour up onto the counter to see if Mabel had any more fried chicken.

15

From the street above, he watched the yellow road-ster nose in between two pickups near the dirt pile. As the couple got out, he pulled his car farther off the street, in among the stand of cypress trees, whose five dark trunks thrust up out of the earth like a huge hand, like the mangrove trees in Florida, where they'd lived for a couple of years. With his car better hidden, he sat taking in the scene below. Did he know the man in the roadster? Why did he look familiar? It was a small village, but he'd lived here only two years. He thought maybe he'd seen him around that upscale car agency, going in and out of the automotive repair shop. Maybe giving the mechanics orders? He liked to buy his beer at the liquor store across the street. Standing in the cool interior, he'd glance over there at the foreign cars in the agency window, thinking what kind he'd buy when they'd made a big enough haul. If this guy was the head mechanic or the owner, then the last name was probably Damen, as on the sign out front. Squarely built, dark, short hair, not particularly good looking. He wondered what the woman saw in him.

The house below him was a one-story stucco with a red tile roof, the typical pseudo Mediterranean of the area. At the far end, a blue tarp had been secured over the roof as if there was a leak there. Weird that they were working on Sunday. How could they hire people on Sunday? Didn't the unions control when men could work?

The garage door was open but from this angle he could see inside for only a few feet. He could hear someone digging in there, and as the couple approached, a strongly built, redheaded man emerged. Red hair, red beard. Plaid shirt and muddy jeans, muddy boots and a shovel in his hand. Behind him the sound of digging continued. Outside the garage beside the tall heap of earth was a pile of broken concrete. Slipping out of the car, he hunkered down beside it, looking. But even at the lower angle he could see in only another two feet.

The cement floor was tracked with mud, as was the drive: spills of dirt, muddy boot prints, and the kind of single, muddy tire track a wheelbarrow would make as they hauled out the dirt to pile in the yard. He wanted to see this drain. He wanted to hear what they might say about it. He wasn't any expert on construction, but he couldn't imagine why they'd dig a drain in a cement-floored garage. From the amount of earth that had come out of it, the thing had to be huge.

Well, they weren't only digging in the garage, part of the dirt must have come from a raw ditch alongside the wall of the house. They'd replaced some windows, too; there was a stack of old windows out front, leaning against a tree. How long did these people plan to stay here on a Sunday afternoon? He wondered if, when they did leave, they'd lock the garage doors. He grew so nervous with the frustration of waiting that he had to use the inhaler again. He hated the bother of carrying it around. *She* said he was lucky to have it. When at last his breathing came easier, and when they were all inside the garage and the digging was louder, as if maybe more than one man was working, he slipped down the hill, staying under the cover of the descending cypress trees, and crouched just above the garage to listen. But then, hunkered among the prickly foliage, he had to wait until the digging eased enough so he could hear.

They were talking about the roof. Soon the three came out again, forcing him to melt back deeper into the stickery shadows. They stood turned away from him, looking up at the tile roof.

The redheaded man must be the foreman. He said the new tiles would be delivered by the end of the week. That made the woman frown. "First of the week is supposed to be clear, between rains. Can't they get them here Tuesday? I'll give them a call Monday morning." The way she talked, you'd think she was the boss on the job. Well, you wouldn't catch *him* working for a woman.

But when she said, "If the gravel and cement are on schedule, we can pour before lunch. This'll be finished easily, Monday afternoon," a nervous excitement filled him. They were going to dump gravel in the hole and then pour cement, and he had to have a look in there, had to see what could be her grave.

He wondered how they could get a gravel truck in under that low roof. Maybe they'd have to dump it on the driveway and wheelbarrow it in? Seemed like that would take all day. He hoped not. If this *was* the place he wanted, then he wanted to see it done quickly, before they discovered anything amiss. He wanted to be finished with it so he could head on up the coast.

Head up the coast alone, he thought with a sudden jolt. His hands began to sweat, and he wiped them on his jeans, tried to concentrate on the business at hand.

The man and woman got back in the roadster and headed away, down the hills. Inside the garage the others kept working, and he settled in among the cypress trees for a long wait, listening to the digging and thinking about her, thinking about the jobs they'd pulled—feeling shaky again.

It was maybe an hour later when two Latino men appeared from the garage and got into the smaller pickup. The redheaded man came out, swung into the bigger pickup and activated the garage door to close it. As the two trucks took off down the hill, he realized that fog was rolling in, it hung low and dense over the village already hiding the rooftops and the sea beyond.

He waited awhile after they'd gone, then returned to the car. He fetched a few small tools from the glove compartment, leaving the shovel on the floor of the backseat, and went down to have a look. Moving around the side of the garage to try the pedestrian door, he crossed the line of fresh dirt where they'd dug along that side. Maybe they'd buried a pipe there. Pausing, he looked up the hill that rose just a few feet from the side of the garage. Maybe they'd laid a pipe to carry away the runoff, as if a deluge of water came down here during heavy rains. Was that the reason for the drain in the garage, to carry away the runoff from the hill?

Curious, he walked around to the back of the house where the hill dropped steeply away.

He was surprised to find another whole floor down there. A daylight basement visible only as you went around the side. It had large windows facing the drop, a smaller window on the side where he stood. When he pressed his face to the glass he saw that the room was finished inside, a big room, plastered and painted white.

But along the bottom of the walls ran a brown stain maybe two feet high where muddy water had come in. And the carpet had been taken up, too, he could see the tack holes in the water-stained, warped plywood. This lower floor had flooded bad, so that *was* what the drain was about. He wondered what would happen if the drain didn't work, if the house flooded again after all this added cost and labor. Wondered who would pay for that. Well, he guessed the woman contractor would, if that's what she was. If it didn't flood, he guessed she'd make a nice piece of cash off this one.

He wondered what would happen to the body if the drain flooded. But with rock and cement holding it down, what could happen? And, he thought hopefully, maybe the contractor knew what she was doing after all.

Returning to the side door of the garage, he fished out his lock picks and got to work. It took him maybe ten minutes, finessing the tumblers, to slide back the bolt and slip inside, locking the door behind him. He stood looking at the drain.

Damned hole was big enough to bury an army. It spanned the width of the double garage just inside the rear wall, running some twenty feet. It was maybe three feet wide and deeper than a man was tall. If this *was* a drain, there'd been a hell of a flood here. Why would anyone waste their time on a house that flooded like that?

But with prices what they were on the California coast, maybe this made sense. The dirt at the bottom of the pit was roughly raked, and a series of four-inch-wide plastic pipes had been laid the full length, disappearing into the earth at either end. He imagined them running underground, connecting to drainpipes that would stick out of the lower hill to dump the runoff. The whole thing seemed like a huge project, more than the heaviest rain could ever require.

There was a window in the opposite wall, over the connections for a washer and dryer. He could as well have come in through there; the window might have been easier to jimmy. But it was not as private, being visible from the street. He saw that he needn't have brought the shovel. They had left all their tools, shovels, rakes. Two electric saws sat on the littered worktable along with empty drink cans, packs of gum, and a wadded-up lunch bag. Down in the pit, an extension ladder had been left in place. Already set up for him, he thought, smiling.

This was exactly what he'd been looking for; he could have spent the rest of the night searching the empty hills and found nothing anywhere nearly as good. These people had dug her grave for him, and now, once he'd finished his part of the project, once the gravel was in and the concrete poured, the body would never be found. She'd have not only a grave but a gigantic and tamper-proof crypt, which, he assured himself, not even a flood would disturb.

Moving to the garage window, he looked out at the empty street and on down the hills where the fog was growing thicker, climbing up past him now into the valleys above. He liked the fog, had always felt safe moving silently through the heavy mist. By nightfall the whole area would be socked in, muffling the sounds of his digging. No cars appeared on the narrow roads, no movement except far down the hill, where an elderly couple was walking along with canes. Most likely they'd soon turn back toward the village or move on to one of the far houses, wherever they came from. With the fog closing in, as evening fell it would be cold, too. The couple sat down on a low stone wall and a small dog jumped up beside them. Strange-looking dog. He watched it uneasily—it moved like a cat. But of course cats didn't go for walks. Turning away from the window, he fetched a pair of coveralls a workman had left hanging on a nail in the wall, folded them inside out to avoid the mud, and, using them as a pillow, he sat down on the cold cement floor opposite the window. Making himself as comfortable as he could, with his back to the wall, he settled in to wait for full dark, congratulating himself that soon she'd be tucked away where no one, *no one,* would find her.

His story that she'd left him while they were on vacation, that they'd had a fight and she'd just taken off, who'd know the difference? They had no children, no close relatives, no one who'd have reason to disbelieve him or to start checking, to follow up on what he told them. By the time anyone noticed a smell in the garage or along the downstairs wall, if anyone ever did, he'd be long gone where no one would find him. Looking across at the fog-shrouded window, he took comfort from the weight of the mist against the glass. It made him feel hidden where nothing could find him, nothing could slip up on him.

16

Lucinda and Pedric Greenlaw paused in their steep climb to sit down on the stone wall where they so often rested. They had ascended at a lively pace, employing their carved walking sticks to help them up the rocky ground. At eighty-something, though the couple was lean and spry, a little help from a good stout cane didn't hurt. Below them the fog had rolled in fast over the village rooftops; above them it blew in dense scarves toward the upper hills and fingered into the narrow valleys. They sat enjoying the misty evening, unaware of anything strange or threatening among the few scattered hillside houses—though neither hiker was unprepared for surprises. Pedric had grown up well aware of human nature. And Lucinda, though her life had been more sheltered, had learned quickly, when the couple had been kidnapped last year, how to take care of herself.

As for their companion, the tortoiseshell cat didn't worry much about life's dangers, Kit met trouble with her sharp claws and her strong teeth or, if she must, by escaping into the treetops. In between, she enjoyed every moment. Coming up the path she had raced ahead lashing her fluffy tail, enjoying the world with every ounce of her wild little soul. Now, leaping to the wall beside Lucinda, she stood watching fog transform the hills and valleys—but she was looking for someone, too. Looking intently up among the hills though she said nothing to her companions. She watched and watched, and suddenly she saw her—a speck so small, so pale within the mist that at first Kit thought it was only a stone.

The two humans, watching where she looked, frowned in puzzlement. "What?" Lucinda said softly. The old woman stared for some minutes before she made out a pale little cat poised high among the fog-shrouded boulders. "Oh!" she said, seeing Kit's excitement. "Who is that?"

Kit glanced at her housemate but didn't answer, she didn't know quite how to explain. Coming up the hills she had sensed the buff-colored cat somewhere up there above them, or maybe she'd only wished the little waif would be there. Now she'd appeared from out of nowhere, just as Kit had hoped.

Kit didn't know what drew her to the pale cat. She knew the young feline was Sage's mate or soon would be, but this had nothing to do with Sage. In this small cat Kit saw her younger self looking back at her, in a wild and curious mirror image, and Kit wanted to talk with her. She wanted, perhaps foolishly, to be friends. This cat was feral, they lived in two different worlds, and Kit knew it would be best to leave the matter alone. But she wouldn't, she was too curious.

Tansy had been on the hills since before dawn, at first hunting with Sage—that was when she'd seen the three cats hunting lower down in the hills and had seen the tortoiseshell one. She knew about Kit from the other clowder cats, knew how Kit had escaped the clowder and run away from the leader Stone Eye. Stone Eye was dead now and the clowder was free again, but Kit hadn't returned.

It was the other cats' talk about Kit and how she lived among humans that helped Tansy remember that she, herself, had not always been with the clowder, that once she had lived with humans. She had been very small when, as a kitten, she'd been thrown away by humans.

Before that terrible time, she'd known a good life chasing dust mice under the furniture; digging her claws into the bright, thick rugs; and swinging on the curtains though she got scolded for that. Little as she was, she had slipped away sometimes into the neighbors' gardens, and even ventured blocks away where the shops began and looked at all the wonders in the bright windows. And once, when the woman wasn't watching her, she had climbed right up a stickery vine to the roof where she could look down on all the world. When she lived with humans she had slept on a soft blanket and awakened to good smells in the warm house, and at suppertime the woman always gave her some of what they ate, even when the man complained—but then the man and woman had a fight over her; the man called her dirty and said she made him sneeze. He yelled at the woman, and the woman cried, and even though Tansy was just a little kitten, the man grabbed her and held her too tight to get free, and he shut her in a box. When the woman tried to stop him, he hit her so hard she fell.

Closing the box tight, he'd put it in his car. She remembered the engine roaring and the car moving sickeningly, and though she clawed and screamed, she couldn't fight hard enough to break free. He drove a long way up into the hills, until she could smell fresh grass and eucalyptus trees, and there he'd stopped and put the box out on the ground and then driven away, leaving her alone there shut inside the box. She mewled and cried, but he didn't come back and no one answered her; she'd heard no sound but the roar of the car growing fainter until it was gone.

It took her a very long time to tear through the cardboard. When at last she could stick her nose out, panting, she gulped fresh air. She was very thirsty. It took longer, then, to make the hole big enough so she could crawl through, but at last she was out. She had huddled against the box, weak and frightened.

She had hidden among some boulders until dawn, then had wandered uncertainly. She wasn't sure how long she was alone, but several nights came and went. She caught and ate some beetles, and drank muddy water from a ditch. And then one morning, just as the sun was coming to warm her, a pale calico female found her, and that good cat had washed her and warmed her and had hunted mice to feed her.

She had gone with Willow to live in the clowder, and that was where she began to talk. She had never dared speak among humans, though she had understood them. In the clowder there was no one to think her strange and different—everyone talked. Clowder life had helped her to forget the cardboard box and the human who had betrayed her; clowder life made her forget for a little while the rich world of humans that was so full of excitement and color and music and soft beds and delicious things to eat.

But then as she grew older, the wonder of that life began to fill her dreams. She would wake thinking about bright store windows and high rooftops, and she began to long for that world. It was not many months until she found the courage to leave the clowder and make her way down the hills and into the village again. The time was early spring. She had gone where there were tall gardens to play in, in the yards of humans. She had let a human discover her, she had made up to the woman shamelessly, rolling over and purring.

She had lived with that human and then with another, lived among humans in half a dozen houses; but each time she found a home, someone would move or go away for many days and forget to feed her. Then another couple "took her in," as they called it. The woman was nice, but then the man had moved away, and then the woman left, too. Left her there alone and, heartbroken, she had crept away from that house and left the village and returned to the dull but safe life of the clowder, to a world without fickle humans.

But she knew humans weren't all alike, and soon she again missed that life. She missed the places of humans, she missed the excitement and color and always something new to intrigue her. Sage didn't like her to miss those things. He'd told her to forget the human world, just as he'd told the tortoiseshell cat to forget it. Sage called the human world wicked, he wanted her to forget her dreams, he said a cat had no business with dreams. This morning when he saw her watching Kit, he'd said she must stay away from those village cats. He said she must obey him, and they'd argued and fought. She said she wasn't his slave, and at last he'd stalked away scowling, his ears back, turning to look at her coldly. That was when she'd fled from him, had raced down the hills to an abandoned barn she knew of. She'd stayed there prowling the empty barn and lashing her tail, wishing the tortoiseshell would find her.

But the barn and the hills had remained empty. She'd stayed there all day. She'd had a nice nap and then caught four fat mice. She was royally feasting on mouse when a yellow car came bumping down the narrow road that wound through the hills, and a dark-haired man and a beautiful, dark-haired woman got out to wander through the barn and outbuildings. She'd hidden from them, but she'd seen another man following them; he stopped his car high above them, beneath thick trees, and sat looking. He was a mean-faced man; he watched the couple the way a coyote watches a little cat.

When the couple left at last in the yellow car, she was sure they didn't know he was there in the trees above them, or that again he followed them.

She'd sat for a long time in the old barn, licking up the last of the mice and feeling uneasy, wondering what that was all about. And then when she'd scrambled up onto the roof of the barn, she'd seen the yellow car parked farther down the hills. She didn't see the white car, but she looked at the big pile of dirt in that yard and the blue blanket over the roof and she was so interested and curious that she'd trotted down to have a look.

The time was late afternoon. She knew it would be dark when she got home and Sage would be angry, and she didn't care. She'd sat concealed in the tall grass thinking that maybe she wouldn't go home at all. There was a narrow canyon between the hill she was on and the place where the house stood, and another hill rose to its right, dense with heavy, dark trees. The man and woman had gotten out of the yellow car and were talking to a redheaded man. She was watching them when she glanced up the hill and saw the white car hidden there among the trees. The mean-faced man had gotten out and stood watching them in a way that made her fur crawl.

It was much later when the yellow car went away. She stayed where she was, waiting and watching as that man came down the hill and walked around the house and looked in, then went in the garage. He was in there for a long time, it was becoming dusk and the fog was settling in over the hills and still he hadn't come out. As she looked down the hill again, past the house, she saw a tall, thin couple coming up the road—and there was Kit, racing ahead of them.

She watched as the couple sat down on the stone wall and the tortoiseshell leaped up beside them. Kit stood very still, looking up the hills, looking straight at her. Tansy reared up, too, so Kit would see her. What would it hurt to go down there? What harm to sniff noses, and talk a little? What harm would that do? She and Kit looked through the fog at each other, and looked and looked, and suddenly they were running, Kit streaking up the hill and Tansy pelting down, both cats running so fast their hind paws crossed beneath their front paws like racing rabbits.

They met nearly head-on, skidding to a stop in the wet grass of the steep hill. At first, neither spoke. Kit's yellow eyes were wide, and she was laughing; they both were laughing, and Tansy knew she'd found a friend.

17

"I am Tansy. You are Sage's friend," the scruffy cat said smartly. "Oh, my. You would have been his mate but you wouldn't have him. You jilted him!"

"Where did you learn that word?" Kit said, amused. "Jilt" was not a word she'd ever heard among the clowder. The stranger was the color of bleached straw, her inch-long coat standing out every which way and tangled with seeds and streaks of mud from the ditches.

"I learned that from humans, when I was a kitten, and later when I ran away from the clowder and came back to live in the village."

"You ran away from the clowder?" Kit knew no other speaking feral besides herself who had abandoned the rule of the clowder and gone to live among humans.

"I wanted music," said the scruffy cat. "I wanted humans to talk to me—though I never talked back. I wanted to curl up before a nice warm fire. I miss that life, I want catnip mice and kind hands, soft blankets and magical stories . . ."

Kit laughed at her but she knew too well that longing, and she could feel a purr bubbling up.

"I was a kitten in the village until a man put me in a box and dumped me in the hills and left me there to die. I nearly starved. Even after I clawed my way out, I was too little to hunt much. But then Willow found me and she washed me and caught mice for me, and I went to live with the clowder. But when winter was over and I got bigger and spring came, I longed for human places, I . . ." Tansy looked at Kit helplessly, as if she didn't know how to describe her dreams.

Kit raised a paw, and looked away toward the village. "Come on," she said softly. And she turned and trotted away.

The scrawny cat followed and was soon trotting beside her. As they passed the stone wall, the old couple remained very still so as not to frighten her. The last Lucinda and Pedric saw of them, the scrawny little cat was sharply silhouetted against Kit's dark, black-and-brown elegance. Lucinda and Pedric looked at each other, and smiled, and the Greenlaws understood perfectly Kit's flick of the ear and lashing of her tail, her silent, *See you later! Don't wait up!*

But then Lucinda frowned, trying not to worry. Living with tattercoat Kit, worry was a given, they never knew what trouble she'd have her paws into. The elderly couple remained sitting on the wall, watching the two cats disappear down the hill to vanish at last among the cottage gardens as they headed into the village. What adventures the two would find, and what dangers, they didn't want to consider. They tried to just fill up on the wonder of the moment and not let themselves think any further.

In the village, Kit led the young cat along her own secret routes through narrow alleyways flanked with little shops, and then up a trellis to the rooftops. They trotted across jagged, shingled peaks and down into the dark crevices among a forest of chimneys. They stood with their paws in the roof gutters looking down at the tourists, then raced across leaning oak branches above a narrow street. They spent nearly an hour peering in through penthouse windows at couples eating supper, at ladies undressing, at children already sleeping in their beds. Tansy couldn't get enough of the exotic world of humans that she had so missed.

As night drew down, they raced up the tiled steps of the courthouse tower to perch high above the world on its narrow balcony. If anyone were to look up and see the two little shapes crouched there, they'd wonder what kind of birds those were that had come to roost for the night. Below them, fog shrouded the cottage rooftops, so the shop lights were blurred into smeared colors along the busy streets. Through the mist, villagers and tourists headed for the little restaurants, and from the restaurants a miasma of smells was rising up: boiled shrimp, charbroiled steaks, and intriguing pasta sauces that made them lick their whiskers and that brought them down from the tower, racing down the long stairs to make their rounds of the restaurant patios. Winding among table legs and people's feet, they paused frequently to fawn on the diners as only a cat can, smiling prettily up into the faces of strangers until they were treated to buttered lobster, rare steak, or roast chicken; and now Kit watched Tansy with increasing amusement. This waif, shy and frightened one minute, was bold as brass the next, employing spry and teasing ways until she got exactly what she wanted—Tansy was not at all as frightened and helpless as she seemed. The flip side of her nature showed Kit a skilled little freeloader. And as they left the center of the village, full of delicious treats, Tansy took the lead, scrambling to the roofs again and heading jauntily to where the village cottages climbed up into the hills.

"What?" Kit said. "Where are you going?"

"*My* neighborhood," Tansy said. "I want to go there to my own street, where I lived. I want to roll in the gardens and smell the flowers. I want . . . That was my home once, and I want to go there." And the small ragged cat raced away across the shingles. Kit followed, silent with amazement. They had nearly reached Tansy's old neighborhood when Joe Grey and Dulcie appeared on a high peak and came streaking toward them. Kit stopped to wait for them. Tansy stopped, too, but she dropped into a wary crouch.

Earlier that evening, Joe had left Dulcie on the rooftops, planning to meet again when night fell, planning on an evening of break-and-enter in the vacationers' empty houses. Parting from his tabby lady, Joe had stood for a moment watching her trot home to her warm supper and to reassure Wilma that she was all right, that she was safe and well. One of the curses of being a speaking cat was the burden of truly understanding how their human housemates worried about them, and the resultant desire to ease their friends' stress. This was a big responsibility for a cat, and one that Joe, in particular, found burdensome. He liked being an active part of the human world, but he also liked his freedom.

Turning for home, thinking that Clyde and Ryan were still house hunting, he expected to find an empty house where he'd have to raid the refrigerator for his own cold meal. There'd be kibble down for Snowball, he thought with disdain. He'd have to be in the last throes of starvation before he filled up on what he considered the equivalent of discarded sawdust.

But when he hit his home roof, he caught the heady aroma of browned pot roast. And when he glanced over the edge to the driveway, there stood the yellow roadster clicking away as its motor cooled. Okay, so they were home from the great house hunt. But how had they had time to cook supper when they'd been gone all day?

Then he remembered the packages of homemade pot roast that Ryan had put in the freezer. Two weeks ago, she had an amazing bout of domesticity. She'd tied on an apron and, with the same efficient dispatch as when she was building a house, she had filled their freezer with enough home-cooked pot roast, spaghetti sauce, tamale pie, lamb stew, and more of Joe's favorites, to last at least until Christmas. The big freezer, a wedding present from Ryan's dad, stood in the laundry room beside the bunk bed where the family pets used to sleep. Clyde's two dogs were gone now, as well as the two elderly cats. Only Snowball was still with them, and now Rock, of course. Both slept on a soft comforter on the couch in Clyde's study, leaving the laundry-room bunk as a handy place to store empty boxes and un-sorted laundry.

Padding across the roof and in through the window of his rooftop tower, Joe pushed into the house through his cat door and onto a rafter, and with a long leap, he hit the desk below. He could hear their voices in some deep discussion, and hear the scrape of forks on their plates. Dropping to the floor he raced down the stairs breathing in the meaty aroma of pot roast, hoping they'd left him some. Only as he approached the kitchen did he slow. Were they arguing? Listening, he paused in the doorway.

But no, you couldn't call it arguing. Just a heated dis-cussion about the faults and merits of one of the houses they'd looked at—sounded like a decrepit heap that wasn't worth firewood but that Clyde was convinced they could turn into a mansion. Lucky thing Ryan knew what she was doing, that she wouldn't waste their money on a wreck.

Or would she? Hoping Clyde's wild enthusiasm hadn't warped Ryan's common sense, Joe padded in trying not to drool from the good smell of supper.

The Damen kitchen was large and bright with its handsome new tile work and new lighting, yet satisfyingly cozy with cushioned dining chairs and, in the far corner, crowded bookcases flanking a pair of flowered easy chairs. Long before Ryan and Clyde were married or even dating seriously, Ryan had done an extensive remodel. Besides adding the new upstairs, she had torn out the wall between the kitchen and the seldom-used dining room, had replastered the walls of the opened-up room and painted them a soft peach, installed Mexican-tile floors and new tile counters with hand-decorated borders. As Joe entered, Rock was snoozing in one of the easy chairs, probably worn out after a long day at the beach with Ryan's dad.

The Weimaraner looked on enviously as Joe leaped onto his usual chair at the table. Rock wasn't allowed to beg at the dinner table, only outside at the picnic table. It was hard for the big dog to bear, that Joe could do what he couldn't. But then, for Rock, the whole concept of a speaking cat was hard to get used to. Life was not as simple as the young Weimaraner had, as a puppy, first imagined it to be. A speaking cat who gave him orders and was quick with the claws if he didn't obey, and yet was a pal to cuddle up with at night, and who had taught him to track a killer, had turned out to be a special kind of friend.

Rock tolerated Joe's household privileges with a rare patience and good humor.

Ryan reached across the table, setting a plate before Joe. The big, round table was so heaped with real estate fliers and newspaper ads, and with Ryan's scattered sketches and her notebook filled with figures, that there was barely room for the couple's dinner plates and for the steaming casserole of pot roast and vegetables.

"What's with the fast service?" the tomcat said.

"We heard you hit the roof," Ryan told him.

"And charge down the stairs like a herd of buffalo," Clyde added.

Before tucking into his supper, Joe studied the scattered papers. In his opinion, this new venture into real estate did not bode well for the Damen household, but what did he know? He watched Clyde dig the plate of French bread out from under some fliers and pass it to Ryan, then Joe licked up his supper. He was not only starved, he was eager to meet Dulcie, half his mind on the Chapman house and the other empty houses of their neighbors.

But the minute he'd licked his plate clean, Ryan leaned over to refill it, and how could he resist? How he'd survived without this woman was hard to remember. She'd even left out the onion from her pot roast recipe, for fear that, as with ordinary cats, the onion would make him anemic. She'd told him she used, instead, red bell pepper, a combination of herbs, and a touch of bourbon.

"Delicious," Joe said, eating with single-minded dispatch. When again he looked up, they were both staring at him. "What?" he said with his mouth full.

"You're in a hell of a hurry," Clyde said.

"Just hungry," Joe said, and bent his head fastidiously to finish his second helping. Trying to look relaxed, he took his time licking gravy from his whiskers and, to humor them, he stepped up on the table and pawed the fliers apart so he could see them better.

There was the vacant ranch they'd talked about, its fences and outbuildings sprawled raggedly across the side of the hill, below a heavy stand of cypress trees. He couldn't imagine they'd want to remodel that whole complex. There were seven other houses, three in the heart of the village and four tucked among the hills. All of them needed paint, a complete yard makeover, new roofs, and undoubtedly expensive interior repairs: new wiring, new plumbing, who knew what else to keep them marketable. He hoped none of them had drainage problems like the job Ryan was working on at present. At least that wasn't her house, it belonged to a client who wanted it saved despite the cost.

Studying their prospective purchases, one of which looked like a real teardown, Joe didn't know whether to laugh or to succumb to serious concern. A teardown, in Molena Point, could go for half a million or more. Half a mil to rip down a house and replace it with a dwelling that might hopefully sell well up in the seven figures. But with Ryan at the helm, what looked like a teardown might, in fact, turn into a real gem—and people were making money saving those old houses.

When Joe first learned he could speak, and was trying to understand the human world, the concept of work for money had meant nothing to him. But as he began to think more like a human, he'd easily absorbed the rudiments. Folks worked at what they liked to do, received promissory dollars for the quality of their skilled or creative efforts, and traded those for whatever goods they chose. To a cat, the concept had been a revelation.

Why, a cat could hunt mice all day, stack them up like cordwood, and trade them for caviar—if one could find a market for the mice. That was the rub, considering that the human appetite didn't really run to dead mice. He glanced out the kitchen window at the night and knew it was time to meet Dulcie.

Clyde caught his look. "You're going out to poke around the Parker house, aren't you? What do you think you're going to find after Dallas and Juana worked the area?"

It wasn't the Parker house he was headed for, but he didn't tell Clyde that. "You're so incredibly nosy."

"You think that guy will come back?" Clyde said. "If the guy watching us was the killer—if there ever was a killer—after we followed him, why would he come back? He'll be long gone."

Joe just looked at him.

Ryan watched them with amusement. She'd learned early on to stay out of these discussions. When Clyde glanced away, she winked at Joe. Joe twitched a whisker at her, and rubbed his face against her arm by way of thanking her for dinner. Then, dropping to the floor, he headed up the stairs to his tower and out to hit the roofs.

18

When Joe slipped out of his tower to the roof-tops, his belly full of supper and his mind on the empty houses, the fog had blown away; the sky was clear, the moon bright as he leaped across the shingles to the neighbor's roof and raced on into the night. He had gone three blocks galloping across the peaks through paths of moonlight when he spotted Dulcie. She stood on a little balcony, rearing up, her tabby coat silhouetted against the white wall of a penthouse. They raced to meet; skidding close together they exchanged a whisker kiss and then galloped away toward the block of Charlie's vacationing clients. Who knew what scent they'd pick up, what details a human might miss?

Hurrying across the village, the streets below them were busy with cars and pedestrians, with couples

186 SHIRLEY ROUSSEAU MURPHY

coming from the restaurants or window shopping. The traffic thinned as they moved onto the residential roofs; soon the streets below were quiet and nearly empty, only a few pedestrians hurrying along. A silent runner passed beneath them as they approached the targeted homes. They were two roofs from the Waterman house when they saw Kit, poised high on a shingled peak. She was not alone.

"What's this?" Joe said. "She's picked up a stray?" A small, ragged, half-grown cat stood beside her.

"That's the cat from the clowder," Dulcie said. "The little cat that Kit was so taken with this morning. She's hardly more than a kitten, what's she doing here? Oh, my. Has Kit lured her away from the clowder?"

As Joe and Dulcie approached, the little female crouched warily. Kit looked down at her small charge in a patient and proprietary way. "Tansy," Kit said by way of introduction. "She lived in the village once."

"I lived in that house over there," Tansy said shyly, pointing her ears at the Waterman house.

"Did you?" Joe said with interest. "That's where we're going. Do you know how to get in?"

"There's a dog door. But—"

"Are you friends with the dog?"

"Oh, the beagle's dead now," Tansy said. "He was old and friendly. He was a little afraid of me," she added, twitching her whiskers.

Dropping into a pepper tree beside the Watermans', Joe crouched on a branch, looking back at Tansy. "Come on, then," he told her. She followed as the four cats moved quickly, trying to remain out of sight among the foliage. To any casual observer this would look strange indeed, cats do not travel in packs, this was not normal feline behavior.

The house was one story with pale stucco walls, the curved tile roof still warm beneath their paws, holding the heat of the day. Below them, the solid wood fence that enclosed the backyard was far higher than necessary to contain the small beagle that had lived with the Watermans.

Dulcie said, "I'm surprised Ben Waterman went with Rita; Charlie said he hardly ever does, that he'd rather stay home, putter around, and play a little golf. But I guess a tour guide is pretty busy, maybe that's why she makes her trips alone."

"It's their anniversary," Joe said. "Clyde worked on their car a few weeks ago; they told him they were either driving up to San Francisco or flying to Greece or the Antilles, they hadn't made up their minds."

"I wonder what it's like," Dulcie said.

"What what's like?" Joe said absently.

"Greece. There are lots of cats, feral cats. I wonder . . . Are there cats like us? Are our relatives there? Have speaking cats survived there from ancient times?"

"Come on," Joe said impatiently. Glancing toward the neighbors' windows, they dropped down onto the six-foot fence and then into the backyard. Half hidden between two mock orange bushes was a dog door into the garage. They slipped inside one by one, Tansy headed through a second doggy door into the family kitchen.

The kitchen corner where the dog bed had been still smelled faintly of the sweet-leather scent of an old dog. There was no sound from deeper within the house. They stood sniffing, seeking any other scent that might seem out of place, and, rearing up, they looked around the bright room for any sign of disturbance.

The kitchen seemed perfectly in order, the cupboards all neatly shut, their mullioned glass doors showing china and crystalware carefully arranged on the shelves within. On the tile counters they could see a stainless steel toaster, convection oven, microwave, food processor, blender, and an expensive coffeemaker with its own grinder. None of those had been stolen, and what else of value would a kitchen contain? "When does she use all those?" Joe said. "She's gone half the time."

"Maybe he cooks," said Dulcie. "Wilma says when she's home they're very social, they're always involved in some local event and they entertain a lot." Turning away, she followed Tansy into the Watermans' living room, a big, square room with a thick white carpet and a high ceiling set with three skylights. The furnishings were white and soft and deep, set against cocoa-colored walls: white velvet chairs, white leather couch, a perfect setting for the beautiful Rita Waterman. Over the fireplace there was an oversize mirror in an ornate silver frame, the glass reflecting the room in reverse like Alice's mirror into Wonderland. Two matching mirrors hung at the other end of the room, on either side of the arch that led into the entry hall.

"Does she have mirrors to to make the room look bigger? Or to reflect herself?" Dulcie wondered. She imagined the tall, slim blonde reflected over and over in endless and perfect images. The room did not look lived in. There was not a book or a magazine in sight, not a pillow out of place, nothing personal left lying around; but when they sniffed the furniture they smelled cat, and could see cat hairs clinging to it. There were three cat baskets, all on low stools, all lined with white plush, all dusted with multicolored cat hairs smelling of the Waterman cats.

"There are cat beds in every room," Tansy said with longing. "I didn't live here long. The other cats chased me away, so I went to another house. I was only little then, and her cats didn't like me much."

Kit licked Tansy's ear, amusing Joe and Dulcie. Kit had found a small and needy friend, a little creature who seemed needy and quite lost.

"But I came back sometimes," Tansy said, "when the other cats were out hunting. They had a housekeeper. Betty. She took care of the cats, but then she retired, whatever that means, and went to live with her daughter. Rita's husband, Ben, he didn't let on, but he didn't like animals much. If Rita ever went away or died, he'd have sent them all to the pound."

The cats couldn't imagine slim, blond, beautiful Rita Waterman dead, she seemed indestructible. She was a strong woman who did as she pleased, who made of her life what she pleased.

Mavity Flowers, one of Charlie's cleaning ladies and Charlie and Wilma's good friend, said that Rita had had a fling with the neighbor two doors down, with handsome Ed Becker. Such behavior shocked Dulcie, though she knew that was unrealistic. She always wanted to think better of humans. In the world of speaking cats, pairing was a serious commitment. Cats did not wander astray; if a cat was tempted, the cat community judged him harshly and sometimes drove him out, to live away from the clowder. A clowder of speaking cats wasn't like a band of ordinary ferals. Speaking cats even hunted cooperatively—they lived by a different set of rules, by a code as intricate and ancient as their own history.

As they padded through the dining room and study, Joe tried to catch any scent that might seem not to belong—hard to do in a strange house. He had a look at the front door, and at a side door that opened to the patio from the small study. Those and the glass sliders to the patio were all locked, and he found no marks of a break-in.

"When Rita was home," Tansy said, "I used to watch her dress or pack her suitcases. I liked to watch her put on her jewelry, all her beautiful jewelry."

"If someone broke in," Joe said, "and they knew about the jewelry, maybe that's where they'd start. I wonder if Charlie looked to see if it was there."

Tansy's eyes widened and she spun away, galloping down the hall. They followed her toward the master bedroom, passing three other bedrooms. All three were large, elegantly furnished in white and cream and pastel tones. Designed, Dulcie thought, as a complimentary background for Rita's blond beauty. The rooms did not seem disturbed, all were neat and did not look lived in. She paused, looking into one at the small stone fireplace, the satin bedspread. Why, suddenly, did she feel afraid? Why were her paws sweating as if something was wrong? She prowled the room, looking, but there was nothing to bother her. Shaking her whiskers, annoyed at herself, she hurried to join the others, trotting down the hall along the thick white carpet.

The master suite was furnished all in white, the windows draped in a sheer white gauze; it was not a man's kind of chamber. Tansy led them across the thick carpet to two large dressing rooms with a compartmented bath between them. "There," she said, slipping into the room that smelled of perfume and was hung with garment bags full of pale suits and dresses.

Built into the end wall was a pair of white, intricately carved cupboard doors with brass hinges, brass handles, and a brass lock. "Her jewelry's there."

When Joe leaped up to paw at the handles, Tansy watched him patiently. He tried, and tried again, but the doors were indeed securely locked.

"On the shelf," Tansy said at last, having let him struggle, amused by his useless tomcat hustle. Leaping onto the dressing table and then to the shelf above the hanging clothes, she reached her paw behind a stack of plastic storage boxes.

She felt around. She clawed deeper. Deeper still, and then pawed the boxes aside.

"It's gone," she said with dismay, looking down at them. She began to move boxes with her furry shoulder, pushing them aside. She was moving the last box when something slithered toward the edge. Her quick paw grabbed it. "Here!" she said, and from her paw dangled a gold chain with a brass key attached.

But then she looked down helplessly at Joe. She knew what the key was for, she'd seen Rita open the cupboard. But she didn't know how to get that tiny key into the lock.

Leaping up beside her, Joe took the key carefully between his teeth. Crawling belly down on the shelf, he shoved himself out until half of him was hanging over space—but even by bracing one paw against the cupboard door, he couldn't reach the lock. He leaned farther, nearly overbalanced. Dulcie jumped up beside him, took the end of Joe's short tail in her mouth and leaned back. Kit joined them, gripping the skin above his flank. He tried again. Holding his breath and carefully aligning the key, he slipped it into the keyhole.

But when he tried to turn it, he overbalanced and fell, pulling Dulcie and Kit with him. They landed in a tangle. Tansy turned away, not daring to laugh.

They tried again, the three females all hanging on to Joe as he stretched out over space. At last he got the key into the lock again, and this time he kept his balance while he turned it. Backing away across the shelf, he pulled the door open. As it swung wide, Kit caught her breath and Dulcie let out a startled "Meow!"

Jewels blazed out at them, a rich array of stones of every color, set in ornately carved works of gold and silver that the cats thought should grace a museum. The broaches and bracelets were arranged on narrow shelves, the pendants and necklaces hanging behind them. Rings and earrings were stored in clear little boxes. Dulcie looked and looked. If ever a cat felt a surge of kleptomania, she felt it now. It had been a long time since she'd had such a strong urge to "borrow" some lovely human treasure.

In the village library, where she liked to prowl at night, she had pored over books of antique collections like this from all around the world and from many centuries. Some of the pieces were set with real jewels and some with paste replicas, but even with those, the settings themselves were of great value. Even in photographs, they were so beautiful that she longed to touch them. The same desire gripped her now, that had so excited her when, as a younger cat, she had stolen beautiful cashmere carves and luxurious satin teddies from Wilma's neighbors. She wanted to reach her paw in and lift out each lovely piece with her curved claws. She wanted to feel each rich necklace around her own furry neck, she wanted to look in the mirror and see that Etruscan pendant gleaming emerald bright against her dark stripes.

"Coral and turquoise," Dulcie said softly. "Lapis lazuli. Topaz. Such beautiful jewelry to set off Rita's own beauty. Even with jeans she wears a silk or cashmere top and lovely jewelry."

"She calls it antique costume jewelry," Tansy said. "She brings it back from all over the world. I've heard her name the places—places *I've* never heard of or imagined!"

"If someone was in here," Joe said, "maybe casing these houses, did they find this cupboard? Did *they* move the key? Or did Rita? And why would a burglar open it but take nothing? If someone was casing these places and planning a burglary for later, what are they waiting for?" Joe thought about the scars on the Chapmans' patio door, about Mango shut away from her kittens, and about the man watching from the hill below and then running. And the cats left the Waterman house, puzzled, wondering if they were on the right track at all, wondering if they were way off base, as they moved on to investigate the other two empty homes.

19

He stood on the hill beside the car hidden by the heavy cypress branches, looking down along the lower roads. There were no car lights, and only a few scattered houselights shone, muted behind closed curtains. People were settling in for the evening, and that old couple with their canes and their weird dog were gone. It had taken them long enough, nothing better to do than sit on a stone wall watching the fog roll in. He'd lost sight of them for a while, and when he looked again they'd vanished. He meant to wait another hour, until there was less likelihood of cars, before he started digging. He didn't want someone taking a late-evening walk and hearing the sound of the shovel or seeing the reflection of his flashlight through the garage window.

Getting in the car, silently closing the door, he sat looking down at the quiet, bucolic neighborhood. Those houses down there, none of them were very impressive, just little wood-framed places, ordinary and small. A strange neighborhood to be putting a lot of work and money into a remodel, particularly with the economy in trouble. Why spend time on the nondescript place, why take the risk?

He didn't let himself think that he was taking an even greater risk—and that he had a lot more to lose than did that contractor.

He had laid the flashlight and tools on the backseat, everything was ready. He wished he could play the radio but he didn't want to chance it. *She'd* have turned on the oldies station, she didn't like to sit quietly when they were together.

Yet she'd lie for hours soaking up the sun, silent and alone and completely happy. He hated that, hated that she'd *liked* being alone.

When he started getting restless, he did turn the radio on, real low, but then nervously turned it off again. Below him, the lights in one house went out, as if the occupants had gone to bed. Or were they leaving, going out? But no car lights came on and moved away. He was about to gather up his tools and get on with the unpleasant work ahead when, far down the hill, lights appeared from around a bend, heading up toward him.

He watched the car getting closer, watched it turn onto the street below and head up the hill, straight for the remodel, making him wish he'd pulled his car even deeper under the trees. As it passed the last lighted house he saw its black-and-white pattern. Black car, white door with MOLENA POINT POLICE stenciled on it. It paused before the remodel, generating in him a jolt of panic.

He could see only the driver, couldn't tell if he was alone. He sat with the motor running, shining the beam of his flashlight over the house and yard. It paused at the dirt pile. He prayed the guy wouldn't walk the property, that he wouldn't try the pedestrian door into the garage, which he'd left unlocked. The thought of a cop going in there made cold sweat prick his neck and shoulders. Was this a routine patrol, or had someone seen him walking around the place and called 911?

The cop's light played over and around the dirt pile for a few minutes but then swung back across the front door and front windows and the garage window. There, again it paused. He expected the guy to get out, maybe walk around the place. If he checked the doors, found the garage door unlocked, would he go inside? There was nothing to see in there. Yet. Would he maybe call the contractor, that the door was unlocked, meet her up here so she could check it out herself?

But the cop didn't get out, he just sat there behind the wheel, looking. As if this was only a routine check after all, and he'd be gone in a minute. He could hear the guy talking on the radio but couldn't make out what he said, his voice was low and the distance too great. Was it something about this house or something else entirely? Maybe only a routine call. It seemed forever before the cop moved on, heading up the hill toward him. As the squad car approached the cypress trees, he slid down in the seat, thinking about the shovel on the floor and the tools lying in plain sight on the backseat.

He watched the reflection of moving headlights, listened to the crunch of tires on the rough street as the unit passed within a few feet of his hidden car. He didn't breathe, couldn't breathe. His blood felt like ice.

But the guy didn't stop, didn't see his car. He remained crouched out of sight, listening to it move on up the hill. Did he hear it stop, up there? Yes, when he rose warily to look, it had paused at a lighted house high on the hill above.

Again he waited, again the cop remained in his car, just sitting there, shining his light around. Didn't he have anything better to do? What, was he checking out a report of someone prowling around up here? Why didn't he get out and walk the properties, then? Was it because he was alone, without backup? Was he afraid to walk these hills alone?

After what seemed like forever, the unit moved on, to disappear over the crest of the hill. He waited, listening. After some time, when he didn't hear it coming back, he eased up, trying to get his breath, sucking on the damned inhaler and then rubbing his legs and arms to warm himself. Shortness of breath always made him cold. Doctor gave him some pills for a really bad attack, but he didn't take them; they made him feel worse than the constricted breathing. He'd dumped them out long ago, and now he wished he had them.

When the law didn't return, he pulled his cap lower, pulled the collar of his dark windbreaker over his face so he'd blend in with the night, and eased out of the car. He headed down the hill staying among the trees, staying in the shadows and trying not to trip on the rough ground.

Moving along the dark side of the garage where the pedestrian door etched a darker rectangle, he told himself it would soon be over and no one would ever find her. In the morning they'd fill in the trench with gravel and pour new cement to replace that part of the garage floor and be none the wiser about what lay under their careful work. By the time the cement was dry, he'd be long gone.

Once he'd laid her to rest, as the obituaries so delicately put it, and before he left the area, he'd have plenty of time to take care of the rest of his business, and by morning, he'd be two hundred miles north.

Letting himself into the garage, he locked the door behind him. There was enough moonlight coming through the window so that he didn't have to flip on the flashlight. He pulled on the gloves he'd brought and took up one of the shovels that leaned against the wall. He was about to head down the ladder when he thought of the coveralls that he'd sat on earlier.

The foreman was bigger than he was, so it was easy to pull the muddy garment up over his pants. He tried on the boots that stood in the corner. The fit was a bit loose, but they'd save having to clean up his own shoes, which he left on the worktable. More important, they'd leave the correct, waffle-patterned footprints in the bottom of the ditch, because who knew what someone might notice before they dumped in the gravel?

Tossing the shovel down into the pit, he descended the ladder. The damp ground had already been loosened with the shovel or a pick and was soft under his feet, the waffled prints showing clearly. He chose the corner that felt softest, and began to dig, congratulating himself on changing into the boots but annoyed that it had been a last-minute thought, that he hadn't planned better. He began to wonder what else he might have missed.

He could think of nothing left undone, he thought he had everything in hand, but still, as he worked, the worry nagged at him. This procedure, tonight, hadn't been planned the way their regular jobs were. *She* hadn't planned it, he thought with sick amusement. Working on his own, he was shaky about his attention to detail—*she'd* seen to the details. Now, without her direction, he had to be doubly careful.

The digging wasn't hard until he hit a layer of soft rock. That slowed him as he stomped the shovel into it—and the scraping sound was louder than he liked. A glint under the shovel caught his eye for a minute, but it was only a silver gum wrapper. It vanished when he tossed the next shovelful on the pile. He had to drive the blade through maybe five inches of rock, which made his breath ragged. Had to stop twice, to breathe and use the inhaler. Digging, he went over his next steps.

Once he brought her down and buried her, he'd swing by the rented garage on the other side of the village, change cars as she had planned, then get on with the night's work. He felt strange, doing the job without her. Strange, and sick, but excited. Almost like a kid doing something new on his own.

He'd been digging for half an hour, was making good headway despite the fragmented rock and the weight of the damp earth. He wasn't used to this kind of heavy work. He'd had to move the drainpipes out of the way, memorizing their position so when he'd finished, he could put them back in the same formation. He was taking a rest when he heard a faint brushing sound, a soft, stealthy noise that turned him cold.

Glancing at the closed door, he ducked down into the darkest corner of the pit, pulling the shovel beneath him so it wouldn't gleam, hiding the pale oval of his face and hoping his dark clothes would blend into the pit's shadows. Had that cop come back?

What else could it be? Not the contractor, not at this hour. He prayed seriously that it was just some animal, a raccoon or stray dog. *She'd* say it was insane to pray. She'd call such determined prayer arrogant and would laugh at him, say he'd already damned his own soul, so what difference would it make? Crouched in the dark corner in the earthen pit he listened again for the soft brushing, trying to envision what might have made the sound.

When it came again he realized it was not from the door at all but from the direction of the window, a brushing and then a scratching noise. *Had* that cop come back and was looking in the window? But no flashlight beam shone in, reflecting through the garage.

The sound continued for so long that he lost patience and warily slipped up the ladder to look, keeping his collar pulled up and his hat low, climbing only until he could just see over the lip of the ditch, could just see the moonlit window.

He froze, his hands turning cold on the ladder rungs.

No human stood beyond the glass. A cat was there, staring in at him, a pale cat crouched and ghostly on the windowsill, pressed against the glass and looking in—straight at him. A white cat smeared with dirt or some kind of smudged markings. Its eyes caught a red gleam from the reflection of moonlight off the glass. Its intent gaze was relentlessly fixed on him, it didn't blink or look away. Swallowing, he backed down the ladder, tripped and nearly lost his footing, his clumsiness causing a metallic clatter that made his heart pound.

When he climbed and looked again at the window, expecting the cat to have been startled and run off, it was still there watching him.

Well, hell, it was only a cat, only a stupid beast. It didn't know what he was doing. And it was, after all, beyond the glass where it couldn't come near him, couldn't rub up against him as cats so often did, as if they knew he hated them and took pleasure in his fear.

Disgusted, he turned back to his digging, kicking the shovel deeper into the earth and loose rock, his breath coming in gasps, and all the time he dug, he could feel the cat watching, feel the icy chill of its stare.

He kept working, booting his shovel again and again into the earth, heaping up the removed dirt at one end of the long excavation. When he stopped to breathe and to measure the depth of the grave with the shovel handle, and then stepped up the ladder to look, the cat was still there. What did it want, why would it watch him? Turning his back on it and measuring again, he determined that maybe six more inches would allow him to cover her solidly. He'd have to make sure the last layer of dirt over her didn't have any rock in it, because the rock all came from deeper in the earth; someone might notice that and investigate. He was tiring, but he kept on stubbornly until at last the hole was deep enough. Setting the shovel aside, leaning it against the pit wall, he started up the ladder. When he looked again at the window, the cat was gone.

20

Frances and Ed Becker's house was a two-story, cream-colored stucco with dark brown window trim and a black slate roof that was always slippery in wet weather. The cats didn't need daylight to know that the lawn was neatly mowed, the bushes trimmed to perfect spheres that they, personally, thought ugly and unnatural—how could one hide or take shelter under a bush trimmed like a bowling ball? Tansy led them straight through the cat door into the garage where dishes of kibble and a bowl of water were laid out beside two cat beds. The Beckers had two orange-and-white cats, and though neither was present, their scent was heavy and fresh. There was no cat door from the garage into the house.

"They don't want mouse trophies under the furni-ture," Tansy said. "Frances can't stand the thought of mouse guts on her imported rugs." She looked up at the pedestrian door that led into the house. "We can try this, sometimes she leaves it unlocked because the garage is locked."

Leaping up, Joe swung from the knob and pawed at the dead bolt, but at last he dropped down again, shaking his bruised paw.

"Come on then," Tansy said, "there's another way." She led them outside and around the house to the front. In the daytime, the front door would be seen from the street, but at night the soft yard lights left it in shadow. There was no one about nor could they see anyone standing at a nearby lighted window.

The front door was flanked by two tall, narrow panels of glass, each covered by a decorative wrought-iron panel. The pale cat, leaping up and clinging to the iron curlicues, reached a deft paw through and pressed at the sliding window until she had pushed it open.

"They used to leave it open for me. *She* did. He wouldn't bother."

Slipping inside, the cats paused in a large entry hall, their paws sinking into a thick oriental rug. A tall, lush schefflera plant in a blue pot filled one corner. A narrow teak table stood against the opposite wall beside a rosewood bookcase holding small, carved boxes. A large, intricate basket stood on the floor before it, in an artful arrangement. The dining room was to their left past the schefflera plant, a formal room with deep blue walls and a pale, carved dining set. Beyond it they could glimpse the kitchen. The living room was straight ahead, blue walls, a high, raftered ceiling, and a bank of tall windows. To their right, past an open stairway that led to the second floor, was a hall and, Tansy said, two more bedrooms. Between these was the door of a locked closet; they could see the dead bolt running through the slit between the door and molding. But Frances had left the key in the lock.

"For the cleaning crew," Tansy said. "She always did that, she wants it dusted. A huge closet, stacked with sealed boxes and long packages wrapped in brown paper. I used to play and hide in there—until once I got locked in. I was so scared. I cried for hours before Frances found me and let me out." She padded into the living room, onto another deep Persian rug.

"Handmade," Dulcie said, flipping up one corner with careful claws and examining the weave. "No machine made these."

"How do you know such things?" Tansy said.

Dulcie showed her the uneven weave. "From library books," she said. "Late at night when the library's closed and no one's there. And my housemate, Wilma, knows about antiques." She admired the sofa and easy chairs, upholstered in tiny, intricate patterns with a primitive flavor. She examined the small carved tables. "Old and handmade," she said, sniffing them. "And expensive."

To Joe, the furnishings seemed nice enough but it was just a handsome room, large and comfortable. Beside him, Kit seemed nervous, peering out the windows, scanning the trees and bushes that flanked the dim patio. Tansy prowled among the furniture, sniffing longingly the scents she remembered. They prowled all the rooms looking for anything that seemed disturbed, for any space conspicuously empty, or for small indentations in a rug where some piece of furniture had been removed, looking for anything that Charlie might have missed. A photograph of Ed and Frances Becker stood on the dining room buffet, Ed tall and darkly handsome and smiling, Frances nearly as tall, a slim, gentle-looking woman with brown hair wound in a French twist. Frances was an accountant, and Ed worked for the California Department of Children's Services.

"He doesn't seem the type to be a children's case-worker," Dulcie said disapprovingly. "Not with those movie-star looks and that too charming smile—and his eye for other women."

"Are all humans like that?" Tansy said.

"Like what?" said Joe, turning to look at her.

"Catting around," said Tansy smartly. "Ed Becker and Theresa Chapman," she said knowingly. "And Ed Becker and Rita Waterman, too, with her fancy jewelry. Do all humans do that?"

"Where did you get that expression?" said Joe sharply.

"I guess from humans," Tansy said contritely.

Joe twitched a whisker and turned away to the hall. They had found nothing in the living room that seemed missing or out of place. He stood considering the door to the linen closet. Leaping up, he swung on the knob until he had turned it, and turned the key, and with a violent kick of his hind paws he swung the door open, revealing a deep space with shelves on three sides, all crowded with brown-paper packages and sealed boxes.

"What is all that?" Dulcie said.

"Frances calls them accessories," Tansy told her. "Rugs and vases and little tables. She loves to change the house all around, move all the furniture, lay out new rugs while she sends the others to the cleaners. Three times when I was here, she rearranged the whole place, even every vase, every book. *He* wouldn't help her, he left the house until she was done."

"But how did she . . . ," Dulcie began, then went silent, listening to a faraway sound from the hills, to the distant yodel of coyotes.

"You won't go home tonight," Kit told Tansy.

The scruffy little cat shrugged. "They're far away, and the moon's bright."

Joe and Dulcie and Kit looked at the little mite, all thinking the same. If ever there was coyote bait, she was it. How could this small waif expect to escape a pack of hungry predators?

"They have pups," Tansy said. "Can't you hear them? The parents won't wander when the pups are learning to hunt, they stand guard, I've watched them. Besides," she said, "I won't be alone, Sage will be waiting for me." And she smiled that cocky smirk that seemed so out of place in the shy little cat.

"He'll be mad, he was mad when I left him there by that house where they're digging, where all the dirt is piled. But even so, he'll wait for me," she said with assurance.

Kit looked at her jealously. Did Tansy know Sage better than she did, even though she and Sage had grown up together? Pulling the closet door closed behind them, she followed Joe as he impatiently headed up the stairs to prowl the four upstairs bedrooms.

The cats found nothing on that floor that seemed out of order. They were thinking this was all a wild-goose chase when Joe caught that elusive scent again, that puzzling whiff that smelled like catmint.

He'd thought he smelled it in the Chapman house, but it was so faint he couldn't be sure. And again in

212 · SHIRLEY ROUSSEAU MURPHY

the Waterman house he wasn't sure, with the lingering smell of the old dog and the scent of Rita's perfume. They galloped back down the stairs and, having found nothing amiss, they left the Beckers' house, slipping out into the night through the wrought-iron grid beside the front door. Sliding the glass closed, they headed for the Longley house.

"We can never get in *there*," Tansy said. "I tried enough times, I even tried the attic."

"But the Longleys have cats," Dulcie said.

"Three," said Tansy. "They're kept inside when she's gone. When she's home, she opens a window, or sometimes the back slider for them. *Then* I could get in. But I was never sure when I could get out again."

Eleen Longley taught at the local college. She was an attractive, lively woman, slim and with long, mousy, fine-textured hair that seemed to catch in every breeze. Earl was an architect; Ryan said his work was all right if he'd stick to the engineering aspects, if he didn't try to design anything new and interesting. When Clyde suggested that her remark was sarcastic, she said, no, that was fact, that many architects weren't talented at both creative design and engineering, and that was too bad.

"There has to be some way in," Kit said stubbornly.

Tansy said, "If we can get in, we'll know right away if something's missing, I know where the treasures are. They have drawings by famous architects and books

CAT STRIKING BACK • 213

locked up in a big glass case and a whole cabinet of little glass domes with pictures inside. Pictures of humans *doing* things," she said, turning her face away with embarrassment. "She calls it porn . . . porn . . ."

"Pornography?" Dulcie said. "A schoolteacher collects pornographic paperweights? Oh, my."

"They talk about how much they're worth. They talk a lot about money and what things are worth—when they're not fighting. They fight a lot, and then the cats hide."

"Come on," Kit said, "I've seen a window at the back, once I watched a mockingbird pecking at the glass." She took off around the side of the house, plunged into a bougainvillea vine, and clawed her way up between its swinging tendrils and sharp spikes. High up, she crawled out again onto a second-floor balcony that was not more than a foot wide. In the thin, shifting moonlight as clouds blew over, she was hardly visible among the balcony's changing shadows. The others swarmed up behind her, under the decorative rail and onto the narrow ledge. Above them was a small bathroom window, maybe four feet wide but only a foot high, that made the cats smile. Joe and Dulcie and Kit had shimmied in through more than one small, high window, always feeling smug at discovering an entrance inaccessible to humans, which was innocently left unlocked.

21

The grave within the pit was finally deep enough. The earth he'd removed stood piled at one end. He climbed out, changed shoes at the edge of the pit, and, just to be safe, he put the boots and shovel against the wall where he'd found them. He'd be back soon, but what if someone came while he was gone to get the car? Moving out through the side door, he left it unlocked. Imagining that cat prowling around, he made sure it was tightly shut.

It was harder climbing back up the hill, he was worn out from digging and the climb took more out of him. The hill was darker, now, too, the moon hidden behind blowing clouds. Were those rain clouds? He didn't like the thought of maybe a heavy rain, of water flooding down the hill into the hole he'd dug. Of water filling her grave before it rose high enough to run out through the drainpipes at either end of the pit. Earlier, he hadn't thought of that.

Scrambling up through the woods, he tripped in the tall, tangled grass. He wondered if, trampling the grass, he was leaving a trail. But why would anyone look for a trail? Why would anyone be interested? In the morning when they entered the garage, they'd see nothing to alarm them. The pit would be just as they'd left it.

Reaching the car, he thought he could already smell the beginning of putrefaction, and that made him sick. But maybe that was his imagination, maybe that was his fear and guilt returning to taunt him.

He waited for some time, watching the area, before he pulled the car down, backed it into the drive close to the garage and opened the trunk. He didn't want to touch her. When he reached to pull her out, the blanket slid off. Her body was stiff but her arms and legs were limp, and she was hard to move. He tucked the blanket around her as best he could, then lifted her. He didn't like this, the changes in her body frightened him. With distaste he carried her around the side of the garage and in through the pedestrian door. Again he locked it behind him.

She was so heavy. She was a slim person, but now her weight seemed nearly unmanageable. He pulled the blanket back around her where it wanted to slide off. Carrying her over his shoulder, he knelt beside the top of the ladder and stepped down. It was hard to balance her and balance himself and swing down onto the first rung. He didn't want to shove her over into the pit, didn't want to hear the body fall. Clinging to the side of the ladder with one hand, with her awkwardly over his shoulder, he was able to carry her down. He tripped on the third rung and nearly fell.

Clumsily he knelt and lowered her into the grave. He left her lying there while he returned to the driveway to move the car.

Getting in, careful to close the door silently, he drove back up the hill to the crest and pulled off the street again, in among the cypress trees. The wind had risen, blowing the clouds away; the hillside and yard below were lighter now, easing his descent but making him more visible. Moving down the hill he tripped on a fallen branch and fell, hurting his knee and hand. Why had he taken off the gloves, stuffed them uselessly in his pocket? Was he bleeding? If the skin of his hand was torn, where he'd carried her, would some infection get into the wound despite the blanket that he'd draped over her? Would bacteria already be growing in her, to get on him and infect him? He was sweating, his shirt sticking to him. He was all nerves, tense and jumpy, afraid someone would come along before he could bury her, before he could shift the dirt back over her, before he could get away. There, by the driveway, did something move?

But no, it was only shadows from the blowing clouds moving across the torn-up yard. Reaching the narrow strip of raw earth along the side of the garage, he moved inside quickly, watching to see that nothing fled in with him, past his feet. Again he locked the door and then changed into the boots. When he looked toward the window, it was empty, there was nothing there to bother him.

But now he wished he could see the cat, could make sure it was there and hadn't slipped inside with him. Or was it outside, sniffing at the door and listening to the small sounds as he descended the ladder? At the bottom, as he picked up the shovel, he glanced again at the window and the cat was back, crouched on the sill staring in at him as it had before, intent and still.

But it was only a cat, a dumb beast. Forget it, pay no attention to it. His hands on the shovel were so sweaty he couldn't hold it right. Trying to move the loose earth to hide her, he spilled more dirt over his feet and into the muddy boots than down onto her body. The weight of dirt had slid the blanket off her. He didn't like to look at her face and bare chest and belly, livid where collected blood had darkened. When he looked up again he was staring directly into the cat's eyes.

The beast's cold scrutiny seemed to elevate his distress at seeing her for the last time, at seeing her slowly disappear beneath his shovelfuls of dirt, seeing her slowly hidden by the weight of the earth, and trapped there. Thinking of her sealed in that small hole that would soon be closed forever, it was all he could do to not abandon the grave and run.

He kept on mechanically shoveling dirt until the grave was filled, and then he carefully arranged the black drainpipes to run the length of the pit, just as he'd found them. Climbing up the ladder, he changed shoes, set the boots at the edge of the pit while he took off the coveralls and hung them up, then set the shovel as he'd found it. Leaving the garage he paused to painstakingly lock the door behind him with the lock picks. He didn't see the cat in the moonlit yard. Quickly he climbed the hill to his car and locked himself in. Foolish, this terror, but he couldn't help it. He began to wonder if the cat could have slipped into the car behind him when he opened the door. The back of his neck crawled as he peered into the backseat and then got out and looked under the seats.

When at last he was convinced that it hadn't followed him up the hill, he got back in the driver's seat. He was alone, the trunk was empty, even the blanket was buried where it wouldn't be found. He was about to start the engine and head out, take the car up to the rented garage and get the RV, when he realized he'd left the boots standing at the lip of the pit, that he hadn't put them back where he'd found them, that he'd taken them off, put on his shoes, and, in too much of a hurry, had left them there.

Planning. Careful planning. She'd been so meticulous about planning. Shoving the flashlight in his pocket he headed back down the hill, his chest tight, his mouth dry.

He picked the lock again, his hands shaking, let himself in, slipped his shoes off at the threshold, moved inside in his stocking feet. Shielding the flashlight with his hand, he shone it on the lip of the pit, picking out the boots, then looked around for anything else he'd left out of place. He was reaching for the boots to put them back by the wall when his beam swung up, catching the white shape at the window. He held the light there in a rictus of fear. The cat's pale fur bristled, its tail was huge, its eyes blazing in the light. Dropping the boots, he snatched up a hammer from the table and in a frenzy of hate threw it hard at the beast. The window shattered with an explosion like gunfire, glass showering as bright as embers and the cat disappeared into the night.

He lowered his light, stood numb and shaken, and couldn't breathe.

At last, steadying himself, he replaced the boots against the wall, and again looked around for anything else he'd left amiss. When he was sure that everything was in place he fled, silently shutting the door, pausing to go through the tedious process of locking it while looking and listening for the cat and praying he'd killed it. When the door was locked, he climbed the hill, started the engine, and hauled out of there, heading for the rented garage.

Down beside the garage, Sage crawled away from the broken glass and the fallen hammer and moved deep among the bushes, easing himself down on the cool ground. He wanted to lie quietly, he hurt bad and he was bleeding. He had never trusted humans and now he hated them.

He'd been hunting, minding his own business and waiting hopefully for Tansy after she'd gone off with those village cats. He was angry with her because she'd defied him but still he'd waited—and now he wished she were there, now he needed her.

He'd been curious when he saw the man leave the parked car, moving so stealthily, and slip down the hill and into the garage. Leaping onto the lumber pile beside the window he'd looked in, had watched him digging, making the pit deeper and then in a little while had watched him carry a dead woman in there and that had frightened him, a naked dead woman with a blanket wrapped around her. He'd watched him bury her, and he knew two things: This secret burial would be very wrong in the law of the clowder. They did not bury their dead secretly, there was always a ceremony. And he knew from the village cats that such behavior was equally against the law of the human world.

Uneasily, he had watched the man bury her, and when the man looked up, his face filling with fear, that had pleased Sage. He had watched him as he nervously filled the grave with dirt, had seen him leave and return. It was then, when the man shone the light on him, that he had bristled up, half angry and half amused by the human's fear, had made himself big and wild, and that was when the man's face contorted with rage and he grabbed the hammer and threw it.

He hadn't been quick enough, the glass shattered and the hammer struck him, and now he lay beneath the bushes hurting very bad and wishing Tansy was with him. Wishing he had someone to care that he was hurt, and to help him.

22

On the high narrow balcony of the Longley house, Kit was trying to claw open the bathroom window when lights flashed along the street below and paused, hitting the edge of the roof as a car pulled into the driveway. The intrusion so startled Kit that she aborted her leap to the window, dropping back to the balcony. Crouching, she jumped higher, hit the roof snatching at the gutter, pulling herself onto the shingles. Joe, Dulcie, and Tansy followed, their hind paws clawing at empty air as they scrabbled up beside her and they trotted to the edge to peer over.

A dark brown recreation vehicle stood below, a compact RV with two camp chairs tied on top. They heard the electric garage door open. The RV pulled in, and the door rolled down again. The cats, directly above, could not see into the cab.

"Is that the Longleys?" Dulcie said. "They just *left* for their vacation. What, did they rent an RV? Has something happened to bring them back?"

"Maybe they gave some friend the key," Joe said doubtfully.

"They would have told Charlie," Dulcie said. "And she would have told us, she knew we were coming here." She cut a look at Joe. "Shall we go in anyway?"

"Are you out of your mind?"

"We could just crack the bathroom window open and listen, find out if it *is* the Longleys. If they come upstairs, we'll hear them talking and we—"

Joe shrugged, and turned, and slipped back across the roof walking softly as he headed for the trellis. They dare not gallop, even a crow hopping on the shingles would be heard from within, in a series of little drumbeats. They were about to drop down to the balcony and try the high window when another pair of lights came up the street, and a second car paused in front of the house. They heard a police radio, and the reflection of a spotlight glanced up through the trees as its bright beam swept the yard.

Slipping back across the roof, the cats looked down on a black-and-white. It stood at the curb, portly Officer Brennan sitting behind the wheel, shining his torch along the house, across the doors and windows. Did he know there was someone here who might not belong?

Brennan got out and dutifully circled the house, shining his light up and down so it glanced along the edges of the roof. Then he eased himself back into his car, looking bored. As if he had found nothing out of order, as if this was only a routine check. That angered Dulcie, that he'd found nothing amiss. "He's just going to leave?" she said angrily, her tail lashing, her ears flat.

"How would he know?" Joe said. "Even Brennan can't see through walls."

Starting his engine, Brennan headed down the street, pulling up at the Waterman house. The cats watched him go through the same routine there. He was simply doing a vacation check, possibly at Charlie's request. When he headed for the Chapmans', they returned to the balcony and its high window.

"Are we going in, or what?" Dulcie said impatiently. "We can't learn anything out here."

"In," Tansy said boldly. "I know places to hide."

"So they see us? We're only cats," Kit said, forgetting times past when such a discovery of unexplained feline entry had led to disaster—when one such incident had frazzled her little cat nerves so badly that she remained jumpy for weeks, flinching at every shadow.

Dulcie looked at Joe. When Joe shrugged, and nodded, the tabby leaped to the little window, her claws in the sill, her hind legs braced against the house. It was an awkward angle, but more swiftly than her companions expected she dug her claws into the window frame, gave one hard jerk, and was surprised to see the glass slide open beneath her paws.

They crowded onto the sill, dropped to the tile counter, and slipped softly down onto the bathroom rug. The bathroom door was cracked open. Crouched in the chill little room, they could hear from downstairs hard footsteps cross the wooden floor, heard someone walking back and forth, back and forth, as if slowly pacing. Then came the scraping of metal against metal, then several little *thunk*s, then a click, as if a door had been opened.

"Stay here," Joe said. "Wait here." And he was out of the bathroom and down the hall before Dulcie could stop him.

The three lady cats followed, to see him disappear down the curved stairs. Pausing on the top step, they tried to see where he'd gone. Dulcie's and Kit's dark coats were nearly invisible on the dark runner, but pale little Tansy shone as bright as the moonlight that was shining in through the high windows. The curved stairway led down to a wide entry, where a cream-colored Chinese rug shone against the dark parquet floor. Arches opened into two adjoining rooms, flanking a carved settee that stood against the wall.

Joe appeared beneath the settee, and paused in the entrance to the living room where moonlight brightened a wall of bookshelves and glass-fronted cupboards. A man stood there, his back to them, opening the glass door of a cupboard, a tall man dressed in jeans and a dark windbreaker.

As he began removing the books within, Joe slipped up behind him and vanished beneath a spindly leather love seat that was stacked with empty cardboard boxes. The door on the other side of the fireplace stood open as well. These shelves were empty, and on a chair nearby, a carton marked VODKA was neatly filled with small, round, glass objects nestled among folds of bubble wrap.

They watched him fill three small grocery boxes with books and stack them one on top of the other. Picking up the cardboard tower, he headed away through the second arch. They heard his retreating footsteps but heard no door open, heard him step from the hardwood onto a nearly soundless surface. Then there was a little scraping sound such as hard shoes might make on concrete. He was in the garage? Even from the top of the stairs they could detect a cold-cement smell creeping up. Joe had vanished, the shadows beneath the love seat were empty.

They heard a car door open, then a sliding sound, as if the man was shoving his boxes into the RV. Dulcie looked helplessly for Joe. The living room had grown darker as clouds floated across the moon. Kit said, "So many books. Can they *all* be worth stealing?"

"And those little glass balls," Tansy said, "with tiny little people in them, naked and doing private things. What did you call them? Who would pay money for those?" Again she dropped her ears. If a cat could blush, Tansy's pale little face would be pink with embarrassment.

They were about to creep down the stairs when they heard the man returning fast, nearly running. Tansy crouched. Kit hissed, her ears back. There was a *bang,* the man shouted in triumph, and Joe came racing in through the arch, the man behind him—he grabbed a heavy ashtray and threw it as Joe dove into the alcove beneath the stairs.

"Go!" Dulcie hissed at Kit and Tansy. "Get out, both of you!" She slapped at them, driving them up the stairs toward the bathroom, and she flew down to join Joe. But Kit didn't leave; she came galloping down alone and pushed close behind Dulcie. Together they bolted beneath the stairs beside Joe.

Joe wasn't there. The dusty space was empty. Dulcie pressed into the darkest empty corner to make sure, then crouched close to Kit, peering out into the living room.

The tall windows had darkened, the moon nearly hidden, the man only a dark, prowling shadow, looking for Joe, kicking into the blackness beneath the furniture.

Why? Why was he so angry? They were only cats.

Terrified for Joe, Dulcie glanced in the direction of the garage. Where else would the tomcat go but to follow the stolen boxes? Perhaps, she thought, chilled, he meant to slip into the RV and ride with the thief to his destination? "Come on," she whispered, slipping from under the stairs. The two cats, flashing behind the man's feet, silently fled for the garage.

The door stood just ajar, the chill air smelling of concrete. They slipped through, dove beneath a workbench, and crouched against the wall, looking out, looking for Joe, and watching the door nervously. The garage was softly lighted by an electric torch that stood on top the workbench, its glow spilling down around them but leaving them in shadow. Both the big overhead door and the pedestrian door to the yard were tightly shut. There were no windows. The walls were smoothly finished and painted white. The usual garage clutter must be hidden within the row of white storage cabinets that lined the far wall. On the other side of the brown RV stood a tan BMW hatchback, most likely the Longleys' second car.

Kit said, "Do you think Tansy got away safe? That she'll get home all right, all alone in the night?"

"Maybe she'll stay close until we come out," Dulcie said, more to ease Kit than because she believed it. Beside her, Kit reared up to look at the lower workbench shelf that ran just above their heads. An assortment of tools was arranged neatly at one end: two hammers, four wrenches, and a dozen screwdrivers of various sizes. All were dusty. The rest of the shelf was taken over by a row of clear plastic containers filled with different size nails. Kit studied the contents of each, from tiny little brads to huge spikes. Focusing on a particular mess of black nails with extra-wide heads, the tortoiseshell smiled. And as Dulcie slipped out to investigate the pedestrian door that should lead out to the side yard, Kit busied herself trying, with stubborn claws, to loosen the lid.

"Door's bolted at the top," Dulcie said softly from across the garage. Kit didn't answer, she was too busy. Why was anything plastic so hard to manage? She heard Dulcie jumping against the far wall, trying to reach the bolt of the side door, and listened to the tabby's little grunt each time she fell back. When the plastic lid popped up, Kit whacked it to the floor, carefully put a paw in, and began clawing out nails.

The nails were heavy, and they wanted to stick in her pads. The points hurt even more when, with a little pile of nails on the shelf before her, she put her nose against them and pawed them into her mouth. Damn things stung her tender mouth like bees. Dropping down to the cement floor, she managed not to swallow any.

When Dulcie returned, defeated by the high bolt— Joe was the master at slipping hard-to-manage bolts— she did a double take at Kit's protruding cheeks. She watched in silence as Kit circled beneath the RV, spitting out a few nails beneath each tire. Seeing what the tortoiseshell was up to, Dulcie smiled and slipped under to help her.

They pawed at each nail until they made it stand upright just beneath the tire. They had nearly finished when they heard footsteps approaching, loud on the hardwood floor. They dove back beneath the workbench as he came down the two concrete steps carrying another stack of boxes; they stared out at his feet as he set the boxes on the bench. They watched him return to the door, heard him lock it. This was the last load, then? Now they couldn't get back inside to find Joe, and Dulcie began to fidget, watching the man nervously.

They still couldn't see his face, unless they came out where he could see them, where they'd be center stage beneath the torchlight. He was putting the boxes in through the RV's side door when they heard a car out front and the voice of a police radio. Had Brennan come back? The man froze. He glanced at the electric torch but daren't extinguish it now in case it shone out beneath the overhead door. He didn't move as the brighter light of the cop's torch skated along the thin crack—but then the crack darkened again. There was a long silence, as if the officer outside was waiting and watching. Had the soft light within the garage alerted him? Or was this, again, only routine? Or was this Brennan's supper break? The cats imagined him sitting in his unit eating a giant burger and sipping from a Styrofoam cup of coffee.

But then at last the unit backed out of the drive and moved on, its purring engine growing softer as it headed up the street. At once, the thief moved to the big garage door and stood with his ear against it, listening. He waited there for some time, but there was only silence from the street. Finally he loaded the last box and silently closed the door of the RV. Slipping into the driver's seat, he activated the electric door with a remote that, at some point, he must have stolen. As he backed out, Dulcie and Kit, feeling the cold night air on their noses, longed for the freedom of the open night. The breeze was like a whisper urging them to run—but Dulcie thought of Joe and she didn't move, she thought only of getting back in the house. Maybe he was hurt, injured by the heavy ashtray the man had thrown. The door started down.

"We can get back in quicker from outside," Kit said. The door was halfway down. "Run!" Kit said. "Run now!"

Dulcie came to life. They fled beneath the closing door, jumping high over the red light that marked the electric eye. The door slammed behind them as they dove into the bushes.

Kit said, "We never saw his face." In the shadowy living room they'd seen only his back. From beneath the workbench they'd seen his wrinkled brown running shoes, his dark jeans, and a glimpse of his green windbreaker.

"What did he smell of?" Dulcie said. She'd memorized his smell as he stood close above them, his personal male scent overlaid with something she should know but couldn't identify. Something akin to catnip, only different. When they were certain the RV was gone, they fled around the house to the back. Dulcie bolted up the trellis and in through the bathroom window, frantic to find Joe, but Kit stopped on the balcony behind her, mewling softly to summon Tansy. She listened, then mewled again. She looked down at the yard, studying the dark and crowded bushes. "Tansy?"

There was no answer and no pale movement among the shadows. She looked away toward the hills, worried that the scruffy little cat had gone on through the night alone. Praying that if Tansy was headed home, she would be wary and cautious and safe.

23

When Dulcie had hissed at Tansy to run, Tansy obeyed as fast as her thin little legs would carry her. The sight of that man chasing Joe jarred to life every terrified kittenhood memory of such cruel men and sent her streaking away up the stairs and into the bathroom, leaping out the window and scrambling backward down the trellis, catching hanks of fur on the thorns. At the bottom she stood shivering, looking out into the night and watching the darkest shadows. She waited a long time for Kit to follow her, and all the while Dulcie's words rang in her head, *Go! Get out, both of you!* And the stink of that man's anger clung to her. As she listened for the other cats to emerge from the house, her heart pounded with fear for them. But she was too afraid to go back. There was only silence from the house behind her. When after a very long time Kit didn't come, when no one came, she fled for the far hills and home, running blindly up through the dark village—until she realized she was lost, was crossing unfamiliar streets through neighborhoods that she had never seen. She was lost and her sense of direction seemed to have abandoned her.

She stood on an empty sidewalk on an unknown street among houses she was sure she had never seen. She listened. She sniffed the scents of this strange place, trying to smell something familiar, trying to find her direction.

At last her pounding heart eased. At last, reclaiming her good cat sense and determination, she scrambled up the nearest pine tree to the nearest roof where she could see better.

Well, of course! There were the hills, black humps like the backs of huge animals, their familiar curves caught in faintest moonlight against the night sky. There were the hills and there was home, and she ran leaping from roof to roof until the houses stood too far apart, then she scrambled down to the gardens. And away she went, racing through weedy grass and up into the open hills, racing for the ruin's jagged and protective walls that rose like a palace against the blowing clouds.

Fleeing for home, she wondered why she had ever gone among humans? This always happened, this violence from humans. Her mouth and nose still reeked of the smell of that man, the smell of human rage. On she raced, her senses sharply alert for predators. She was passing the house with dirt piled in its yard when she smelled something other than a predator. She smelled death.

Human death?

She froze in place, looking all around. Why would there be a dead person here? She was frowning, studying the house when she saw something pale stir on the hill above, a small, feeble movement. She crouched warily, looking. She reared up, stretching tall, scenting the air, and it was then that she smelled him. She ran straight up the hill to him, streaked up through the grass and crouched beside him, her paws going cold. "Sage? Oh, Sage."

He didn't move or speak, he lay unnaturally hunched. But he was alive, his eyes looked into hers, filled with pain. When she snuggled carefully beside him, touching him with her nose, he pressed against her shivering, his body rigid and tight.

"What?" she said softly. "What happened?" She looked around into the night, but she saw nothing, now, that could have attacked him. She could smell no coyote or other animal, and certainly no human—except for the stench of a dead person that came from the house below.

Above them a raft of clouds blew past, again freeing the fickle moon, and down the hill, the house and the pale drive and the walks brightened. The dirt pile lit up along its side and the tiled roof became a tangle of curved shadows. The smell of death sickened her, and then the wind came straight at her and she smelled that man, too. The man she had run from. How could he be there when he was down in the village in that house?

"A human hurt you . . . did this to you?"

"He's gone," Sage said. "A long time ago."

"What did he do . . . what happened?"

"He threw a hard tool at me, a hammer. Threw it through the window where I was watching him. It came through straight at me, broke the glass, I wasn't quick enough."

"Why did he?" She licked his face. "What did you do to make him so mad? To make him hurt you?"

Sage rose stiffly and started down the hill, limping badly.

"Stay still, you'll hurt yourself more."

Ignoring her, he headed for the house, every line of his body showing pain and anger. She followed him until, approaching the garage, the smell of death hit her so hard she turned away, gagging.

"Come where the window is," he said impatiently. "Mind the glass. Come where we can see in." Crawling painfully up onto the stack of lumber, trying to avoid the jagged shards, he put his paws on the sill, looking in between knives of glass. She hopped up beside him.

"See that ditch?"

She looked at the deep fissure. "Why is there a ditch there?" She looked at the dirty concrete floor where earth had been hauled out, at the muddy footprints.

"There's a dead woman down there. That man went down in the ditch and dug the hole deeper, then he brought her in his car and carried her down the ladder and covered her up with dirt." Sage turned to look at her, the pupils of his eyes huge and dark—with fear, with anger. "That's not how humans bury their dead. Even I know that. This was sneaky, stealthy. When he saw me watching, he went white and grabbed the hammer and threw it."

Tansy looked back at him, surprised not so much by what the man had done—humans would do anything— but because, maybe for the first time in his life, Sage was paying attention to something outside the clowder; he was enraged by something that was not a part of *their* world. From Sage's standpoint, the hiding of a dead human would have nothing to do with a cat's proper business—until the man had hurt him. She guessed that made it his business.

She said, "I saw him earlier, in the village. He was stealing from a house, we watched him. He threw something at Joe Grey and chased him."

Sage's eyes widened. "Did he hurt Joe?"

"I don't know," she said, looking down in shame. "I ran . . . I should have gone back. But I must go back," she said. "I have to see if they're all right, I have to tell them that he came here and that he buried someone. Why would he bury a woman? Unless . . . Did he kill her? That is a crime in the human world, humans will want to find him and punish him. We—"

But now Sage turned reluctant. "This has nothing to do with us. This is not a matter for cats."

"Then why did you show me?"

"Because he hurt me. I'm going home where it's safe."

She sat looking at him. "You spent weeks among humans when you were hurt before. Humans cared for you, they pampered you, gave you nice things to eat, made soft beds for you—humans saved your life, Sage!"

"Come on, Tansy." He eased down from the sill and off the lumber pile with a grunt of pain. "We need to go. This is human business." Expecting her to follow, he limped away, heading up the hill.

Tansy did follow. She dare not let him travel home alone when he was nearly helpless—yet she was ashamed to let him stop her from what she must do. If they didn't tell the village cats what Sage had seen, maybe no human would ever know that a dead woman lay there hidden in that ditch. Somewhere, a woman was missing. And no one would ever learn where she had gone.

24

Earlier in the Longley house, when Dulcie and Kit dove into the recess beneath the stairs, Joe Grey had slid around the corner and into the shadows of a hall, stopping, dead ended, at a closet door. Frantically he had pawed it open as the man searched the living room. Slipping inside and beneath a tangle of coats, he pulled the door closed with a hasty paw, thanking the great cat god that the hinges were silent. He didn't dare let it latch, even the smallest click would crack like a rifle shot. This wasn't smart, shutting himself in such a trap. If the guy jerked the door open, he'd have to be quick to get out, to save his furry neck. The closet stunk of damp wool, and of dog urine on the tip of an umbrella that was propped in the corner.

As the man's heavy footsteps approached, he leaped up between a trench coat and a black peacoat, digging his claws into the thick wool. Hanging there with the claws of all four feet busily engaged, he hoped the damn rod wouldn't give way.

The footsteps paused just outside. The door opened and the man knelt, looking in beneath the coats. He picked up the umbrella and poked it into the dark corners. Then he gave a cross "Hmph," shut the door, and went back down the hall.

Dropping carefully to the floor, Joe pressed against the door. He listened for some time to the guy searching for him. Finally he must have given up, because Joe heard him return to filling his boxes with books. He imagined Dulcie and Kit watching from beneath the stairs—he'd heard Dulcie hiss at Tansy to run, had heard the smaller cat's racing footfalls on the floor above.

He waited, it seemed, for a very long time before he heard the guy walk heavily away toward the garage, as if loaded down with another stack of boxes. When he'd gone, Joe leaped at the knob, grabbed it between his paws and swung until he could kick the door open. Peering out, he whispered for Dulcie.

There was no answer. He waited, listening. There was no sound. When the man didn't return, he was about to slip out and look for her and Kit when he heard the garage door rise and the RV pull out—and a chill hit him.

Had they followed the guy and slipped into the RV intent on shadowing him, on finding out where he was taking the stolen property?

That would be like them. Both females were as nosy as a bloodhound on the scent. Frightened for them, he raced up the stairs and out the bathroom window, hoping to see which way the RV headed, thinking to call the station and report the burglar, get a be-on-the-lookout started. He could think of nothing else to do.

Racing across the roof to the edge, he saw the dark vehicle moving slowly away, up the street. He fled across the shingles after it, with a giant leap to the next roof, and the next, praying that Dulcie and Kit weren't inside being hauled away to who knew where. He was scorching down a pine tree, where the roofs were too far apart, when the RV slowed and pulled into the Beckers' drive. As he fled through the bushes for the Beckers' yard, he heard their garage door open.

The RV disappeared inside, and the door rolled down again. This guy must sweat every time the sound of an electric door broke the night's silence, as he hastened to conceal his intrusion. How did he have openers for these houses? How, for that matter, had he known these particular houses were empty? Joe approached the Becker house beneath a low-growing pepper tree. Within seconds he was clinging to the wrought-iron grille beside the Beckers' front door. Though his big paws weren't as clever as Tansy's, with persistence and with tomcat muscle he soon slipped the window open and bellied inside.

Leaving the window open for a quick departure, he listened for sounds from the garage. A sudden scurrying behind him made him spin around.

Dulcie came sliding through the window and into the dark entry hall, uttering a little mewl of relief at finding him there. Kit exploded through behind her. Both cats were panting.

"Might as well try to catch a racehorse," Dulcie said, "as to track you. You must have flown across the roofs. What . . .?" She went quiet at the sound, from the direction of the garage, of a knob turning.

They heard the inner door creak open. Footsteps approached fast, as if he was certain the house was empty—and as if he was familiar with the layout. There was no handy place to hide from him, and the cats fled in three directions. Joe spun toward the stairs and up out of sight. Kit leaped onto the rosewood bookcase, where she froze between two decoratively carved boxes, her mottled coat blending with both. Dulcie slipped into the African basket, her dark stripes melting into its patterns. The burglar had traversed the short distance to the entry hall, where he paused within touching distance of Dulcie and Kit, noticing neither camouflaged cat.

From the shadowed stairs, Joe peered down into the living room, thanking the great god who had effectively crippled human night vision. He had sensibly tucked his head down to hide his white paws and chest, hoping, if he was seen, that he'd resemble one of those life-size cats that people brought home from the gift shops of airports—wouldn't that be a shocker if this guy picked him up expecting a stuffed replica and got a fistful of fighting tomcat.

Again the burglar was well prepared, with a stack of empty boxes. Moving on through the foyer, he began to strip the living room of all the small pieces, intricately patterned handmade pillows, small carved chests. For nearly an hour the cats posed, unmoving, rigid in their grandstand seats as the busy burglar packed up rugs and accessories, carved side tables, and the paintings from the walls. He even had newspapers to pack up the expensive-looking porcelain and protect the delicate tables, and he seemed to know exactly what he wanted. Dulcie imagined a computer inside his head ticking off dollar signs, toting up the value of each separate piece. When he seemed about to finish in the living room, Joe left his perch on the stairs and the cats crawled uncomfortably beneath the lowest shelf of the teak table. A tight squeeze but a better hiding place, putting them at eye level with his shoes as he made trip after trip carrying his treasures to the garage. This guy had planned with care, from acquiring the garage door openers to inventorying the contents of the designated houses. There seemed to be no hesitation, no misstep. The question was, how did he know these houses so well?

They could hear him out in the garage loading the boxes into his RV, which must be getting pretty full. Returning, he went through the rest of the rooms, upstairs and down, carrying away the nicest treasures. Last of all, he opened the hall closet and started loading up the packages and sealed boxes.

The deep closet, crowded with Frances's wrapped treasures, proved her to indeed be an avid collector. Dulcie guessed she had to be a topflight accountant to afford the luxuries with which the house was furnished. By the time the burglar had made only two trips carrying taped boxes and brown-paper packages, Joe had worked out his plan and was tensed to spring into action. As the man headed away on his third trip, Joe slipped down the stairs to have a look at the closet door.

The doorknobs on both sides were simple round ones. The lock was installed above the knobs. There was no corresponding bolt inside, not your usual safety arrangement. If you were inside, and someone locked the door, you'd be trapped. And that made the tomcat smile.

Rearing up beside the open door, he could just reach the key. The door was heavy, most likely a solid core, and hardly moved under his weight. With a quick paw, claws gripped around the key, and twisting his whole body, he was just able to turn it—the dead bolt slid noiselessly out. When he turned the key again with another hard, shoulder-wrenching twist, it slid back. He heard the guy returning and dove back into the shadows beneath the table, pushing in between Dulcie and Kit; and the minute the man left with another load, the tomcat laid out his plan. "I'll be the bait," he told them.

"No," said Kit, "you're stronger. *I'll* lure him inside. You and Dulcie shove the door and turn the lock, I can dive out faster!"

"No!" Dulcie and Joe said together—but they heard him coming back and it looked like this would be the last load, the closet was nearly stripped of packages. "No!" Dulcie hissed again as Kit dove into the closet, concealing herself behind the remaining boxes like the good hunter she was, waiting for her victim.

25

Kit waited deep in the closet, crouched and still. As the burglar stepped in and reached to take the last boxes she leaped at him, exploding in his face with a bloodcurdling yowl that made him stumble backward and fall, crashing into the shelves, thrusting out his hands to ward her off—she looked twice her size, fur standing out, bushy tail lashing. When she screamed again, he scrabbled at the shelves as if to climb away from her. She advanced on him, forcing him back as Joe and Dulcie crouched to leap at the door. Their timing had to be fast and exact, Kit racing out and the door slamming closed. *Run now!* Dulcie thought, wanting to scream at her. *Run out now!* Her muscles quivered, primed to leap the moment Kit bolted through.

But now, instead of trying to escape from Kit, he grabbed a long package and began to beat at her. She dodged and he missed. As he swung again, Joe and Dulcie sprang at him, forgetting the door. He yelled, knocked the cats off with hard blows and bolted past them out the door, hitting Joe as he slammed it in their faces.

They heard the key turn, the dead bolt sliding home.

Joe staggered up and jumped at the door, clawing uselessly at the knob. He fell back to the floor, staring up where the inner knob of the lock *should* be. They were locked in, they were trapped. They pushed close together, fear gripping them, and Kit began to pant.

At first they heard no sound from without, but then, pressing against the door, they could hear him breathing—as if he was standing just outside. Already the air felt close and hot, already the walls were pressing in. They thought about cats trapped in the holds of airplanes, about kittens falling into some hidey-hole where they couldn't get out, about cats locked in abandoned houses. They stared at the heavy door, wanting to claw through it and knowing cat claws couldn't penetrate an inch of solid wood.

The fact that they'd meant to imprison the burglar as they were now confined, made them feel all the more helpless, made their plight all the more horrifying. Theirs had been an honorable plan. They hadn't meant to leave him here to die, they'd intended that he be rescued.

But what did he intend? Was he smiling, hoping no one found them until it was too late?

He stood staring at the locked closet door, feeling smug that he'd trapped them but shaken by their attack. He leaned against the wall, fishing in his pocket for the inhaler, and found he'd left it in the RV. Where had those cats come from? It couldn't be the same three as in the Longley house, but they looked the same. And how would they get into either house? Cats didn't go through locked doors, he thought, shivering.

Earlier, as he'd hurried to load up the books and paperweights, could they have smelled his stress and fear? Could that have made them follow him? He'd always believed that the smell of fear would make a cat come after a person. He was still so sick from their attack that even after he returned to the RV, when he couldn't find the inhaler, he could only sit miserably behind the wheel gulping air, trying to get his breath. When at last he could breathe again he searched under the seats then moved into the back, searched frantically among the boxes and packages that he'd loaded, searched every inch of the floor that he could reach. He wanted to go back in the house, to look in all the rooms, but there wasn't time.

He remembered when he'd watched that couple from above the empty ranch, he'd had the inhaler then, he remembered using it, the comforting feel of knowing it would help him. And he'd had it when he buried her, had used it then. Before he hauled her down the ladder he'd taken it out of his pocket, didn't want it falling out as he bent and dug and heaved dirt. He remembered laying it on the worktable. He couldn't remember his hand on it again, couldn't remember putting it back in his pocket.

It wasn't only that it was a prescription inhaler, that he couldn't stop in a drugstore and pick one off the counter. It was that his fingerprints would be on it. He looked again through the glove compartment and the console, but it wasn't there. He'd have to go back to the remodel, go in the garage again where he'd buried her, see if it was on the worktable. Yes, he was sure of it, when he grabbed and threw the hammer, he'd been so upset he'd forgotten it.

These last two houses would take only minutes and he'd be done and could go get the inhaler. In these houses, all he wanted was the small stuff, and in both cases the collections were all in one place. The jewelry wouldn't take any time to gather up, and Theresa's miniature paintings would fit in a couple of boxes. He didn't want to leave those, there were some name painters in there who would bring a good price. Get the stuff quick and he'd be done. Swing by and get the inhaler, then hit the road.

Starting the engine, he activated the garage door and backed out, shutting the door behind him. With the successful completion of the major part of his plan, with *her* put safely to rest, and when the sound of those cats clawing the door could no longer reach him, his confidence returned. Couple of hours from now he'd be up the road, tucked comfortably into a motel under another name, a drink in his hand and his stash safely locked in the RV, ready, in the morning, to trade for cash and a new start.

He had no notion, thinking about his plans, that when he returned to the empty house he would again be watched. If he'd known, he might not have gone back, he might have left the inhaler and prayed that no one would pay attention to it, that it would be tossed out with the rest of the trash.

26

"I'm getting really paranoid when Joe isn't in for the night," Ryan said.

"Shank of the evening," Clyde said as he turned out the living room lights and they headed upstairs accompanied by Rock and Snowball. "You have to learn to live with it."

"You don't worry?"

"I worry all the time. I put it on the back burner, like a dull toothache."

"That is really very encouraging," she said, moving up the stairs beside him.

In the master bedroom Clyde lit a fire and pushed the sliding doors open between the two rooms so they could enjoy the cheerful blaze from the study. His desk was littered with the car ads he'd placed in various newspapers and magazines, with the "car collectors" columns from various newspapers, and with faxes and notations of phone calls to answer.

Ryan had set up a folding table next to the couch to serve as a temporary work space. This was stacked with real estate fliers and notes on the dozen pieces of property they were considering. The two of them were so jammed into the small study that neither one could move their chair without disturbing the other. Sitting down to sort through their prospective purchases, she looked up at the newly installed door that led into the new construction, eager to be finished and move into her spacious new studio. The big space was dried in, the roof on, but there was the tile floor still to lay and the rest of the interior to finish; she could hardly wait, she wanted her work space, wanted to get on with the bids on two new jobs plus whatever project she and Clyde decided on. As she considered the real estate material, Rock came to nose at her hand, restless and needy.

The big dog had paced the house since supper, and it was obvious he was looking for Joe, returning again and again to the downstairs cat door to sniff hopefully for any new scent. Now he looked pointedly at Ryan then directed his gaze to the rafters above, to the high and unreachable cat door that led out into Joe's tower.

254 • SHIRLEY ROUSSEAU MURPHY

"Why's he fussing?" Clyde said. "Joe's out at night a lot, Rock never paces like this. Or does he only want a run?"

"He's been with Dad and Lindsey all day, walking. They must have done ten miles, up in the forest."

"I thought Lindsey didn't like hiking in the rough outdoors."

"She likes to hike with Dad," Ryan said, smiling complacently. She was very much in favor of her widowed father's romance. "What she doesn't like is overnight camping—all the bugs and cooking on the bare ground and no shower."

"But with an RV—"

"An RV isn't camping. I mean real camping, that's what Dad likes, but that isn't for Lindsey." She shrugged. "He doesn't care, they do everything else together."

Lindsey Wolf had only recently come back into Mike Flannery's life after a long absence. He'd been working a cold case for the department, the ten-year-old murder of Lindsey's fiancé. That case soon involved a second murder—it was the cats who'd discovered the body. Without their nosiness, Ryan thought, and without their stubborn efforts to bring that hidden grave to the attention of the law, that victim might never have been found, might have moldered among the Pamillon ruins until the world ended.

But with Joe's involvement in the case, nudging the law to follow his lead, the gray tomcat had been stranded alone in a strange area fifty miles from home. A plight that, by the time they'd found and rescued him, had driven Ryan to tears though she seldom cried.

Now, as she and Clyde worked, silent and preoccupied, Rock at last gave up pacing, climbed up on the leather couch, and flopped down with a huge sigh. He left just enough room for Snowball, curled up at the far end on the afghan. The white cat woke long enough to lick the big dog's nose, then went back to sleep. But as Clyde worked at getting the best prices for his collectors' cars, and Ryan estimated the cost of a major remodel for her favorite of the houses they were considering, both remained tuned to the roof, listening for the sound of soft feet trotting across the shingles and for the flap of Joe's cat door.

There remained only silence, Joe did not appear on the rafter above their heads yawning and demanding a late snack. It was an hour later that the phone rang, startling them both. Clyde glanced at the caller ID and picked up. Turning on the speaker, he imagined Wilma sitting up in bed with a book in her lap, her white hair loose around her shoulders, a cup of cocoa by her side, a fire burning in the cast-iron wood-burning stove.

Her voice was crisp with tension. "Is Joe home? Have you seen Dulcie or Kit? Lucinda just called, they haven't seen Kit since their walk up in the hills late this afternoon."

"Well, that isn't—"

"Pedric's worried, too, and he seldom worries. Lucinda said they were somewhere below Ryan's remodel when Kit met up with a new cat, one of the ferals. She said the two went racing off toward the village. She'd thought that when it got dark, Kit might bring the little thing home, not let her go back alone to the hills, but . . . Clyde, a clowder cat has never come to the village like that, except when there's trouble, when there's some urgent need.

"The Greenlaws haven't seen either cat since, and I haven't seen Dulcie or Joe since Charlie came by, around noon. Have they gone up among the ferals in the middle of the night? I can hear coyotes and they sound pretty close."

"I expect they're all right," Clyde said reassuringly, trying not to telegraph his concern. "Ryan's here, the speaker's on. Have you called Charlie?"

"I was about to. It's so foolish to worry, but . . ."

Ryan moved closer to the phone, leaning into the speaker. "It gets no better, does it? Over time, you don't worry less?"

"I still worry," Wilma said reluctantly.

"Call Charlie," Ryan said. "Then call us back."

"Yes," Wilma said, and hung up.

They waited, Clyde uneasily shuffling papers. Rock had left the couch and resumed pacing, with that quizzical Weimaraner frown on his face that made Ryan even more uneasy. Why were they all so tense? The cats were gone many nights, hunting. Joe would come in, in the small hours, and hop on the bed, nosing at her, his cold muzzle smelling of raw mouse—she was getting used to that. Now, watching her good dog worry and wondering what he sensed, she felt like pacing, too. When Rock looked at her again, the worry on his face even sharper, she went into the bedroom, turned off the gas logs, and stepped into the closet to change her slippers for jogging shoes. She had pulled on a sweater and was getting Clyde's coat when the phone rang.

Clyde switched on the speaker. Charlie said, "I'm in the car. This afternoon, before we chased that guy, Joe and Dulcie were really focused on the vacation houses, asking a lot of questions. I think . . . I have keys. You want to meet me there?"

"Yes," Clyde said. "We're on our way."

Ryan tucked the afghan around Snowball and turned off the desk lamp. Clyde turned on the stairway lights and they hurried down. Grabbing Rock's leash that hung by the front door, they headed for the roadster, which was handier on the narrow streets; with the top down they could better watch the yards and rooftops. Ryan wondered if they were being foolish, were overreacting. On the seat behind her, Rock paced from one side of the car to the other, staring into the night and up at the rooftops, sniffing the wind with such intensity that he made her even more nervous.

27

The night was still, and the sky was clear, now, above the Harper ranch, the stars glinting where, an hour earlier, rain clouds had threatened. The silence was broken only by the rhythm of the sea away beyond the pastures and below the cliffs, and by the distant singing of coyotes in the hills to the north. In the barn the horses dozed. In the house only one lamp burned, near the flickering hearth fire. Max Harper sat in his favorite chair watching the flames, an open book on the table beside him, the two big dogs sprawled on the hearthrug. Charlie's chair was empty but still warm, her half-empty cup of tea forgotten beside the mystery novel she'd been reading. Before she'd rushed away, setting the phone down beside her book, the world had been perfect, just the two of them in their own corner of the universe, a rare evening when Max had gotten home early for a leisurely dinner and a night, he'd hoped, without interruption.

Frowning, he picked up his book again and poured the rest of his beer into the glass, his movements spare and deliberate. He stretched his lean frame, easing his feet nearer the fire, careful not to disturb the two fawn-colored half Danes. He was a tall man, lean, with the leathery look of a horseman, his face pleasantly lined from the sun. He'd be coming up on retirement soon—unless the city council extended his time past their usual retirement age for law enforcement. He'd been chief of Molena Point PD for over fifteen years, good years, all of them. Sometimes he looked forward to retirement, sometimes he didn't like the empty feeling it gave him; it even scared him a little, though he'd never tell Charlie that.

He didn't look forward to what went with retirement, to getting old. As long as he could do the ranch work, was healthy and could do the things he liked, age didn't matter, it was the going downhill that could scare a guy. He didn't like to see it in the men he knew, and he wasn't going to like it in himself.

He wished Charlie hadn't had to go out. She'd hurried away frowning and so tense, jingling her car keys, her jacket over her shoulder. He hadn't liked her urgent need to hurry down to the village for what he thought was no sensible reason. The phone call from her aunt still puzzled him.

Answering the phone, Charlie had moved away with it so as not to be talking in his ear. "They haven't?" she said. "None of them? But they often . . ." A pause, then, "They are? They did?" She'd glanced across at him. "It's possible. The way they . . . Yes, I have keys. I'll go right down. . . ."

Another pause. "Yes, please do. No. I'll bet you're in bed, reading. No, stay there, there's no need. It's cold out. Yes, that'll be fine. Tell them I'll see them there."

Hanging up, she'd said only that Wilma thought her cat and maybe Clyde's and the Greenlaws' cats were locked in one of the empty houses. She didn't say how Wilma would know that, and it didn't make sense to go racing down there. Those cats could be anywhere, they wandered all over the village, no one could keep track of them. And why did she have to race down there in the middle of the night? If a cat got shut in somewhere, it would be fine until morning.

She'd said vaguely that someone in the neighborhood had heard a cat crying in one of the empty houses, as if it was shut in. But that could be any cat, most of the families in that neighborhood had cats. Why the hell would it be Clyde's or Wilma's cat?

Well, hell, he thought more reasonably, Charlie's concern hadn't been so much for the missing cats as for her aunt Wilma, who was inclined to worry over that tabby cat. It was nearly midnight. If Wilma was still awake, then most likely she was worrying. And when Wilma worried, Charlie worried. That, plus her concern for her clients' empty houses, was hard on Charlie though she'd never admit it. He'd be glad when she sold her business, he hoped that would take the pressure off. There was always something, a broken waterline, the resultant damage to attend to, a leaky roof . . . Now that her books had found a growing market, Charlie's Fix-it, Clean-it was becoming more headache than pleasure, its many disruptions offering more stress than she needed.

Well, he guessed he was being cranky for no reason, out of sorts because a couple of cats had dragged her away on the one evening in weeks that he'd been able to come home early. But he had to smile, too, at her going down there to roust out a couple of cats. He'd grown to like those cats, and he sure wished them no harm. He'd gotten used to having them around the station, particularly Joe Grey, taking over like he owned the place, bumming Mabel's lunch, sleeping on his desk. If that cat wanted to nap on a court order, you had to remove him bodily—independent as hell, and mule stubborn.

Looking into the fire, watching the big dogs twitch in their sleep, he thought again about retirement, about being home with Charlie, riding together, cooking together, working on the place. And while Charlie was writing, maybe he'd take a stab at writing his own book. He'd thought about it some. Something related to law enforcement, maybe a few suggestions for civilians on how to keep themselves safe in an increasingly dangerous world.

Or maybe they'd buy a few more horses, get some classes going for the local kids, get them away from TV and video games and too much computer time—help them *do* things rather than sitting around letting the spectator media numb their minds. Get them outdoors and make them responsible for a horse, help them see how strong they could be and how satisfying it was to become proactive in shaping their own lives.

The ringing phone brought him back. Glancing at the caller ID, he picked up.

"We've had a break-in," Charlie said. "I called the station, told Officer Baker I'd call you. Davis is on her way. You don't need to come, I just wanted to—"

"I'm on my way," Max said. "I don't need to tell you—"

"Not to touch anything," she said impatiently. "They didn't ransack the house, but Theresa's miniature paintings are missing, and I'm worried about the other houses, Frances Becker's beautiful antiques and Rita Waterman's jewelry."

"You're still in the Chapmans'? Get out, Charlie. Get out now. And stay out. Keep your phone on, don't hang up."

"I'm already out, I just—"

The phone went dead. Scowling, he rang the station, told the dispatcher to get two more cars over there. Quickly he turned off the fire and raced for the door, snatching up his jacket and hardware, was out the door and swinging into his pickup, heading down the hills.

28

Entering the Chapman house, Charlie had gone into the laundry room first to check on the mama cat. Before she'd switched on the light, a low hiss greeted her. She'd paused, then thrown the switch for the single light over the washer.

Mango stood just outside her blanket-lined box, boldly facing Charlie, her tail lashing, her ears flat, shielding her kittens with a growl so businesslike that Charlie hadn't approached her.

"Someone was here," she said softly. "Someone scared you, Mango." Nothing but intrusion by a stranger would have frightened Mango so. She peered around Mango to see if the kittens were all right. They seemed to be, two of them nosing at their mother, the other two curled up, yawning.

The laundry window was closed, as it should be. The room was as she had last seen it, nothing seemed different. Mango continued to face her, too upset to settle in again with her kittens. Leaving her alone to calm down, Charlie moved into the kitchen, her hand concealing her pepper spray.

Nothing seemed disturbed there, the small electrical appliances and the kitchen TV were all in place. But as she'd entered the dining room, she'd stopped cold and backed against the wall, scanning the living room and the hall beyond, then looking around with dismay.

The walls were no longer bright with the jewel-like rows of miniature paintings that she'd so enjoyed. All three walls were bare except for rows of small picture hooks marching across like dark insects poised in some miniscule military maneuver.

Warily she'd moved on through the house knowing she should leave, should go back outside and call the department. Removing her shoes and switching on lights as she entered the silent rooms, she'd slowly scanned each area, walking in the center, away from the cupboards and cabinets that a thief would have examined and where he might have left minute debris from his shoes.

She'd found nothing else disturbed beyond the missing paintings. No closet door had been left open, no drawers with their contents spilling out. The sliding glass door with its pry marks was securely locked; she used a tissue around her fingers to make sure. At last, certain that no one was there, she'd called out to Joe Grey and Dulcie, at first using only, "Kitty, kitty," in the silly, high voice that she sometimes used to tease Joe, and that he hated. She'd called Joe's name, and Dulcie's, but there was only silence.

What if the cats were hurt, unable to answer her? Moving carefully from closet to closet, using a tissue to turn the knobs, she searched for them knowing Max would be furious that she'd prowled the house like this, playing cop.

When she was certain the cats weren't there, and having found nothing more out of order besides the missing paintings, she'd hurried on to the Waterman house, stopping to fetch gloves from her Blazer. She was at the Watermans' door when Clyde and Ryan pulled up.

"Chapmans were robbed," she told them. "Looks like they took only Theresa's paintings, but it makes me worry about the cats. I want to look in the other three houses before we call the department."

"Not a good idea," Ryan said. "Call the department now, Charlie."

Charlie looked at her and knew she was right. She called the dispatcher, then she called Max. The phone went dead while they were talking, but that wasn't unusual in this hilly area. She sat in the car with Ryan and Clyde, and Rock, waiting impatiently and worrying about the cats, worrying that the thief might have hurt them. It was a given that if those cats spotted the burglar, they'd followed him into the houses. Though they were only cats and shouldn't draw his attention, those three had a way of attracting trouble.

When Detective Davis arrived, Charlie gave her the keys to the four houses, and they waited while Davis and four other officers cleared each house. Charlie wanted to go in with Davis, but only when all four houses had been cleared did Juana take her through, so Charlie could tell her what might be missing. Juana had found no sign of a break-in. When two more units arrived, Juana sent two officers to canvas the neighborhood.

In the Waterman house, Charlie found nothing out of order until, wearing gloves, she retrieved the hidden key for Rita's jewelry cabinet. When Davis opened the carved door, they stared in at empty shelves.

"Rita's beautiful jewelry. Her baroque and Byzantine pieces, the lovely cloisonné." She turned to look at Juana. "That seventeenth-century faux emerald necklace I so liked." She stood very still, touching nothing, her anger sharp and hot.

The house wasn't torn apart as if someone had seen Rita wearing such jewelry and was looking for it.

This thief knew not only where to look, but must have known the location of the key. Leaving the master bedroom, they went through the rest of the house again but Charlie could find nothing else disturbed, everything seemed to be in place. Certainly the electronic equipment was all there, televisions, the music system, and the computers. As they walked through, Charlie innocently called the cats, saying, "Kitty, kitty," so they'd know she wasn't alone.

No one mewed, she heard no clawing at a door, no faint cry of a cat in distress. She had a sick feeling that the burglar might have discovered the cats following him as he made his thieving rounds, that maybe Joe had followed too closely on his heels and the burglar had turned on him. Had an edgy thief, finding the big cat stalking him through the dark rooms, been startled into cornering Joe and hurting him? And what about Dulcie and Kit? Had the three cats been together, all three witnesses to the thefts? All three victims?

She watched Juana, wearing cotton gloves, open each closet. They found just the usual household contents, some cupboards cluttered, some neatly arranged. At last they left the Watermans', moving on to the Becker house, where Juana had found much of the furniture missing, indentations on the carpet where little tables had stood, empty picture hooks on the walls, bare places on the hardwood describing the absence of Frances's small imported rugs.

The house was cold, too, from a draft through the open window just beside the front door. "He didn't get in this way," Juana said. "He may have forced the window and reached through, not knowing it was a double bolt with no key in the lock."

No, Charlie thought. *No burglar could have entered. But a cat could.*

"You want to record what's missing?" Juana asked. Charlie nodded, Juana produced a small tape recorder, and Charlie followed her through the rooms inventorying as best she could remember every missing rug, carved table, painting, and piece of porcelain. They had circled the living room, the dining room, and the kitchen, had returned to the front hall and were headed for the main-level bedrooms when a yowl brought them up short. Charlie spun around. Davis reached to open the closet door, which shook with thuds. Joe yowled again, louder, and Dulcie and Kit mewled frantically.

Juana pulled the door open and the cats were all over Charlie. Joe Grey hit her shoulder, clinging with demanding claws. Dulcie and Kit climbed up her jacket, mewling and lashing their tails with indignation that they'd been locked in. But even as Charlie hugged and cuddled them, Kit leaped free again, streaked out through the open window and the wrought-iron grille and disappeared into the night. Dulcie tensed to race after her, but Joe laid his ears back. His look said, *Let her go.*

Dulcie scowled at him as if thinking Kit could use some help, and before he could stop her she, too, was gone. Joe and Charlie stared at each other, the tomcat's yellow eyes burning with annoyance. Davis looked on in silence. Neither Charlie nor Joe dared wonder what she was thinking. After a moment, she said, "What about the closet?" The shelves were nearly bare.

"It was full," Charlie said. "He cleaned it out. Everything was wrapped, I can't itemize those pieces. I think they'd be similar to what we listed."

Carrying Joe, Charlie returned to her Blazer. Ryan and Clyde were parked behind it, Rock asleep in the backseat. As Charlie approached the convertible, Rock woke and lunged up to nose with delight at the tomcat, slobbering in his face, making Joe grimace.

One squad car had left, and Davis was still in the Becker house. Watching carefully to make sure they were alone, they sat in the roadster listening to Joe's whispered and condensed version of the night's adventure.

"He could have killed you," Clyde said. "Could have killed all three of you."

"Four," Joe said, reminding them of Tansy's part in the action.

"And the burglar?" Charlie asked. "Did you get a better look at him?"

"Not a good look," Joe said. "But I'd know that smell, the same as around the swimming pool." He tried to describe the scent, which seemed to him a cross between catmint and maybe mouthwash. "How did he get openers to all four garages and the door keys? And what made you come looking in the middle of the night?"

"So strange," Ryan said. "All at once we got worried about you three. Rock was pacing and fussing, and then Wilma called. We all felt that something was amiss." She frowned, her green eyes puzzled.

Joe Grey shrugged. He didn't think it strange that a few perceptive humans could sense when their friends were in danger, he was surprised it didn't happen more often. He was about to express his opinion when, seeing two officers approaching, he curled up in Ryan's lap and closed his eyes.

29

Kit ran up through the hills shying at every sound, dodging every changing shadow as the moon came and went, the land pale one moment and inky the next—and empty. Nothing moved. She could see nothing crouched, waiting. Where *was* Tansy? Had she headed home by herself, so small and alone? She could almost hear the smaller cat crying out to her. She didn't understand their strange connection, she only knew it was like the bond between sisters.

She couldn't remember her own sisters, she didn't know if she'd ever *had* sisters or brothers. What would that be like, to grow up in a real family, with siblings to play with and squabble with, all of them connected by a bond that was like no other?

Racing through a black valley, her heart pounding, she bolted up the side of a hill as the moon showed itself. She could hear the coyotes, off to the south near the Harper ranch. When she reached the crest, almost winded, there was Tansy high above her, poised atop the next hill, the pale little cat rearing up to look. Another cat lay beside her, just as pale, but very still.

Sage. It was Sage. He didn't rise or move. Flying up the hill to them, Kit was cold with fear. Oh, what was wrong? Sage was like her own brother. Once, she'd thought he would be more than a friend, that he would be her mate. Now he lay unmoving, his head resting against Tansy's paws.

She slowed and padded silently up to them; she couldn't stop shivering. Sage moved a little, then, and opened his eyes to look up at her.

Tansy mewed, "That man . . . He threw a hammer at Sage, he hurt him bad."

Kit crouched next to Tansy, her nose to Sage's nose, feeling his quick, shallow breathing.

"I found him just above that house where they're digging, I wanted to go for help but he's so . . . He insisted on going home but then he hurt more and was weaker, and I don't know what to do."

Kit touched Sage's shoulder gently with a careful paw. When she stroked his side he jerked away, catching his breath. She didn't touch him again. She thought of Dr. Firetti and the animal hospital but Sage hated that place, even though John Firetti had saved his life. And the hospital stood so far across the hills, clear at the other side of the village, too far for Sage ever to walk there. How could this have happened, after all the pain he'd already suffered, the broken and crushed bones, his long recovery in a cast, his long time among humans as he tried not to fear the human world? How could this be fair?

But life wasn't fair, and that made her all the more angry. "I'm going for help. The road is just down there, Lucinda and Pedric can drive that far, and we—"

"No," Sage said. "I don't want humans, I don't want a doctor, I don't want to be inside a building." He tried to scramble up, then lay back. "I can walk, I just need to rest awhile."

Kit imagined broken ribs, bones puncturing vital organs if he moved, internal bleeding, all the terrifying things she had learned about in the human world and wished she hadn't. She was reaching to touch his back leg, to see if the old, healed injury had been damaged, when a rustle in the grass made her spin around.

Dulcie stood there. She looked at Tansy, looked at Sage's still form, and then crouched over Sage as Kit had done. When she felt him as Kit had, he flattened his ears and gritted his teeth but didn't flinch. "Can you get up?" she asked softly.

"In a little while." He lay quietly looking at them as Tansy snuggled beside him, her face next to his, shivering against his stillness. Around them the hills were silent, even the yipping of the coyotes had ceased. Above them the moon went in and out of the clouds, throwing running shadows across the frightened cats, and Kit licked tears from her nose.

But at last Sage stirred, and rose, leaning against Tansy. "I want to go home. I want the clowder, I want my own cave." Limping, he started away up the hills. Slowly the three females walked with him, supporting him as they made their way toward the fallen mansion that was home, his and Tansy's home.

On the street of the robberies, lights burned in all four houses and in the neighbors' houses, where people stood in their yards in little knots asking questions of one another and watching as officers secured the four yards with crime tape. Police cars crowded the street, their radios cutting through officers' voices. Two detectives and three officers worked the houses, searching, photographing, lifting prints, vacuuming for trace evidence. One burglary might not have commanded this degree of attention. Four, with a possible link to murder, was another matter. The Becker house, where Charlie had released Joe and Dulcie and Kit from the closet, seemed to have fared the worst, stripped of all the smaller furnishings.

Juana had emerged from the Longley house when she took a call from the dispatcher. Glancing up at Charlie, in the roadster, she gave her the thumbs-up then stepped over to the car and punched in a single digit on her cell phone, turning on the speaker.

Max was saying, "I'm on my way, just turned off Ocean."

"You'll like this," Juana told him. "Prints from all four burglaries match those from the swimming pool."

Max chuckled. "Very nice. Charlie's okay?"

"She's right here." She handed Charlie the phone.

"Fine," Charlie said. "I'm fine." Down the block, lights turned onto the street, moving toward them, and in a moment Max's pickup double-parked beside a police unit. As Charlie hurried to the driver's window, and Davis returned to the Longley house to finish lifting prints, behind Clyde's and Ryan's backs, Joe Grey slipped out of the roadster and through the shadows, and into the house behind Juana.

What he'd like to do was stroll casually up to Davis and say, *I told you so! I told you there was a body at the bottom of the swimming pool! And I had a pretty good idea, all along, that our burglar was the same guy!*

But of course Davis *had* listened to him, as the detective always did. She might complain about the anonymity of the phantom snitch, but she paid attention. And now, with the matching prints, with burglary and apparent murder linked together, both detectives would be working different aspects of the case. Following Juana into the master bedroom, he slipped under the dresser to watch her lift prints in the adjoining bath, handling with gloves the cosmetic bottles, the toothpaste tube, though these were items the burglar probably hadn't handled. The bath was done in shades of cream-colored marble; countertop, floor, shower, and the walls were painted a pale cream. Slipping up behind Juana, Joe used his nose to work the scene in his own way, sniffing for the elusive medicinal scent that so resembled catmint. If the smell *was* of a medicine, and if he could find one bathroom among the four houses where it was stronger, that might be the best lead yet. It was the combination of crimes that was the teaser.

Did this guy kill the woman because she knew he was planning the burglaries? Maybe she confronted him and threatened to call the law? Or had it been an accident, had she found out and confronted him, he'd lost his temper, hit her, and she fell? And then he was too scared to call for help, didn't want to tangle with the cops? Maybe he had a record, maybe he was on parole. So he'd hauled her out of there, hosed down the pool, loaded up the body, and . . . and what?

Where was the body now? He had to stash it somewhere before he proceeded with his burglaries. Or was the corpse tucked away in his RV all the time, while he loaded the stolen goods in with it?

He watched Juana leave the room, then he trotted into the bathroom to sort more carefully through the scents. If the scent he was looking for was medicine, maybe he should check all the bathrooms. Here he smelled lemon soap, mint toothpaste, spicy shaving lotion—he thought he caught the catmint scent but, mixed with everything else, he couldn't be sure. He checked the other two bathrooms, then headed for the Watermans', intent on covering all the bathrooms in the four houses if he could avoid the two detectives and the officers, who wouldn't take kindly to a tomcat walking through the evidence.

It was an hour later when, having accomplished his task but gained nothing, Joe saw Clyde coming up the street, peering among the bushes looking for him. The time was well after midnight, pushing dawn, and Clyde was yawning. Joe, scrambling up a pepper tree, didn't intend to go home. Vanishing into the roof's shadows, he raced away over the neighbors' roofs toward the hills. Kit's hasty retreat, and then Dulcie taking off so fast, had left him increasingly uneasy as he prowled the four houses. Kit was so charmed by that half-grown kitten—if Kit had gone after her, Dulcie would have followed; and a sharp nervousness filled his belly, a shaky unease that sent him flying toward the dark hills.

30

Joe was high up the hills making his way through a tangle of fallen oaks when the wind shifted and he smelled the stink of coyote. Slowing to a trot, he scanned the slopes around him. He didn't see the beast, and he caught no glimpse of Dulcie or Kit. The rolling mass of open land remained empty, and he went on warily through the dark, tangled grass.

When he smelled the coyote again it was way too close, somewhere in the black valley just below him. Ducking into a maze of boulders he backed into a hollow between them just as the beast lunged. He backed deeper, pressing down among the granite rocks. The coyote pushed its nose in and began to dig, reckless and fierce. Joe raked him twice. The beast ignored him and kept digging. When Joe struck for its eyes and bit its black nose, it yowled and backed away. He was poised to charge out at it when the coyote spun around and ran.

Slipping out to look, Joe watched it race away with a cluster of cats clinging to its back, raking into its thick coat. Joe stood up on a boulder, laughing, as the beast went tearing off into the night with its unwelcome passengers. Then Dulcie was there beside him, frantically nosing at him.

"Are you all right?"

"I am now," he said. They heard the coyote scream, heard dry bushes breaking, saw the beast vanish over the high crest.

Moments later a dozen cats emerged from the night, crowding around them. These were the clowder leaders: white-coated Cotton, tabby Coyote with his tufted ears, and pale Willow of the faded calico coat and green eyes.

"Come on," Willow said. "That was a yearling pup, three of them are off hunting on their own and it isn't safe. We were hunting wood rats for . . ." She paused uneasily. "To take back to the clowder when we saw him stalking you."

"Hunting wood rats for who?" Joe said. Only a sick or injured cat didn't hunt on his own. "What's wrong? Where's Kit?"

"She's fine," Dulcie said.

"Tansy, then?" he asked, thinking guiltily of that scrawny little mite who had led them through the empty houses and then run away so frightened.

"Sage is hurt," Dulcie said. "I think he found the missing body, I think he found the killer." She turned, and she and Joe followed the clowder cats up the hills toward the Pamillon mansion, Joe filled with questions that she insisted must wait.

As long as they could remember, the mansion and its acreage had stood abandoned, home for raccoons, deer, the occasional bobcat, but more recently for the wild clowder. Soon they were crowding in through the fallen front wall of the two-story house, where the parlor, and the nursery above, stood open to the world like a vast stage ready for a theatrical production.

To the wild clowder, this shelter was a palace. The slate roof was sound, the rooms dry enough, and not only did the big house offer protection, but its acreage with all its cellars and outbuildings provided uncounted places for a cat to hide from danger and to hunt the smaller beasts that sustained them.

The parlor's flowered wallpaper was peeling off in long strips, the tables and beds and upholstered furniture sagged with rot, their stuffing pulled out by generations of long-deceased mice and rats. Dulcie led Joe across the cluttered room to the back where, behind a moldering couch, Tansy crouched beside Sage. The young tom lay on a cushion that was little more than cotton stuffing but that looked warm and soft; he was very still, his eyes closed, his breathing quick and shallow. Kit sat nearby, her ears down, her tortoiseshell face grim with worry.

Joe sat down beside Sage, and the clowder cats crowded around, resuming a vigil they had left when they went to hunt. Four cats carried dead wood rats, which they laid beside the couch where their scent might tease Sage's appetite. Outside the broken wall the night darkened as the clouds shifted, and the wind blew cold off the far sea, intruding into the abandoned room, unwelcome and bold.

Joe could smell Sage's distress and fear. "What happened? *Where* did you see the body? What—?"

"Let him rest awhile," Willow said. "The wind was knocked out of him, maybe some ribs broken. He hurts here and here," she said, lifting a careful paw but not touching Sage. She looked up when an orange tomcat slipped in beside them dangling a wood rat from his jaws. When he held it right in Sage's face, Sage's eyes opened and brightened, and he struggled to sit up, wincing as he reached out with a gripping paw and pulled the wood rat to him. He was soon gulping down the welcome meal, his enthusiasm strengthening with each morsel.

When he'd finished he rose and stretched, and clearly he felt stronger. He clawed at the sofa and then limped around the barrier and stood looking across the ruined parlor through the wide vista of broken wall, to the hills below. Far away, the moon hung low above the sea, half hidden by low clouds.

"The pain's not so bad now," Sage said. "My side doesn't hurt so much." He looked at Joe Grey, in awe of the older cat, thinking about the time, in the animal hospital, when Joe and Dulcie had let a doctor take their own blood so that he could live.

Joe came to stand beside him. "What happened tonight?" he repeated.

Lying down again for a little rest, Sage told Joe about the pit inside the garage and how the man had buried a woman there, how the man saw him looking and went pale and snatched up the hammer and threw it, how the glass had shattered and he was knocked off the lumber pile. As Sage spun the tale, the clowder cats all crowded around, their minds filled with what, to them, was indeed a threatening but fascinating scene. The speaking cats might fear humans, but the strangeness of the human world never ceased to stir their wonder. There was a link between the two worlds that would forever fascinate them.

"That man left the same smell," Tansy said. "The same as the man who robbed those houses."

Joe Grey looked at her with interest, then trotted to the edge of the broken floor and stood looking down toward the remodel tucked among the lower hills. "Ryan will dump gravel in the morning, they'll fill in the pit and then pour the concrete." He looked around at Dulcie. "We can't let them do that." And without another word he trotted out through the broken wall and headed away toward the village. As Dulcie and Kit galloped to join him, behind them, Sage rose.

"You're too weak," Willow said.

"I'll go just a little way," said Sage. "I want to see . . ." He turned to look at her. "I'm stronger, I want to go just a short way . . ." Willow looked at him, puzzled, but she said no more. She and Tansy followed him, unwilling to let him go alone. Soon the whole clowder was moving down the hills, surrounding Sage to shelter him, but filled with curiosity, too, wanting to see this strange grave, this cruel and lonely disposal of a human person.

It was very late when Clyde and Ryan headed upstairs, Clyde still complaining because Joe had raced away into the night. Ryan dropped Snowball gently on the bed and set her cup of cocoa on the nightstand. Crossing to the fireplace, she knelt to light the gas logs. There was a little pop, and bright flames licked up, silhouetting her slim form through her translucent gown. She rose, turning, her dark hair tumbling across her cheek. She picked up her cell phone from the dresser, and before putting it in the charger she checked her messages.

She looked up at Clyde, frowning. "Gravel won't be there until ten. They're usually more reliable. Scotty said he called the concrete company and delayed that delivery so they wouldn't sit waiting. Damn. I'd hoped we'd be finished by noon."

"Call Charlie. Maybe, before you go to work, you can help with her phone calls."

An hour ago, when they'd parted from Charlie, leaving the robbery scene, she'd been trying to reach the four families, to find out what instructions they would have for her once the police had released the scenes. And to find out if anyone else had had keys to any of their doors. She'd had no luck reaching any of the four couples. She'd headed home so irritated, and concerned, that Ryan wondered if she'd be up all night dialing cell phones that had been turned off. What worried Charlie the most was the possibility that one of the few employees who'd left her, or one of the two she'd fired, might have copied her keys on the sly.

But maybe by the time Davis finished canvassing the nearby houses, they'd have some leads. That was a close neighborhood, maybe someone had seen a stranger or a strange car. Everyone for blocks around had to know those four couples were on vacation, and they were inclined to watch out for one another. Ryan dialed Charlie's cell, got a busy signal, and left a message: "My delivery's delayed for tomorrow morning. If you haven't reached your clients, call me. I'll make some calls for you before I head up to the job."

Clyde sat down on the edge of the bed, watching Rock and Snowball, the small cat curled up tight against the Weimaraner, happily purring. "Such a sweet and innocent little cat," Clyde said, reaching to gently stroke Snowball. "*You* don't go chasing off in the middle of the night after burglars." He wished Joe would learn to stay in at night—and how unrealistic was that?

Ryan finished her cocoa, set her cup on the dresser, and went to brush her teeth. Getting into bed, she slipped her feet carefully around the sleeping animals. "At least everything was insured—except maybe Theresa's paintings. Insurance on pieces of art is ridiculously high." She looked at him bleakly. "I don't know if I can sleep, worrying about Joe. I've worried before, but not like this. You'd think, after they got themselves locked in that closet, they'd be ready to call it a night."

"Not those three." He switched off the lamp and stretched out.

"Did he tell you what, exactly, they were doing? Tell you how they got locked in? Were they tailing the burglar? Why did they let him get so near that he shut them in? And what good to run surveillance," she said crossly, "if they go off in the night and don't *tell* anyone what they found?"

Clyde sighed, and shook his head. "We just have to live with it." He drew her close. "Do we have a choice?"

31

He was sweating as he headed for the highway. He couldn't stop seeing that cat watching him through the window. What had made it stare in at him so intently and then stare straight down at her grave, almost as if it *knew* what he was doing? He thought about that big gray cat watching him, too, while he was packing up the last of the books. He couldn't figure how it had gotten in there. Why had it and those other two followed him to the next house? Evil devils, all of them. Evil.

Well, he'd taken care of them. With any luck, they wouldn't be found in that closet for weeks—found dead from thirst and starvation. He smiled, thinking of them locked in and slowly dying, and a chill of pleasure filled him, a sharp and satisfied lust.

But then he couldn't get his breath. He had to find the inhaler. He felt all his pockets again, felt around on the car seat. *Had* he left it on the table by her grave, where he was headed? If he'd left it in one of those houses . . . Oh, God. When those cleaning people found the paintings gone, found the furniture and rugs cleaned out, the books and paperweights, there'd be cops all over those rooms. He couldn't let them find the inhaler with his prints on it. Couldn't . . .

He had to get hold of himself. He searched his pockets yet again, squirming up in the seat as he drove. Found his handkerchief that she'd always ironed and folded just so. His pocketknife, the gloves he'd used. The four sets of keys, which he would dispose of somewhere along the highway, toss them off the cliff into the Pacific. But no inhaler.

But even if they found it, found anything of his, what would it matter? He was a neighbor, a friend, he was in and out of those houses all the time. The cops could find his fingerprints—which they wouldn't because of the gloves—and it wouldn't make any difference. And yet, heading for the remodel, he knew he'd feel easier not to have left it in one of the houses. Before he searched the remodel, he knew he had to go back to the houses he'd robbed, even if he had to leave the RV sitting right there all loaded up . . . Oh Christ . . .

But he'd feel better when it was done, when he'd found it. Winding along the hillside roads, back onto the residential streets, half of him knew he was being paranoid—the neighborhood was quiet and dark, everyone was asleep, there was nothing to worry about. This wouldn't take long, and he'd feel easier, maybe it *was* there somewhere. Swinging into a U-turn he headed along the hillside street above his street, where he could look down there before he approached. Or maybe he could park up there, walk down the hill, find the inhaler, and then hit the highway, and not have to go back near her grave.

Head for the city, make contact with the fence, collect his money, and then across the Golden Gate and on up the coast, just another tourist in his beat-up old RV. Drive slow and easy up through the little lumber towns, on into Oregon and then inland to eastern Washington for a while before he headed home—returning alone and devastated from their vacation, where she'd left him. Had taken her bags and walked out on him, cleaned out their bank account, and caught a plane to the East Coast.

He'd take care of the electronic deposits on her laptop, transfer the funds to her household account. He didn't know yet how he'd manage withdrawals from that account, he'd figure that out later. He'd tell people she had a lover, that he'd been so shocked and hurt, heartbroken. And then to find they'd been robbed, that would nearly destroy him.

Calling the cops about the robbery, he'd wonder aloud if she had come back and cleaned out her treasures, stashed them somewhere before she caught her plane. He wouldn't be certain this was a burglary until he learned that the other houses had been robbed. Then he and his neighbors would share their misery.

Winding along the hill's steep crest on the dark and narrow street a block above his, he was rehearsing the poignant scene with his neighbors when a tire blew. The RV lurched, the steering wheel jerked in his hands, and the suddenly unwieldy vehicle headed for the drop. There was no guardrail. It was all he could do to pull the RV over onto the opposite side, against the rising hill.

He got out, shaken, looked along the dark, empty street where it was too steep for houses. The three houses high up on the cliff were dark. He walked over to the edge, looked down the steep drop to his own street, below . . . Quickly, he stepped back.

The street was filled with lights. Car lights, lights on in all the houses. More cars approaching, cop cars. He could hear men's voices and the distant mutter of police radios. What the hell was this?

Had someone seen the RV enter or leave one of the garages and, unable to mind their own business, called the cops? The garage door openers had been *her* idea. Over the past year, using one excuse or another to be in each garage alone for a few minutes, borrowing tools or a dab of paint, he'd used the electronic duplicator she'd purchased through a special catalog to program duplicate garage door openers. It had worked like a charm.

Two more police cars arrived, pulling up in front of the brightly lit houses. He could see half a dozen uniforms searching the yards, their flashlight beams cutting into the shadows of trees and bushes. Their predatory search panicked him. Helplessly watching, wanting only to get away, he turned nervously to attend to the flat tire.

He didn't want to use the flashlight, not with all those cops down there, one of them was sure to look up the hill, and they'd be on him like a bunch of damned commandos. He hadn't changed a tire in years. He found the spare under the floor in the back, just inside the door, but it took him a while to figure out how to release it. She'd tripped up there, not to have gone over the manual with him. In all the five years they'd had the RV, parked in that rented garage or off on short trips, the tires had never even gone soft on them, and they'd sure never had a flat.

When he released the spare and bounced it, it was soft, too. It took him awhile to find the hand pump. He was almost convinced there wasn't one, until at last he found it down in the well where the tire had been housed, jammed way to hell down under the bracket for the jack and other tire tools.

He got the tire pumped up, his heart pounding, his breath short. After two tries, he got the jack set, lying under the RV so he'd be sure to get it right under the axle. He'd started to jack up the vehicle when he remembered he hadn't set the brake, or loosened the lugs before taking the weight off. He had to ease the wheel down again, set the brake, then start over, and that angered him.

When he removed the nuts, he nearly lost them before he thought to put them in his pocket. He hadn't changed a tire since he was in his teens. The one time more recently that her car had had a flat, he'd called AAA, had let the emergency road crew do it. Tires didn't go flat now like they had years ago.

He was sweating and nervous when he finished, anxious to get away. When he looked over the edge, the cops were still all over the place. He thought he saw the chief of police, Harper. And the woman who ran the cleaning service, that was his wife. Regular family affair. He could see that woman detective, too.

For an instant he felt a belly-wrenching fear that some-how they knew he was up there watching them. But that was stupid. He was tired, that was all. Worn out from changing the tire, breathing hard. He needed that inhaler. Turning away, he checked the lug nuts again, but they were tight. He'd screwed them on hastily in the dark, wanting to rest. It had taken the last of his breath to get them all good and tight.

Shoving the wheel he'd removed into the back of the RV and laying the tools beside it, he carefully eased the door closed so it made hardly a click. His hands shak-ing, he got in, started the engine, and headed slowly up the dark street using only his parking lights. Squinting through the windshield at the sheer drop, he saw again in uncomfortable memory that pale cat staring in the window at him, watching him bury her, watching him lay her down in the grave and clumsily scoop earth over her, shovel by slow shovelful. He couldn't stop think-ing that the cat knew he had killed her.

When he was around the first bend, he switched on the headlights. Driving slowly across the hills, his thoughts were filled with the inhaler that he seemed to see clearly now, sitting on that contractor's worktable among the hammers and screwdrivers. Driving the dark and winding residential road toward the freeway, he turned right at the top of the hill, crossed over the freeway, and headed for the empty remodel.

This time, he parked right in front of the place, right beside the dirt pile. He'd be there only a minute. The houses below were all dark, not one light; he'd just pick the lock, get the inhaler, and he'd be out again and gone.

Letting himself in, he searched the table, then the dirty floor under the table. The inhaler wasn't there. He stood at the edge of the pit shining the flashlight's beam back and forth across the raw earth, but he picked out only the black drainpipe and the boot prints. He turned to search the rest of the garage, along the wall where he'd sat on the floor, everywhere he'd been; once in a while he glanced up at the broken window, thinking about that cat, hoping he'd killed it.

The window remained empty, the cold air scudding in. He didn't find the inhaler. The cat didn't appear again. At last, trying to figure out where he could have left it, he locked up again and headed for the RV, taking a moment to circle the yard to see if he might somehow have dropped it there. Cupping his hand around the flashlight, directing only a thin beam onto the ground, he approached the broken window. Across the lumber and on the earth around it, shards of broken glass blazed up at him, scattered among deep paw prints. For an instant, he lifted his beam to the window.

As his light hit the sharp teeth of glass, the pale cat exploded out of the blackness straight into his face, its eyes ablaze, its pale fur standing out like licks of white flame. It landed in his face, raking and biting him. He stumbled backward and fell, and a second cat was on him, cats all over him in a tangle clawing him, so many cats their weight held him down. They screamed and raked him and the pale cat was right in his face. The dark cat with a white stripe down its nose was at him, too, so fierce he was terrified they'd blind him. Blood ran into his eyes. Wild with terror, he drove them off enough to stagger up and run, cats clinging to his back and shoulders and throat. As he knocked them away, he could swear he heard a voice say, "Leave him, let him go." He spun around to see who was there, saw no one in the blackness. He'd dropped the flashlight, its beam shining uselessly along the ground picking out shards of glass. The cats had drawn back but they crouched on the lumber pile as if to leap again. He ran and stumbled and nearly fell again as he made for the RV. Flinging open the door, he bolted in, slammed and locked it, leaned against it, shaking.

Someone was out there, someone had spoken, but he'd seen no one. Fearing a witness, he started the engine and took off with a squeal of tires, heading for the highway.

32

The truck had backed up to the garage of the re-model, ready to dump its gravel. Joe, Dulcie, and Kit, watching from the tall grass on the hill above, shifted from paw to paw, and every few minutes Joe Grey reared up, scanning the road below. Still there was no sign of Ryan.

The pickup belonging to the two Latino laborers was parked beside Scotty's pickup, the two men sat in the cab smoking cigarettes, waiting to haul gravel and spread it evenly across the pit. Only Ryan could stop the work, she was the only person the cats could tell, her uncle Scott didn't know the cats' secret. Though Joe thought that with his heritage, with that mysterious turn of mind the Scots-Irish seemed to have, the truth might not come as such a shock. But they didn't need anyone else to know, too many people already shared their secret.

Watching for Ryan, fidgeting nervously, Joe knew he should have gone home, should have woken her before dawn and told her to stop the deliveries, told her what the gravel and cement would be burying.

None of the three cats had been home. After they attacked the killer, they and the feral band had spent the few remaining hours until dawn licking bruises and hurt places on their bodies, licking blood from their cut paws and carefully pulling out small shards of glass with their teeth. Glass that they'd dropped into a little hole and covered over, as they would cover anything vile. As the first light of dawn grayed the sky, most of the ferals had headed home smiling with pleasure at their night's adventure; Sage's retribution had been sweet. Only Sage and Tansy had remained with the village cats, Sage wanting to see what would happen next. He and Tansy rested higher up the hill, well hidden among the weeds and grass.

One thing for sure, Joe thought, glancing up at them, *that man won't mess with a cat again. If he didn't fear cats before, he fears us now.*

Down in the yard, Scotty stood in front of the garage talking on his cell phone. With the wind blowing and the big truck's engine running, the cats couldn't hear much. It seemed to be a one-sided conversation, as if he was leaving a message, most likely that they were going ahead with the work. It would cost a bundle to keep the gravel truck waiting, and would cost probably far more to delay the cement truck. In the few months Clyde and Ryan had been married, Joe had learned quite a lot about the construction business. These delivery folks charged by the hour, and they charged a lot. Where *was* Ryan? She'd known the deliveries would be early, she'd said she hoped to be finished by noon.

Joe watched Scotty close his phone, scratch his red beard as if perplexed, and then turn to speak to the driver, a skinny man, and stooped. He had rounded shoulders that made his khaki shirt hang in folds across his chest, and big, protruding ears beneath a striped cap. They watched him step to the cab, and in a moment the truck bed began to tilt up from the front. As it lifted to its maximum height, the gravel slid out with a grating thunder into a pile before the open garage. At once the two Latino laborers began to shovel it into the wheelbarrows to be hauled into the garage and dumped into the pit, further covering the buried victim. The tomcat watched the road impatiently.

Ryan was never late to a job. Soon Joe was not only impatient but getting worried about her, thinking about wrecks and illness, fussing as nervously as his house-mates fussed when he didn't show up at bedtime.

"We could stand in the pit, stand over the grave," Kit said. "They wouldn't pour gravel on *us*."

Joe snorted. "And Scotty wouldn't pick us up and throw us out of the garage? And you don't think that little protest would make him wonder?"

Dulcie glanced back up the hill, watching the tall grass ripple where Tansy and Sage crouched. She was interested to see that Sage, after last night's fine vindication, still wanted to hang around and see that the body was found. She wondered if he really cared, or if he was, after all, simply too hurt to go home. That worried her, but the good thing was that Ryan would be here soon. If he *was* badly hurt, she could get him to the vet despite his reluctance.

They could hear the older laborer, Fernando, in the garage, dumping his wheelbarrow load into the pit. He was the shorter of the two, with grizzled gray hair. The two worked one at either side of the gravel pile, so they didn't get in each other's way. A mist of gravel dust filled the air around them like thin smoke.

"They'll have to dig it all out again," Dulcie said.

"Let's hope Ryan's willing," Joe said. "Sage is the only one who saw him bury the body."

"She won't refuse! Ryan knows Sage wouldn't lie."

Moving the load of gravel seemed to take forever. Long before the two laborers scraped the last bits of rock from the driveway, the driver had handed Scotty an invoice, gotten back in the cab, and rumbled off down the hill. Still there was no sign of Ryan, and half the deed was done, the body in the pit entombed beneath a thick blanket of crushed rock.

The cats had been waiting for over an hour when Dulcie said, "Looks like they'll have to dig out a lot more than gravel. Here comes the cement." They watched the cement truck struggle up the hill, its big, round belly rotating as it churned, mixing its load. Kit said, "I left my paw prints in the neighbors' fresh cement once. Then I ran." She smiled. "My prints are still there, maybe they'll be there forever." She looked at Joe, her eyes widening. "*Can* Ryan dig that up again, after it gets hard?"

"With a jackhammer," Joe said.

The cement truck turned its nose into the street and backed up to the garage. The driver got out, Scotty checked over the order, and they set the chute in place. The cats watched the thick, muddy-looking cement begin to slide down the chute, eased along by the men's shovels. Soon Scotty disappeared inside the garage; the cats listened to the gritty, wet stroke of shovels, imagining the red-bearded foreman and his helpers distributing the wet concrete like cake batter that would harden into man-made stone.

When the pour was finished, the driver hosed down his chutes and stored them. He carried an invoice in to Scotty, got in his truck, and pulled away. Within the garage, the sound of scraping had changed to a slick slushing. Joe envisioned Scotty floating out the cement with a wide, flat tool on a long handle, working it to a smooth finish. He had seen Ryan do this when she poured Clyde's back patio. "Come on," he said, and he headed down the hill into another stand of tall grass where they could see into the garage, but could still see the road.

Inside the garage, the cement was a dark lake, lying even with the old floor. The cats had hardly gotten settled when Ryan's red truck appeared far down the road, coming around a curve, hurrying up to the job.

Manuel, the younger Latino laborer, carried the float and the shovels out to the yard and began to hose them down. The moment Ryan's pickup pulled in and parked, before Joe or Dulcie could stop Kit, she was gone, scorching straight to Ryan, leaping up on her as she stepped out of the truck. As Ryan gathered Kit in her arms, Joe crouched to follow, but Dulcie's gentle claws pulled him back. "Let her go." The tabby sat down beside him. "Let her do it, she won't give us away to the men."

"She's so . . ."

"Enthusiastic," Dulcie said, smiling.

Ryan stood holding Kit, laughing—but then her expression changed to puzzlement. She cuddled Kit across her shoulder, close to her ear, and wandered away from the garage toward the far end of the house where they wouldn't be heard. The cats watched Kit look all around and then whisper in her ear. Ryan was very still—then she spun around, carrying Kit, and headed for the garage.

Moving inside, she stood looking down at the smoothly finished cement. She stroked Kit, looking at the tortoiseshell then looking back at the concrete, then glancing out to where Scotty was hosing off his boots.

Standing at the edge of the finished floor, Ryan thought about digging it up again, about doing it right now, before it hardened. She could just hear Scotty, whose Scots-Irish temper matched his red hair. What the hell could she tell him? What possible excuse could she give him?

She didn't imagine Kit was lying, any more than she would think Joe Grey or Dulcie would lie to her. If they said Sage had seen a body buried there, and if *they* believed Sage, then she had to believe them. This was one moment when her still limited experience with speaking cats strained every fiber of her good sense, one of the moments when she felt she'd fallen into Alice's Wonderland. And yet she hadn't imagined Kit's frantic revelation, certainly she didn't imagine the imperious, yellow-eyed gaze Kit had turned on her, demanding and expectant.

But what about Sage? What if Sage *had* lied, for some unimaginable reason? Sage was wild, his band was feral, he might have very different scruples from the village cats. What if they spent the rest of the day shoveling out the heavy, wet cement, and then hauling out heavy gravel, then moving the drainpipes and digging down into the earth, and found nothing?

She was still debating what to do when Scotty came into the garage behind her. "Nice work," she said unnecessarily, indicating the cement. "I thought they weren't coming until ten."

"They had a last minute cancellation, so they just came on." He reached to stroke Kit. "What's Greenlaw's cat doing up here?"

"Lucinda and Pedric walk up in this neighborhood. I guess she saw the activity and got curious, she's a nosy little thing."

Kit narrowed her eyes at Ryan, and her claws tightened a little against Ryan's shoulder. Ryan grinned, and stroked her, and looked back at the wet cement wishing she had X-ray vision, wishing she could see through the dirt and gravel and concrete, see what was down there.

"What?" Scotty said. "What's wrong?"

"The job looks great," she repeated. She laid a hand on his arm. "This morning before they dumped the gravel, did you look into the pit?"

"I made sure nothing had fallen in, if that's what you mean. Saw that no lizard or mouse had gotten trapped down there, made sure the drainpipe connections were tight."

"And the pit looked the same as last night?"

"The same," he said shortly, frowning at her.

"Footprints?"

"My boot prints," he said, scratching his beard, perplexed.

She scanned the worktable, then looked above the washer and dryer hookup to the broken window. "When did that happen?"

Scotty did a double take. "What the hell? How could I miss that? When *did* that happen?" He stepped to the window to look more closely at the jagged shards of glass, as sharp as skinning knives, sticking out from the wooden frame.

She said, "You were busy pouring and finishing, your mind was on the job."

"That's no excuse." Scotty turned to look around the garage.

"Were the footprints in the pit all yours?"

Scotty was silent, visualizing the bottom of the pit. "They were mine."

She waited, stroking Kit, feeling Kit's anxious little heart beating hard against the hollow of her shoulder.

Scotty said, "What's this about? Who the hell was nosing around here?"

She said, "I had a call this morning that someone broke in last night. That they dragged something heavy into the garage through the side door."

"The door was locked when I got here, I had to unlock it. A call from who?"

"I don't know, he wouldn't tell me. Said he watched a man haul a heavy bundle in, that he looked in through the window, watched him wrestle it down the ladder into the pit. A long, thin bundle wrapped in a blanket. Said he'd unloaded it from the back of a car, that he dumped it in the pit, then pulled the car up the hill, in among those cypress trees. That in a little while he walked back down, went in the garage, put on the boots that were in the corner and the overalls—your boots and overalls—picked up a shovel, went down the ladder into the pit where he'd left the bundle, and started digging. Caller said he couldn't see down into the pit."

"Why didn't this guy stop him?"

"Maybe he was scared. I don't know. A stranger digging in the middle of the night . . . He said that after about twenty minutes the guy came up out of the pit without the bundle, leaned the shovel against the wall, took off the boots, was taking off the muddy coveralls when he glanced up at the window and saw the caller. Said the guy went white, scared to death, grabbed a hammer and threw it, shattering the glass."

The two were silent, looking at each other. Scotty scratched his red beard, and then put his arm around his niece. "You've come up with some good ones, my girl. This one takes the frosting." He headed out of the garage and around to the side to look for the hammer. Ryan followed him, still carrying Kit.

At the side of the garage they stood looking at the broken window, at the teeth of jagged glass. On the lumber pile and on the ground, smaller shards of glass glittered in the morning sun. A ray of sunlight caught Scotty's missing hammer.

When he reached to pick it up, Ryan grabbed his arm, pulling him back. "Fingerprints," she said.

He was silent, looking at her. "Who the hell called you?"

"I don't know who. But, with the broken window, and the hammer right here, I don't think we can ignore it." She hoped Scotty wouldn't notice the smudged paw prints all among the glass, or that he would think they'd been there before the window was broken. "I think," she said, "we need to get that cement out before it sets up. And then we need to call Dallas."

Scotty glanced out at Fernando and Manuel and shook his head. "You want to tell them? Or shall I?"

33

Sitting at the big, round table in the ranch kitchen, still in her old plaid robe and with her first cup of coffee, Charlie tried again to reach her absent clients. She didn't understand why no one was answering their messages. She didn't care if she woke them, but even that seemed impossible. Did they all turn their phones off at night?

Most likely they did, she thought crossly, at least when they were on vacation. As she listened to yet another recording, looking out across the window seat to the ranch yard, she watched the sky lighten into a clear dawn. She could hear Redwing in the barn pawing at her door, wanting her hay and wanting to be turned out. It wasn't quite feeding time, but the mare had seen Max leave earlier and had decided she'd been forgotten.

Charlie hung up the phone after getting another "not available"; no point in leaving another message. She had risen to refill her coffee cup when her phone rang. Turning hastily back to the table, spilling her coffee, she saw that the number on the screen was Ryan's. She picked up, grabbed a towel, stood with the phone to her ear, mopping up coffee.

"I got Carl Chapman," Ryan said. "He'd just turned his phone on. When I filled him in, he didn't sound eager to tell Theresa about the paintings, said she was still asleep. He gave me the number for their insurance agent, asked if you'd call him. He's hoping you can take the adjuster in the house for a look, give him a tentative list of what's missing. He asked me to check on several other items in the house, he gave me a list. You have a pencil?"

Dutifully Charlie copied down the list, thinking that this whole thing was more of a pain than she wanted, that she'd be glad when she'd sold the business. At the moment she had only one serious prospect: a woman who, at one time she'd not have trusted to take over the service she'd so lovingly built, a woman she'd thought was dishonest until she'd learned that she was working undercover on the side of the law.

"I'll keep trying the Beckers," Ryan said. "Any luck with the others?"

"Not yet. I tried until well after midnight. Knowing Frances Becker, I expect when you get her, with half her antiques missing, she'll head right home."

She'd hardly hung up when the phone rang again. She picked up to Earl Longley's dry voice. "Eleen's out shopping," he said. He sounded even more irritable than usual. He spent considerable time cross-examining her about just how many books were missing, and which ones. He didn't seem nearly as upset over Eleen's paperweight collection, which, Charlie thought privately, was understandable. The loss of a closet full of pornographic paperweights really didn't stir her.

She must be on a roll, because the next call was from Ben Waterman. They were in Greece, had flown in that morning. It was cocktail hour, Ben said Rita was just getting out of the pool. When Charlie told him about the break-in, and described the events of the previous night, he startled her with his anger.

"What the hell were you doing? Don't you lock up your keys? Who had a set, how many of your people? I hate to tell Rita, she's going to be mad as hell."

"Ben, I don't blame you. But let's concentrate on finding this guy, on getting the jewelry back if we can. Does Rita have some kind of inventory?"

"She has a full inventory," he said coldly. "She has a photograph of each piece, with written descriptions and appraisals. You know the gems were all paste? But the settings were antique, some very old, and they didn't come cheap."

"Are the photographs and inventory in the house where we can find them? If the department can get copies to identify—"

"Why would they be in the house? So they could be stolen, too? Or burned up? It's all in the safe-deposit box."

"Does anyone else have access?"

"Of course not."

"And your insurance agents. Do they—"

"I'll call our agents and give them your number. I'm not sure what Rita gave them." He hung up. Charlie sat holding the phone, swallowing back her anger. Did he have to be so cross? Now, if the department arrested a suspect and the jewelry was on him, they'd have to wait nearly two weeks for a positive identification. She was fixing herself some breakfast when Ryan called back to say she'd gotten Ed Becker.

"Guess I woke him. He was pretty cranky. He said, 'How many people did Mrs. Harper tell we'd be out of town?' I told him that wasn't very realistic, that everyone in the neighborhood knew they were gone. He accused your crew of loose tongues and carelessness with the keys, of possibly copying the keys. Complained because you hadn't come by in the evenings to turn on the lights, which, I pointed out, you hadn't arranged to do. I suggested several things they could have done, like automatic light controls. He said Frances wouldn't do that, that she was afraid one would short out and cause a fire."

"Well, that's all four couples notified," Charlie said noncommittally, "and only half of them critical. I'll be so glad when I sell the business. Thanks for helping, and thanks for the moral support."

"Gotta go," Ryan said. "I need to check on two jobs in the village and be up at the remodel when the gravel and cement arrive, around ten. Clyde says—"

Her phone went dead. Charlie hung up and waited, supposing Ryan was out of range. She waited quite a while, but Ryan didn't call back. When she dialed her she got an "out of service" message, so maybe she'd forgotten to charge her phone. That wouldn't be the first time—though it was about the only inattention to detail that Charlie had ever noticed in her efficient friend.

Putting Max's dishes in the dishwasher, she warmed up a slice of cold bacon and her scrambled eggs, and made some toast, preoccupied with the robberies. The whole scenario was strange, she couldn't shake the thought that she was missing something, was overlooking some crucial element that should be perfectly obvious.

Setting her breakfast on the table, wanting to hurry and go feed the horses, she realized that part of her unease was the phone calls themselves. Neither she nor Ryan had talked with any of the four wives, they had spoken only with their husbands.

In all four instances, there were good explanations: Rita in the pool; Theresa asleep, and probably Frances Becker, too; and Eleen shopping, maybe for more paper-weights. She was reaching in the drawer for a fork when she stopped. Stood looking down into the drawer, at the new rubberized fabric with which she'd recently lined it, but seeing Theresa Chapman's kitchen drawers.

Leaving her breakfast to get cold, she picked up the phone to call Max.

The dispatcher said he was out, so she talked with Detective Garza. "Dallas, Theresa Chapman had keys for maybe half a dozen neighbors, all those with pets. She sometimes took care of the animals if someone was delayed at work; and she would sometimes let a work-man in. She kept them in the kitchen silverware drawer, underneath the wooden divider and the liner."

"We'll have a look," Dallas said. "How many others, besides the neighbors themselves, knew that?"

"I don't know. She told me she was very careful, didn't let anyone see where she kept them. She let the workmen think she had a key just for the day. The keys weren't marked, the names weren't on them. They were all different colors."

Hanging up, she warmed her plate in the microwave again, and returned to the table, opening the morning paper. She was just finishing breakfast when Dallas called back.

"Keys were here. I've printed them and will take them with me." He laughed. "You want me to feed the cat? She's playing up to me shamelessly. Those kittens are pretty cute."

"Yes, feed her," Charlie said, amused. "Cat food's on the washer." She guessed Joe and Dulcie and Kit were not only good at sleuthing, they were skilled, as well, at expanding the horizons of a dedicated dog person. Dallas had had pointers all his life, mostly German shorthairs. He was a bird hunter, a gun-dog man, and until recently he'd had no use at all for cats. She hung up, smiling at the change in him, wondering if he'd like to make a home for one of Mango's little kittens.

Ryan and Scotty stood looking at the broken window, at the hammer gleaming up at them among the fall of shattered glass. Scotty made no comment about the paw prints; she hoped he thought they belonged to some prowling neighborhood cat. "*Someone* was here," she said. "Someone broke into the garage and threw your hammer out through the window." She looked at him helplessly. "Just like the caller told me."

Scotty shrugged and scratched his beard. "We won't know for sure until we've dug out the concrete. You're willing to take his word for it, whoever it was?"

"I don't see that we have a choice. The department *does* have a report on a missing body. The lab has identified human blood, human hair, and human skin in the drag marks. And now someone says there's a body buried here? You think we have a choice?"

"Come on, then. The cement's setting up."

As she turned away to the garage, Kit squirmed in her arms and jumped down. Ryan watched her trot away and leap into the bed of her pickup. The labor and expense of digging out the concrete and of a new pour lay totally on the word of one small cat who, by sensible standards, could not exist at all.

Well, hell, she thought, moving into the garage and taking up her shovel. She watched Scotty fetch a wheelbarrow and give Manuel and Fernando their orders. Manuel looked as if Scotty had gone mad, but obediently he fetched a heavy pick. Small Fernando of the scarred face didn't move, stood frowning at Scotty.

Scott Flannery was a big man, broad shouldered, a bit wild looking with his thick red beard. But he was a quiet man, and patient—until his temper kicked in.

Now when he grabbed a second pick, Manuel backed away.

Scotty tested the hardening concrete with the pick, and then lit into it, swinging so hard he sent damp, crumbling debris flying. He handed the pick to Manuel.

"Dig now! Dig here, dig now, or you'll have no job to come back to and no pay." He repeated his orders in fractured Spanish.

Soon the two men were digging out the setting cement. With Scotty and Ryan working beside them, it didn't take long to clear away the carefully poured floor and rake the debris into a heap to be hauled away. Ryan couldn't stop thinking how embarrassed she'd be if, after they moved the gravel and dug down into the earth, they found nothing. No grave, no body. It hurt her to see the men's faces as their careful work was destroyed, as the nice smooth cement job was trashed into rubble.

She thought life might have been simpler if they'd quit work after the pour, paid the men, and sent them home for the rest of the day, and then she and Scotty had done the digging alone. She hoped to hell the missing corpse was down there so she wouldn't come up a liar. She was dismayed that she could never tell Scotty the real source of her information, that she had to lie to her uncle. Scotty had helped Dallas and her dad raise her and her sisters after their mother died, they were family and they seldom kept secrets from one another.

Through her goggles she watched patches of dark gravel appear, mixed with cement. Soon, Fernando and Manuel started heaving the gravel out, piling it against the garage wall where, later, it could be shoveled back into the pit—after the body had been disinterred.

If there was a body. And if there was . . . She thought about Dallas or Davis and the coroner working the scene; about the long wait of perhaps weeks or months until the case was resolved and they could close up the pit again, and pour fresh cement. She thought about her clients who were waiting anxiously to move in, who expected the work to be finished promptly—now, she was going to have to pay a steep penalty. Not envisioning this kind of delay, she'd deviated from her usual contract and allowed a time restriction to be written in, docking her a hundred dollars a day for every day over the agreed-upon finish date.

Earth began to show beneath the gravel. As Fernando reached to move a black drainpipe aside, Scotty reached to stop him, and Ryan fished her phone from her pocket. Time to call the department, they didn't want to disturb anything more until they had Max or a detective on the scene.

The two men climbed up the ladder. Glancing at each other and at Ryan with renewed skepticism, they stood waiting at the edge of the pit to see what would happen next. Despite their boss's crazy female notions, they were too curious to walk away. No one noticed that beyond the open garage, in the bed of Ryan's pickup, the three cats sat in a row, half hidden beneath the tarp, also waiting for the victim to be revealed. No one could have said whether the four humans, or the three cats, were the more curious and impatient.

34

Dispatcher Mabel Farthy clicked on the phone, answering Ryan's call. Ryan pictured the hefty blonde speaking through her headset, sitting in the open cubicle formed by the reception counter, her cluttered desk, filing cabinets, and shelves crowded with radios and the fax and copy machines. "I'm up at the Cowen remodel," Ryan told her. "On Blakely. Max and Dallas know where. We had a phone tip this morning, guy said we have a body buried up here, down in a drainage ditch—into which we'd just finished pouring fresh cement," she said wryly. "We've dug that out, dug out the gravel. We're down to raw earth and don't want to go any further."

Mabel didn't ask questions. "The chief's out. Hold on, I'll buzz Detective Garza. You okay? You sound pale."

"I'm fine," Ryan said, smiling at Mabel's turn of phrase. In a minute, Dallas came on. She said, "You know the ditch we dug inside the Cowen garage?"

"Yes, the second Panama Canal?"

"I got a phone call this morning that there's a body buried there."

"What kind of call? Who was it? What time? You get the name of the caller?"

"He wouldn't give it. It was . . . I was on my way up to the job, it was about ten. He gave me the message, said, 'The detectives and the chief know me,' and he hung up."

Dallas was silent for a long time, undoubtedly thinking about the department's anonymous snitch, the voice from out of nowhere, to which they had all learned to listen.

"Dallas, I believe him. You . . . You're cutting out," she said, not wanting to be interrogated.

"I'm on my way," he said shortly, with considerable irritation. "Don't do anything. Wait for me." When he'd hung up she stood outside looking around the property, wondering how much their careless coming and going this morning, so many people back and forth, had destroyed of the tire tracks and footprints. When she glanced up the hill, where the grass was swaying, she was startled to see Tansy and Sage slipping away over the crest as if headed home. Her phone rang and it was Dallas. "We're just turning onto Cohen." In a moment she heard cars approaching up the narrow road, crunching bits of gravel beneath their tires. Dallas's tan Blazer appeared, and Max's truck behind it. As they parked, she glanced at the bed of her pickup where the tarp was rippling in a quick, scurrying movement. For an instant, Joe Grey peered out, then vanished, and the tarp went still.

Joe watched Dallas swing out of his tan Blazer. His small SUV was a few years older than Charlie Harper's red model, and showed far more wear. The dark-haired Latino detective wore jeans, a white shirt open at the collar, and a leather jacket. Max Harper, stepping out of his pickup, was dressed in uniform this morning, as if he might have been in court. The two men headed into the open garage, stepping as carefully as they could between piles of wet cement and cement-covered gravel. As they stood looking down into the pit, talking with Ryan and Scotty, the two Latino laborers moved away.

Max said, "When did you get this phone call? Was it on your cell? Where were you?"

"On my cell. I was coming up the hill. Scotty and his men had just finished working the cement. You think I didn't want to strangle the guy? You know what concrete costs? You know how long it takes to finish it? And look at the mess we have to clean up."

Max said, "I'm surprised you tore it out. You queried this guy? What exactly did he say?"

"I asked him how he could know this. Told him I wasn't digging up that cement, that I'd have to have proof to do such a crazy thing. He said he saw the guy bury the body, that the only proof he could offer was the body itself. If we wanted to be sure, we'd have to dig."

"And you took his word for it," Max said. "Where did he say he was? Did you ask him to come in, give a statement?" That was a futile question. The cats knew it, and Max knew it, he knew their unknown snitch wouldn't do that.

She said, "The guy hung up, Max! I thought it could be a crank call. But then I thought about your snitch, I know he doesn't wait on the phone to answer questions. I had two choices. Let it go, let the concrete cure, and forget I ever got that call. Or dig it up and call you."

In the pickup, Joe Grey smiled.

"Are you going to hang around while we dig? Or are you going to laugh at me and leave?"

Max tried not to grin as Ryan's temper rose. He exchanged a look with Dallas, who spoke with Fernando in Spanish, which none of the three cats understood except for the occasional familiar word, including Manuel's interjected, half-joking "loco" as he glanced across at Ryan.

That made Dallas laugh. "Maybe not loco at all," he said in English. "We'll have to wait and see."

Max flipped open his phone and in a moment was speaking with the coroner. That cooled Ryan down, the fact that he wanted John Bern on the scene before they uncovered a corpse.

In Ryan's pickup the cats settled in to wait, curled up for a little nap beneath the warm canvas. They were all three fast asleep when a car woke them, pulling up to park. Looking out from under the tarp, they watched John Bern step out of his white van.

Bern was young, slim, prematurely bald, his fine-boned face was unlined by the depressing nature of his job, as if the mysteries he set himself to unravel, in the cause of death and the identification of a body, far outweighed the grimmer aspects of the profession. Wiping his glasses, he entered the garage and stood talking with Ryan and Max and Dallas, looking at the lumps of gravel and the messy pile of slowly hardening cement.

"You did all this on the word of a guy you don't know and who wouldn't identify himself?"

"I believed him," Ryan said shortly. "We've blown a whole morning and a bundle of money on this. He'd better be telling the truth." She was losing patience and losing confidence. She wanted to get on with the dig, either to be vindicated or to stoically endure her embarrassment.

Bern climbed down the ladder into the pit, and Dallas followed. Max stood looking on, a little amused, a little put off. The cats couldn't see to the bottom, could see into the garage only as far as the lip of the pit, where Ryan stood watching. They could hear the soft scrape of slow, careful digging, could see Fernando and Manuel just inside the door, idly shuffling their feet, waiting to witness Ryan's embarrassment when all this digging turned up nothing—or perhaps to experience a macabre thrill if a corpse was uncovered. Soon the sounds of digging grew more tentative, there was a long, muffled discussion, then the cats could hear only soft scratching, such as their own careful paws might make. Dallas's exclamation was sharp.

Ryan stepped closer. Fernando and Manuel moved forward to look but then Manuel backed away, his face pale. Fernando stood looking, and then nodded at Ryan and gave her a shy smile

She grinned back but looked at the two men with concern. "You guys okay?"

"Okay," Fernando said. Both men were looking at her now as if she possessed some magical power, as if she were some kind of witch to have known that there was a body buried there.

She said, "You'll have to wait for the detective to take your statements, then you can go on home, take the rest of the day off with pay."

That seemed to revive Fernando. Manuel gave her a lopsided, gentle smile. Down in the pit, Garza said something the cats couldn't make out. Joe Grey wondered how many bodies Dallas Garza had helped to disinter over his twenty-five years in law enforcement. He wondered if it ever got any easier to deal with a victim of violence, to look on a battered or mutilated body and think about the cruelty that existed in one's own species. The tomcat burned to slip out of the truck and move closer where he could see if he knew the woman, but Dulcie's armored paw on his shoulder drew him back. She was always so afraid people would wonder why they were watching. He didn't want to admit she was right.

It was some time before John Bern and Dallas finished bagging evidence. Joe, having at last lost patience, had left the pickup despite Dulcie's protests and slipped into the garage behind the pile of cement. He had to smile when Dulcie and Kit followed him, crouching beside him where they, too, could see down into the pit but not be seen.

They could see Dallas's back where he knelt beside Bern, but couldn't see much of the woman, only a glimpse of her arm and one bare, tanned leg. They jerked to attention when Bern said, "These look like cat hairs."

The cats lived in fear of cat hairs being found at a scene, hairs that could give them away, and would certainly generate questions. But why were they flinching now? They hadn't been *near* this victim, they hadn't *been* in the pit. There was no way . . .

"Hairs stuck to her skin," Bern said. "She's oily, smells like suntan oil. She's tan all over, not a pale mark on her. Was she in the habit of sunbathing naked?"

"I don't know," Dallas said dryly. "I never had the pleasure."

Bern lifted a cat hair with forceps, to view it though his magnifying glass. "Yellow. Sure looks like cat hair. Maybe it came off her clothes, or . . . I wonder if those same hairs are stuck to the killer's clothes?"

The cats crouched, frozen. A yellow cat? There were no yellow cats in that neighborhood except Theresa's cat. Oh, this wasn't Theresa. They felt as if they'd been kicked in the belly.

Max said, "Charlie has clients a couple of blocks from the empty swimming pool where we're working that missing body. I think one of them has a yellow cat.

I'll get Charlie over to the morgue, see if we might get lucky and she can ID her."

Frightened for Theresa, already grieving for her, the cats slipped out of the garage and across the drive to the shelter of Ryan's truck. Crawling up beneath the tarp, they pushed close together, Joe and Kit pressing their heads against Dulcie.

"Oh, it isn't Theresa," Kit mewled. "No one . . . It mustn't . . . It *can't* be Theresa."

"Not Theresa," Dulcie said. "They're wrong, it can't be." She pressed hard against Joe, her ears down, her eyes closed, and the three cats clung together, mourning Theresa as they had seldom, in all their lives, grieved for a human person.

35

When he woke in the motel, it was broad daylight. Christ! Looking blearily at his watch, he saw it was nearly noon. What had made him sleep so long? His mouth tasted bad and his face felt worse. Gingerly, he touched his cheek, his whole face was covered with deep claw wounds, and probably some of them still had glass in them. He'd picked out a dozen bloody slivers last night that he'd gotten when he lay facedown below the window, trying to protect himself from their dirty claws. He was still bleeding, there was blood all over the pillows and sheets. His stubble itched bad already, and he wouldn't be able to shave. A razor would take half his face off, what was left of it.

He hadn't crawled into the musty-smelling bed until after three by the time he'd changed the tire and then gone back to find the inhaler. Never had found it and that was when it hit the fan, that was when everything went wrong.

After those cats attacked him, after he got away and locked himself in the RV, he'd tried to clean up. Found a towel in the back and, half blind with blood and pain, had tried to wash and doctor the filthy wounds, squeezed on some salve he'd found in the kitchenette, that *she'd* put there in case of some emergency. She hadn't guessed what kind of emergency. Bleeding all over himself, he'd headed for the highway, wanted only to be out of there, to be as far away from that cursed house and the cursed village as he could get. But then he'd driven only as far as Santa Cruz when he knew he had to sleep. Caught himself twice jerking awake, knew he had to find a motel where he could pull the RV out of sight and get some rest.

He'd driven around the fusty little town for some time before he found a motel that would suit his purpose. He'd had to ring for ten minutes before the manager came stumbling out in an old bathrobe, none too pleased even if the place was nearly empty, only five cars parked in front. It was after three o'clock when he'd finally checked in and fallen into bed. Hadn't slept well, kept waking, his face hurting, and feeling those cats all over him. Would jerk up in a rictus of terror then, sweating, then fall into sleep again.

His muscles ached. He was stiff from digging, from hauling her up out of the pool and heaving her in the car, then later moving her into the RV and then into that garage and down the ladder. He wasn't a laborer, he worked out some to keep in shape, but not that kind of abuse. He'd already been sore when the tire blew. Changing that had nearly finished him. And then to be attacked—that monster exploding in his face and then a whole pack of them erupting in a horror, like his worst nightmares. Where had they come from? And why?

Getting out of bed, he found a coffeepot in the small bathroom. Pot so stained and dirty that if he didn't die from an infection of cat bites he'd likely die from the accumulation of bacteria that it had collected over who knew how many years as the hotel maids wiped it out with their dirty scrub rags.

He couldn't have picked a skuzzier motel. It was in an old, run-down district, a two-story, dilapidated stucco building that must have been constructed early in the last century, surrounded by a neighborhood of small wooden houses with peeling paint, ragged lawns, and junk cars in the yards and narrow driveways. But it had what he wanted. Before he checked in he'd driven around behind the building where he found a narrow alley that would serve him well. Returning to the front and checking in, he'd asked for a room at the back, told the clerk it'd be quieter back there, away from

334 • SHIRLEY ROUSSEAU MURPHY

the street. He could pretty well choose his own room, empty as they were. Taking his duffle up, he'd opened the window, draped a towel over the sill to mark which room. Then he'd moved the RV around into the alley, parked it among the garbage cans just below, pulled it up against the building so no one could open the side door. Had hoped, if anyone tried to open the locked driver's door, he'd hear them. Carrying his coffee, he opened the window and looked down.

RV looked all right, he could see in through the side windows that it was still full of the boxes, just as he'd left it. Turning, he surveyed the fusty room with its faded brown wallpaper and ragged curtains. Some send-off for a trip that they'd meant to be fancy. A trip *she'd* meant to be an upscale vacation, spending the money they'd pocket from their neighbors' treasures. They'd set it up so well. And she had to go and ruin it.

Ever since they'd moved into that neighborhood they'd been friendly with the neighbors, had made it a point to be. Three other couples they'd gotten along with well, they'd made a good group. He sat down on the bed, drinking his coffee.

He wondered if, when his face had healed and things cooled down, he *could* return home, keep on in the same vein with the neighbors and no one the wiser. Act grateful for his friends' condolences about her leaving him, exchange sympathy with them about their mutual burglaries, keep right on enjoying their company. They'd had some fun parties, the eight of them. Potlucks, card games, cookouts. He wondered if he could get away with that as smoothly as they'd pulled off other jobs, in other cities. *She'd* say that what someone didn't know would never hurt them.

He missed her. Why the hell did she have to be so clumsy? He thought again that he could have called the paramedics. But that wouldn't have saved her, she was dead seconds after her head hit the tile coping. He could have called the cops, told them she fell, but who would have believed him? Believed he didn't push her, that he hadn't murdered her even if it *had* been her fault?

He had to quit thinking about it. It was over, she was gone. Buried where no one would ever think to look. He had to get on with it now, and he could sure use the money, would need it if he decided not to go back. He didn't know how that would play out, that would depend on what the cops found, on what he read in the papers—if it was all reported. If the damn cops didn't hold something back, trying to trap him.

Biggest problem was, he'd laid no groundwork in the neighborhood for her leaving him, he hadn't planned on this. He hadn't dropped hints that they might be having problems, and she would have no reason to say that. He'd made no big withdrawal from her account for the cops to discover, as if she planned to leave him. No secret plane reservations on her Visa. He'd have to say it was a spur-of-the-moment blowup, that they'd had their little tiffs but he'd never dreamed she'd get mad enough to leave, to just walk out on him. Have to say they'd kept their differences to themselves, that they'd had a far worse argument than usual. By the time he got up to Washington State he'd have worked out the details to make it look reasonable. He'd have to do this tedious stuff on his own, now, working out all the picky details.

Last night after changing the tire, after pulling away in the dark, leaving his lights off until he was clear of the cops below, he'd felt physically ill at their presence down there. Heading toward the highway he'd felt ice cold, and his stomach had been churning. Who the hell had called the cops? What had someone seen? Had they seen *him*? Seen the *RV*? Right now, was every CHP on the highway watching for an old brown RV that wouldn't be hard to spot?

Rising, he went into the tiny bathroom where he showered, trying to keep the hot water off his face. It stung like hell, and he didn't want it bleeding any worse. He wasn't hungry but he thought he'd better eat. Maybe some breakfast would make him feel better.

He badly wanted to see a newspaper, see if the burglaries were in it. Molena Point wasn't that far away.

Before checking out, he tried the TV but by the time he turned it on there was no more news, it was all daytime programs, as murky as the oily dregs in the coffeepot. He finally found a local channel with some news. He watched that for nearly an hour but there was no mention of Molena Point. His stomach awash with coffee, he knew he had to eat.

Leaving the room, he walked past the elevator to where a window was open at the front of the building, stood looking out through the greasy curtains, up and down the street. He could see nothing like a restaurant, not even some kind of hole-in-the-wall grocery that would have packaged snacks and newspapers. Maybe better to hit the road, find somewhere to eat on his way to the city. Approaching San Francisco, there'd be plenty of restaurants.

Returning to the room, grabbing the small duffle that he'd brought in with him last night, he walked down the one flight, stopped at the desk to pay his bill. The clerk was young and pudgy; she avoided looking at his face. When he told her he might be back that night, she wanted him to make a reservation, and that made him laugh. As if they were expecting a big crowd, were booked solid with upscale tourists or some medical convention. The quality of this place, they couldn't count on a convention of second-rate hookers. Paying his bill in cash, which the clerk didn't question, he went around to get the RV.

No, nothing had been disturbed. When he slipped in, locked the driver's door, and went to look in the back, the boxes and furniture and rolled rugs were just as he'd left them. Starting the engine and moving out to the street, he stayed in the scuzzy neighborhood, driving the narrow streets looking for someplace for breakfast. Once he'd eaten he meant to return to Highway 1, stay on the coast, away from cops and traffic. As soon as he'd taken care of business in the city, dumped the RV and bought a car, he could move north on any route he chose, he wouldn't be recognized then. Meanwhile, the day was clear and bright, the sea reflected the sun cheerfully, and he might as well enjoy the ride. After a week or two, he'd decide whether to go back and say she'd left him, or to keep moving.

36

The three cats watched from Ryan's truck as Dallas and John Bern emerged from the pit with the wrapped body on a stretcher and lifted her into Bern's van. She was fully covered by the body bag, and the cats were relieved not to have to look on her face in death. They wanted to keep their own picture of Theresa, her eyes laughing down at them, her hands gentle and warm as she stroked them, her round cheeks pink with health and life. They didn't want to remember her sunny face as the waxen face of a corpse.

As the coroner's van pulled away, Dallas followed in his dusty Blazer, leaving the house encircled by crime tape. Max had already left to return to court and then to pick up Charlie, to head for the morgue. As soon as everyone else was gone, Ryan stepped to the bed of her truck and pulled aside the tarp where the cats were huddled.

"Come on, you three," she said gently, reaching to stroke sad little Dulcie. She looked into their eyes, so miserable. There was nothing she could say to ease their pain over this woman she'd never met. While Charlie knew the four couples well, she didn't know them at all. "I'll take you home," she said softly, "if that's where you want to go. Come up front with me, where it's warmer."

Joe hesitated, crouching lower.

"Those boxes could shift, Joe. I don't want you hurt. I can drop you in the village if you'd rather." She tried to stroke the tomcat, but his miserable glare made her pull her hand back. She picked up Dulcie, who pressed against her. When she took Kit in her arms, Kit pressed her face into Charlie's shoulder. Carrying the two lady cats, she turned away toward the cab. "I'm not starting the truck, Joe, until you come up front."

In the cab, she started the engine, turned on the heater, and left the door open for Joe. As Dulcie and Kit crowded against her, she thought of many things she might say to try to ease their pain, except anything she said would sound patronizing and insincere.

At last Joe appeared, slipping up into the cab beside Dulcie.

The cats snuggled together trying not to think of Theresa wrapped in the body bag and headed for the morgue, but able to think of nothing else. No one spoke as they moved down the hills on the narrow, winding road, they were silent all the way to the village. On Ocean, Ryan pulled to the curb, reached over, and opened the passenger door. "This okay?" she asked, trying to hide her worry over them.

"Fine," Joe said. Dulcie and Kit nosed at her by way of thanks, and the cats leaped out to the sidewalk. She'd started to pull away when a portly man in a brown tank top banged on the truck door, shouting that her cats had escaped. Already the cats were gone, flowing up a bougainvillea vine to the rooftops, heading for MPPD. Behind the fat man, his frumpy wife stood staring up, shouting and pointing.

Ryan rolled down her window. "It's all right," she told the meaty tourists. "They do that all the time. They like to ride into town, then go off on their own. They'll be home for supper." They stared at her, shaking their heads in disbelief. She smiled and waved, and pulled away.

At Molena Point PD Detective Juana Davis sat before her computer typing up her field notes from the burglaries and from her interviews with eight of the neighbors. She had slipped off her uniform jacket, revealing a white shirt open at the collar. Beneath her desk she had loosened the laces of her regulation shoes and slipped them off, too. The divergent observations she'd collected were the usual tangle, from which she must try to separate facts from imagination. Civilian witnesses weren't trained in accuracy. Too often their minds, at the moment in question, were half on other matters. Listening for the kids sleeping in their beds, hearing the TV or a ringing phone, wondering if they'd turned off the stove. Few folks remembered clearly what they'd seen and heard, particularly when they didn't realize at the time that those moments would later be important.

Leaning back in her chair, she sipped her cold coffee, thinking about the burglar. He knew the neighborhood, knew it well enough to know exactly what he'd wanted to steal and, apparently, where it was in each house. He—or she—hadn't rooted in the drawers or torn apart the closets, he'd gone right to his objectives. He had copies of all four garage door openers and access to the house keys. Whether keys had been kept hanging in some of the garages, or he'd had duplicates of them all, was yet to be determined.

Every one of her eight interviewees had said that, as far as they knew, none of the four couples kept extra garage door openers in the house, that there was just the usual button inside each garage, and an opener in each car, some of those programmed directly into the cars' electronic systems. She thought it likely that the guy had one of those programming gadgets available online to your everyday thief. As she set her coffee cup down, a movement in the bookshelf along the far wall startled her.

She looked up, frowning at Joe Grey. "When did you slip in here? I'm no more observant than our witnesses." That disturbed her, that she hadn't seen an intruder cross her office, even if it was only a cat, that she'd been so focused she'd noticed nothing. "At least you're not armed, you little bum," she said, grinning companionably.

What she hadn't seen was Dulcie and Kit melt behind the small easy chair that sat at an angle at the end of her desk. By stretching, standing on their hind legs, their claws in the back of the chair for support, the two lady cats could just see Juana's computer screen, though at an angle that made it hard to read.

The interview she was typing was with a Raymond Atwater, who lived at the south end of the block. Atwater was a widower and lived alone. Sometime between his supper and his bedtime, he saw the lights of a car pulling into the Becker garage. He thought they might have delayed their vacation, and he didn't question that. He didn't recall the time. He said he tried not to mind the neighbors' business. He'd gone on to bed, to read, and hadn't seen the car leave. He'd been deep in his book when he heard the scream of a cat, said he'd assumed a couple of neighborhood cats were mating.

Well, he *heard us yowling in the closet,* Joe thought. *Would he eventually have come to rescue us? Maybe, maybe not. We could have died within earshot, and some people wouldn't care.* In order to read the report, to avoid a glare on the screen that wiped out the message, the tomcat had to move along the bookcase and crane his neck. He was waiting for Juana to finish up with Atwater and get on to the next witness when the phone rang.

Juana glanced at it, and picked up. "Yes, Chief." Juana Davis was old fashioned enough that she didn't much care for a speakerphone, she was never sure who might be out in the hall listening, an arrestee on his way to an interview, a felon being escorted back to lockup.

Behind the chair, Dulcie was content to listen to the one-sided conversation, but Kit wanted to climb up on the desk where she could press her ear against the receiver. Dulcie's look drew her back.

After a moment, Juana nodded. "I hope you can get an ID." She paused, then, "I'm just getting to the last interview. A Mrs. Edmond Turner, four houses down from the Chapmans' . . . Nancy Turner, yes. She said she stopped by the Chapmans' Saturday around noon to loan Theresa a book she'd wanted to read on vacation. She said Frances Becker was there, that Frances said she was on her way out for a quick walk, that she and her husband were leaving that afternoon. That before they left, she'd wanted to see the kittens. The two women were in the laundry with the kittens, she said Frances was making a real fuss over them. It surprised her, that Frances was down on the floor playing with them like a kid."

Another pause, then, "Yes, she did. Said both women were wearing shorts and flip-flops, that only young women could dress like that in this weather. She said Frances walks a lot, usually on weekends.

"She said there was a rolled-up blue towel lying on the floor next to Frances, looked like a beach towel. Said the kittens were all over it, playing and clawing it." Davis had a satisfied smile on her face. "Yesterday at the swimming pool, the threads I bagged? Some of them were blue. Blue threads stuck to the coping, some of them with blood."

She listened for a few minutes, answered, "Yes," then, "No. When Mrs. Turner left Theresa's, Frances was still there."

The cats could hardly be still. Dulcie and Kit were fidgeting with interest, and Joe Grey watched Juana intently. Had Frances stopped by Theresa's on her way *not* to walk but headed for the abandoned pool? Carrying her beach towel, intending to strip and catch a little sun before leaving? Joe thought about the towels that Clyde had used as cat beds, how they quickly got matted with fur. He imagined Frances beside the empty pool, stripping off her shorts and shirt, lathering on suntan oil and stretching out on the blue towel—where every yellow cat hair would have clung to her oily skin.

Was it Frances Becker who died? And not Theresa?

Across the room, Dulcie's heart was pounding. Kit could hardly keep from lashing her tail. *That was* Frances *with cat hairs stuck to her suntan lotion! Theresa isn't dead? That was Frances Becker who'd died in the pool, not Theresa?*

Juana said, "No, she didn't. Yes, let me read it." She looked at the screen to quote Nancy Turner. " 'She likes to take long midday walks alone. Sometimes she wears a Walkman, listens to classical music. Frances does a lot of her work at night. I can hear the CDs she plays. She's very dedicated in her accounting jobs, I see her office light on very late.'

"That's most of it," Davis said. "She couldn't tell me which way Frances went when she left the Chapmans', she said she'd gone right home, that she didn't know where Frances usually walked once she left the block."

Resting his chin on his paws, Joe thought about Frances Becker, so sensible and low-key. Was she the kind of person to sunbathe naked? How much did they not know about her? He thought about her charming husband—her philandering husband—and how much they didn't know about him, either.

Was Ed Becker capable of murder? If he was a womanizer, Joe thought, then why wouldn't he be just as capable of stealing? Had Ed Becker planned those thefts, Frances found out and tried to stop him, and he'd killed her?

Joe thought about Ed following her to the abandoned pool, killing her, getting rid of the body, and then moving on as he'd planned, to steal from his neighbors. Proceeding just as glibly as when, behind Frances's back, he stole the attentions of his neighbors' wives.

This scenario made sense. And yet as relieved as he was to hope that Theresa was alive, still a dozen questions rattled in his head and wouldn't let him rest.

"Yes," Davis said. "You're headed there now? If she's from the neighborhood, Charlie will know her. Yes, I'll be at the autopsy first thing in the morning."

As much as the tomcat liked to be in on every aspect of a murder, when he imagined Davis photographing the autopsy, he was willing to bypass this part of the investigation. Dissecting a human body was not the same as eviscerating a mouse.

Well, it shouldn't take but a few minutes for Charlie to identify the victim, and for Max to call Davis. He watched Dulcie and Kit curl up behind the chair to wait, and he stretched out along the bookshelf, closing his eyes. Praying, as coldhearted as it might seem, that that was Frances Becker up there at the morgue, and not Theresa.

37

Leaving the county morgue beside Max, Charlie slipped into the passenger seat of her Blazer, happy to let him drive. As soon as he turned the key she rolled down her window, turning her face to the wind, hoping to blow away the smell of formaldehyde and death that clung to her. The stink seemed to have seeped into her every pore, and every fiber of her clothes. Were they depositing the smell in her Blazer, too, so it would never again be the same? Would her nice SUV, which had been a gift from Max on her last birthday, forevermore smell like a grave?

How did John Bern stand it? She'd wondered more than once what made a person like Bern embrace that particular profession. He was young, strong and intelligent, and nice looking, his premature baldness seeming only to add to his attractiveness. He'd told her once that it was the challenge, that he was fascinated by the precise procedure, of unraveling the mystery of how someone died. He said that if it was a murder, he got completely caught up in helping to discover the killer.

She looked back at the cream-colored, four-story stucco building, its roof fluted with red tile, thinking about the chill and antiseptic morgue in its basement, about the physically cold, visually cold viewing room with its unadorned walls, chill gray terrazzo floor that could be easily scrubbed, and its hard metal chairs. A room that hadn't offered much in the way of emotional comfort as Bern rolled out the cold metal gurney bearing Frances's covered body.

"We've done preliminary testing for drugs," he'd told them. "My guess is she died from an intracerebral bleed. I don't want to make a final judgment yet as to whether she was struck, or if this occurred naturally, from a fall. Looks like she fell at least several feet, from the contusion and the specks of grit and cement embedded in the skin."

They had discussed the autopsy for the following morning, which Detective Davis would attend, and before they'd left, Max had called Mabel to put out an APB on Frances Becker's white Honda Accord, which was the car missing from the Becker garage. Now, pulling out of the parking lot, Max said, "You okay? You're pale as hell."

"Fine," Charlie lied. "I'm fine."

"The smell will go away," he said, wondering if she was going to be sick. "If it was her husband who killed her, then is there no one to notify? She had no family?"

"Not that she ever mentioned."

"Davis will go over the house again, maybe she'll find an address in her files, some relative."

"One thing about Frances," she said, "she was a neatnick, everything in order. It shouldn't take Davis long to find an address, if there *were* any relatives."

As Max turned onto the freeway, Charlie said, "John Bern says Frances has been dead at least thirty-six hours. When Ryan talked with Ed Becker this morning, he told her that her call woke Frances."

"What is he going to do, tell her Frances can't come to the phone right now because she's dead?" He flicked on his emergency flashers to get a car off their tail, watched the guy pass on their left. The driver wouldn't take such a liberty if they were in a patrol car. "If Becker turns out to be the burglar as well, then he apparently changed cars, switched to the dark RV. He could have put the jewelry and paintings in Frances's Accord, but not the furniture and boxes of books." He looked over at Charlie. "Switched cars, hid the Accord somewhere, maybe in a storage unit or rented garage."

Charlie tried to remember if Frances had ever mentioned a locker or a rented garage. But if Ed was stealing, surely she didn't know about it. Did they own a rental house somewhere, and he'd stashed the car there? That didn't seem likely when they'd lived in Molena Point only about two years. "Maybe there *was* a storage unit, maybe they still have unpacked boxes, maybe part of Frances's furniture collection. But if Ed was the burglar . . ." She looked at him, frowning. "He loaded up all that furniture from his own house to throw you off the track?"

Max shrugged. "Again, what else could he do?" They were turning off the freeway toward home when her phone buzzed. It was Ryan.

"We're just getting back from the morgue," Charlie told her. "I won't turn the speaker on, there's too much traffic noise. The dead woman is Frances Becker. You want to tell . . . Clyde?" Meaning, *Will you tell Joe Grey?* She knew the cats would be grieving for Theresa.

Ryan said, "They just walked in, all three of them, grinning like Cheshire cats." And, more softly, "They were there when Max called the station."

Charlie hid her smile.

Ryan said, "You want to run down here for supper? Beans and corn bread, and we'll show you pictures of the house we've decided on."

Charlie covered the phone, looking at Max. "Go down for a quick supper?" In truth, she didn't feel like eating, she wasn't sure she'd ever eat again, not sure her mouth would ever stop tasting like something dead.

But maybe a comforting meal of beans and corn bread would stay down. When Max nodded, she said, "We'll just run by home and take care of the horses, we won't be long." Part of her would like to stay home, but she wanted, even more, to reassure the cats that indeed Theresa was just fine. Approaching the village, Max turned up the hills toward the ranch; the minute they turned into their long private road, the two big dogs saw them from the pasture and came barking, racing along inside the fence. The four horses galloped beside them, all of them wanting supper.

While Max fed the livestock, Charlie hurried to brush her teeth and lay out clean clothes. She took a quick shower and washed her hair, pinning it back wet. Max showered and changed, they threw their clothes in the washer and were out again in half an hour, headed for the village in the truck, leaving the Blazer in the stable yard with all the windows rolled down, hoping the sea wind would sweeten that clinging smell.

The village streets at dinnertime were busy with tourists crossing back and forth looking in shop windows or pausing before the small restaurants, reading the posted menus. Turning down the Damens' street and parking, they caught the comforting scent of Clyde's favorite bean recipe. Wilma's car was parked in the drive beside the Greenlaws' gray sedan. "What's this?" Max said. "I thought we were just running down for a quick bite."

"I don't know," she said innocently. Because Dulcie and Kit were here, it would have been only natural for the Damens to invite the cats' housemates. Rock barked at the door to greet them, and Clyde handed them each a beer. Everyone was gathered around the fire, the three cats sprawled on the mantel, warming themselves safely above the cozy blaze. Charlie paused to stroke them. They smiled up at her, their eyes filled with delight that Theresa was alive. They might feel sad for Frances, but not as sad as if they were grieving over their real friend. In front of Max, Charlie could say nothing, she stood petting them, trapped in one of those maddening moments when she and the cats longed to talk, but could say not a word. Of everyone present, it was only Max—the most keenly attuned to the subtleties of body language and behavior—who didn't know the truth.

38

Eighty miles north of Molena Point, traveling the narrow two-lane along the edge of the cliff high above the Pacific, there was hardly any traffic. Above him the sky was clear, not a cloud, just the way he liked it—except that the sea was too bright, its flat surface metallic with reflected sun, that shot through the windshield at an angle that he couldn't block with the visor.

The road was so narrow that when an occasional car did approach him, he had to press the RV precariously close to the rocky cliff that rose jaggedly on his right. His face hurt like hell and he kept thinking about infection. Cats were dirty creatures, and he was sure there was still glass embedded in the wounds, so deep he might never get it out. Every few miles he checked himself in the mirror to see if he was bleeding again.

He'd put flesh-colored Band-Aids on only the worst wounds, otherwise his whole face would be covered. He felt better, though, with some breakfast in him.

In the steamy, boxlike restaurant with its dark-stained plywood walls smelling of the fishing wharf, he'd ordered ham, three eggs over easy, potatoes, and three biscuits, washing it all down with a big carafe of coffee. His bandages and bloody scratches had gotten wary looks from the half dozen tourists sitting in the plywood booths. One skinny woman in a purple sweater had looked so shocked that she half rose to leave, then glowered at her husband when he pulled her back into the booth. Two locals at the counter—wizened old men dressed in leathers that stunk of fish, their faces wrinkled and dark from sea and sun, had given him darkly amused stares. Both of them were drinking beer that was colored pink by the red wine they'd poured into it. Four empty wineglasses were lined up precisely beside their beer bottles. The waitress, an overweight redhead with a checkered apron pulled tight over her belly, took one look at him and asked, smartly, if he'd been in a catfight. He'd eaten quickly, didn't tip her, paid his bill, and left.

Now, moving north up the precarious coastal two-lane, he glanced at his watch. One thirty. Not too bad considering how late he'd slept. He'd be in the city by three, unload the goods with the fence. Be out of there with the money and on the road again with plenty of time to dump the RV, leaving it on some back street where the homeless would strip it to sell for parts. Plenty of time to catch a bus to the nearest out-of-the-way car lot, some small operation where the salesman wouldn't get fidgety if he paid in cash. Pick up a nondescript vehicle and head on north.

If he was ever questioned about the car that was now in the rented garage outside Molena Point, he'd say *she* took it when she ran off and left him. That he didn't know why she'd taken it back there. He could get rid of it later, slip back into the village, drive it off to some chop shop.

As he plied the narrow highway north of Half Moon Bay, most of the sparse traffic was moving south, hugging the road above the sheer drop, detained from some fatal misjudgment only by occasional short lengths of guardrail. He kept the windows open, letting the cool, damp air soothe his burning face. The echo of the sea far below crashing against the rocks pleased him, he liked its wildness, he liked the thrill of danger. It was the same as the thrill of their thefts, they skirted the edge but always moved on unharmed. She'd loved that, loved the excitement that they *could* get caught but never did. She'd loved selecting their targets beforehand from within an intimate group, she'd loved their duplicity. *She* was the one who insisted they slip away with only the items she'd chosen and take nothing else. They'd had a good thing going. Live in a neighborhood a few years, get cozy with the neighbors, join the local organizations, go to the concerts and amateur plays, even the school functions when the neighbors' kids were involved—that was key, getting involved. During that time while they were settling in, listening to their neighbors' problems and sometimes trying to help, babysitting their kids, they could often pull a few jobs in some previous neighborhood if it was close enough. Pick a time when there was a funeral or a wedding that would involve most of the residents. Then afterward allow enough time to lapse so everyone grew complacent again, thinking the thieves had moved on. They had done this on the East Coast, too, before they'd come out to California. To rip off their adopted neighborhood, that was the thrill, and they'd planned their moves carefully.

And then she'd gotten in one of her moods, had to have one more fling sunbathing, and look what it got her, she'd messed up everything.

Taking his time around the hairpin turns, wary of some approaching driver trying to pass another on the narrow road, he played the radio, pushing the buttons for a new station whenever he got bored, selecting alternately the talk shows, the hourly news, some nutcase discussing alternative medicine, and a station that specialized in UFO sightings. Anything to keep his thoughts moving, not dwell on her. And not dwell on those cursed cats last night. The sea air was calming, but then going around a curve the wind hit his face hard, making the wounds burn like fire, so painful that he felt the cats on him again, clawing and biting. Even with the distraction of the radio, he kept seeing them exploding in his face, their eyes like fire. When he took his hands off the wheel, they were shaking. His stomach, full of breakfast now, was getting queasy again as it had last night. Last night he'd lain awake for hours sweating, seeing that pale cat bursting out at him through the broken window, feeling enraged cats all over him. That kept him awake until he got up, found the sleeping pills they sometimes used, took two, and then at last dozed off. But even then, he slept fitfully, would jerk awake, his face burning. Once he woke seeing Poe's cat plastered inside a wall staring out at him, and then saw *those* cats screaming up from her grave letting the whole world know where she was buried.

Trying to pass a slow-moving truck on the two-lane, he pulled his thoughts back to the road, looking ahead as far as he could to negotiate the curve. He couldn't drive these hairpin curves with his mind obsessing over cats. The road was precarious here, the drop precipitous, straight down maybe a hundred feet. He'd passed the truck without mishap and was headed downhill when the steering wheel jerked in his hand, jerked again, back and forth. Oh, Christ, not here, not another tire! Wheel felt like it was alive, nearly pulling itself from his grip. He steered into the cliff to slow the heavy vehicle, afraid to apply the brakes and make it skid. But when he tried to edge it into the cliff to make it stop, the wheel jerked harder, he hit the cliff too hard and careened away, and *had* to use the brakes. He hit them only gently but the vehicle dropped hard in the left front where he'd had the flat, far more out of control. What was wrong? The way it wobbled back and forth, it felt like the whole wheel was coming off. He had a flash of changing the tire, of putting on the lug nuts wondering which way they should go, which way he'd removed them. Feeling in the dark the sharp corners on one side, the rounded corners on the other. Had he got them wrong, or not tightened them sufficiently? Had he put them on backward, and they'd worked loose? The RV careened toward the edge so hard he could no longer steer. Felt like the wheel was half off, wobbling bad, the RV skidded straight for the edge, the steering wheel in his hands useless. He grabbed at the door.

The car was out over space, falling and rolling in midair as he fought the door. When he got it open, it swung and hit him. He managed to kick free and jump, the RV falling beside him. Its heavy bulk bounced against him and then he was under it, trying to swim through the air to get away from the hurtling vehicle. It twisted and came down on him and hit the sea—he hit the water on his back, the RV on top, driving him down, the jolt was like hitting concrete. Explosions of unbearable light shot through his head and then that pale cat exploding in his face; the whole world filled with cats screaming and raking him, and then *her* face, *her* face laughing at him and she had the blazing eyes of a cat. Her face was the screaming face of the cat closing over him . . .

The weight of the RV drove him deep, forcing water into his mouth and nose and lungs as tons of metal carried him to the bottom and crushed him against the seafloor. He knew no more. Nor would he ever know more, the sea roiled and shook the drowned vehicle, and after a long while the RV eased up again, releasing him as a limp floater.

39

With the hillside remodel now a crime scene and Ryan's work halted, and with the completion of two other jobs she'd been juggling and their satisfactory final inspections, Ryan and Scotty turned their attention to finishing Ryan's studio. She could hardly wait to move into her own bright space. She started work in the mornings before Clyde was out of bed, was still at it when he shouted up to her that supper was on the table. The house was filled with the pounding of hammers, the whine of the Skilsaw, the *thunk* of the staple gun, and the intermittent purr of its generator. The whole house, upstairs and down, smelled of sawdust, of drywall and then of plaster, of paint and tile adhesive. With all the fumes and noise, Ryan took Snowball up to Dr. Firetti to board and to have her annual checkup and shots.

Ryan's dad was more than pleased to share his time, his bachelor pad, and his lady friend with Rock. Only Joe Grey remained among the chaos, coming and going at his pleasure, but sleeping in his rooftop tower with the sea breeze blowing through, unassaulted by toxic fumes. Long before Ryan finished the studio, the Chapmans and the Longleys returned from their vacations.

The Chapmans arrived the day after Charlie called them, Theresa rushing straight to the laundry to see to the kittens, hugging and snuggling the babies and Mango. She was distressed by the loss of her miniature paintings, which had not been insured, but that didn't matter in comparison to her concern over her little cats, she'd wanted only to hold the cats and love them, making sure they were well and safe.

The Longleys returned the next day. Earl Longley was still angry with Charlie and threatened to sue her for negligence, but she didn't think that would happen. She thought he'd cool down when he'd collected what promised to be a large insurance settlement based on the appraisals that he had kept current of his rare books. The Watermans remained in Greece. Rita talked with their insurance agent and filed their claim by e-mail, then put the matter aside to enjoy their vacation. There were as yet no viable leads to any of the stolen property, no response to the police fliers from

364 • SHIRLEY ROUSSEAU MURPHY

any fence or from legitimate dealers. There were no leads to the whereabouts of Ed Becker.

Two weeks after the murder, Ryan finished her studio. That Sunday she and Clyde and Scotty moved her desk, her blueprint cabinet, her drawing board, and her computer from where they'd been crowding the guest room, up the stairs and into her bright new space; then she and Clyde threw a Sunday-night party.

Wilma arrived carrying Dulcie, wearing a new embroidered denim jacket over a red sweater and white jeans, her long silver hair clipped back with a bar of gold and coral. The Greenlaws walked from home, across the village. They arrived with their canes, Kit trotting eagerly beside them, just as Dallas pulled up in his old tan Blazer with Detective Davis. Everyone had a tour of the solarium-like studio with its high ceiling, its three skylights supported between the heavy beams, its glass walls, Mexican-tile floor, and Ryan's treasured antique fireplace that she and Clyde had brought home from their honeymoon trip. The mantel's hand-painted tiles featured pictures of cats, and the rearing cat in the center matched exactly the carved cat that graced the old Pamillon mansion where the wild clowder now lived; but that was a story of its own.

Ryan's dad arrived with Rock on a leash and Lindsey Wolf on his arm. Lindsey wore pale jeans, sandals, and a honey-toned cashmere sweater that complemented her honey-brown hair and hazel eyes. Her infectious smile shone comfortably, and often, on Mike Flannery. When they let Rock loose, the big silver Weimaraner moved quietly among the guests, graciously accepting any and all offerings, working the room as adroitly as were the three cats. Snowball was the only antisocial little soul among the five animals. She was thrilled to be home from the vet and was happy to see her friends, but she soon retired upstairs to the master bedroom, away from the crowd and the noise.

The Chapmans had been invited, and when they arrived the cats wound around Theresa's ankles purring so extravagantly that both Charlie and Ryan gave them looks that sent them padding away again. But they looked back at their friend lovingly, saying little cat prayers that she was safe. She was wearing a pink T-shirt that set off her pink cheeks, and pale jeans and sandals. Her long brown hair was tied back haphazardly, and was streaked from the coastal sun. Carl Chapman, always quiet, stood smiling complacently as Juana Davis asked about Mango's kittens; Joe and Dulcie watched, amused. Had Juana weakened after all this time of living alone without a pet? Did she finally mean to give in to the pleasure of a feline companion? The squarely built detective, in her dark uniform, made Theresa look even slimmer and somehow more ethereal. As they discussed the basics of responsible kitten care, they joined the others gathered around the big kitchen table, taking up plates, dishing up helpings of the casseroles and salads. Max Harper was loading his own plate when his cell phone rang.

Answering it, he stepped into the guest room where he could hear without the din of conversation. His back turned, he didn't see Joe Grey slip into the room behind him. When the tomcat leaped on the small writing desk and lay down at his elbow, the chief scowled at him, then grinned and stroked Joe as he talked, mildly amused by the tomcat.

The Damen guest room had recently been redone, with plantation shutters, furniture designed in a combination of wicker and golden oak, and bright primitive rugs. Joe, stretching out just inches from the phone, could hear only half of what the caller was saying; soon he sat up straight, closer to the cell phone, nearly pressing his ear against it. If Clyde saw his nosy display, he'd kill him. The caller was Captain Jim Cahill of the CHP.

Joe knew Jim, he was a nice guy, he used to stop in the station when he was dating a woman in Molena Point. Good build, tanned, nearly bald, but with the remaining hair shaved clean, brown eyes, and always an easy smile, even when his thoughts might be less than complimentary. Max had known Jim since their days at San Jose State, before either hired on with their respective departments.

From what Joe could make out, the CHP had just pulled an RV out of the ocean, somewhere along Highway 1. Cahill was saying, "Driver's dead. His description matches that on your dispatch, the prints belong to an Ed Becker, Sacramento address. He's about six one, maybe two hundred pounds, black hair. We have a mug shot, I'd say he was a good-looking guy before his face got all scratched up."

"Damage from the wreck?"

"No, this happened earlier, before the RV went over the side. Band-Aids still half stuck to him. RV was three-fourths underwater, on its side. A fisherman spotted it about four hours ago. We had to get divers, heavy equipment up there to get it up the cliff. No plates on it, and the divers couldn't find any."

"Anything inside?"

"It's loaded, Max. Furniture, small imported rugs, looks like everything you describe. Everything soaked, the cartons of miniature paintings and books soaked through. The antique jewelry is all tangled together, and the seawater could cause corrosion." He laughed. "The paperweights aren't damaged."

"What were the scratches?" Max said, returning to the detail that puzzled him.

"Don't know, but he's a mess. Maybe the coroner can shed some light."

"And you have the body and the RV where?"

"Vehicle's impounded at San Mateo PD. Body's in a mortuary there until we can send it down to your coroner."

Max jotted down the phone number and address of the mortuary. "I'll make arrangements and get back to you." They talked for a few minutes about personal matters. Jim still had bird dogs, five English pointers. His wife had just retired from her job as a hospital nurse and planned to take a few private cases. She wasn't a hunter, but she liked to fish, and they were planning a trip to Alaska. Thanking Jim and hanging up, Max finished up his notes then sat looking at Joe Grey, who lay innocently stretched out across the blotter. He scratched the tomcat's ears for a moment, then rose and returned to the party. Joe waited a while, so as not to seem too obvious, and then followed him back to where supper was being served.

In the kitchen, as Max picked up his loaded plate from the counter where he'd left it, he frowned at Dulcie and Kit. "You haven't been sampling my dinner?" The two females sat in the bay window not inches from the plate. They looked innocent enough, and he had to admit that the plate didn't look as if they'd been at it. Only when Joe Grey jumped up on the counter and padded across to sit beside the other two did Max get that uneasy feeling these cats sometimes gave him, a puzzled sense of missing something, that he could never quite figure out. He looked up as Charlie came to stand beside him, putting her arm around his waist.

She looked narrowly at the cats. "They weren't sampling your supper?"

Max laughed. "Not as far as I can see. Sometimes . . ." He frowned at Charlie. "Sometimes these three make me uneasy, for no reason." She just looked at him. "Their stares," he said, "are more piercing than any judge I ever faced."

"Piercing?"

"Haven't you ever noticed? Don't they look, sometimes, more aware than a cat should be?"

Charlie laughed. "I never noticed that. They're sweet and smart, but I don't see anything unusual. What was the phone call?"

"Jim Cahill. The CHP found Becker, dead. He went over the cliff and into the ocean north of Santa Cruz. Driving a brown RV, with the stolen goods in it, maybe the whole lot. Everything's soaked through."

"Oh, Theresa's paintings. Oh, I'm sorry." She couldn't feel sorry for Ed Becker. He was a thief and a killer. Was she supposed to grieve for him?

"They had to get heavy equipment up there, to pull it out of the water. I don't know what happened to the guy before he went over, Cahill said his face was covered with deep scratches, something that happened before the wreck because he was already bandaged."

Charlie glanced at the cats before she could catch herself. Joe looked away, Dulcie glanced down, and Kit blinked. "They're looking at your plate," she said. "Poor things. I'll get them some supper." She turned away to the table, certain that the cats had been at the man, or some cats had. She could hardly wait to hear the rest of that story.

Max watched her filling a plate of delicacies for the cats with the attention most people gave to their children. He picked up his own plate and headed into the living room, making for the one empty chair, Joe Grey's clawed and fur-covered easy chair that was the last anyone wanted to occupy. He was happily enjoying his buffet supper, hoping to keep the cat hairs out, when Charlie appeared, followed by the cats. She set their plate on the mantel, watched them leap up and tuck into their supper. She did have a way with cats, an empathy he admired—but that sometimes made him as uncomfortable as did the cats themselves.

Across the room, the gray Weimaraner watched Charlie and the cats every bit as keenly as did Max—

though only with greed. To Rock there was nothing startling about the three cats, he'd learned early on that these were not ordinary cats. Being only a dog and not driven by the complications of human logic, he had no reason not to believe what, to him, was perfectly obvious. These cats were different. He'd learned to live comfortably with their bossing him and expecting him to mind them.

Bringing her own supper, Charlie sat down on the arm of Max's chair. He was relaying to the little group what Jim Cahill had told him. The Chapmans didn't want to believe that Ed Becker had been a liar and a thief, that he had turned on people who'd been his close friends, that he could ever have been vicious enough to kill Frances.

Theresa said, "To break in like that, break into our houses where he'd made himself at home and was always welcome. They were friends with everyone on the street . . . Or we thought they were. They were always there for us, they babysat for people's children . . ." She looked sadly at Max. "He *killed* her? Because she found out he planned to steal from us?" A tear slid down her cheek. Quietly Carl put his arm around her.

Max said, "A lot of questions still unanswered. We have, apparently, no one to prosecute, but that doesn't mean we won't still dig for answers. For one thing,

Becker's MO could fit a whole string of similar un-
solved burglaries, we'll be working on that."

On the mantel, the cats looked so satisfied at the
resolution of the case and at the death of Ed Becker
that Clyde glared at them, and Ryan raised a warning
eyebrow. Turning away, they wiped the smug little cat
smiles off their faces and leaped down.

But as Joe went to sit behind Clyde's chair, out of
sight, a look of triumph returned to his gray-and-white
face. Dulcie, as she leaped to the arm of Wilma's chair,
was purring. Only Kit, as she snuggled on Lucinda's
lap, looked not quite at ease with herself, looked as if
she was still filled with questions.

Later that night, when Dulcie and Wilma were home
again by themselves, Wilma told her, "You cats are
getting careless, you looked way too interested tonight.
When you learned that Becker was dead, all three of
you looked much too alert, far too pleased."

Dulcie said nothing. She watched Wilma turn back
the bedcovers and kneel to light a fire in the wood-
stove. As Wilma tucked herself up under the quilt with
her book, Dulcie jumped up on the bed beside her, but
still she said nothing.

"Do you want to spoil everything?" Wilma asked,
stroking her. "You want to blow this exciting life you're

living? You want to spend the rest of your lives trying to be no more than clueless housecats, not daring to do *anything* interesting?"

"We don't want that," Dulcie said contritely.

Wilma opened her book, and held up the comforter. Quietly Dulcie slipped in under it, and put her head on the pillow beside Wilma's where she could clearly see the pages of the new mystery they were reading. Why was it that these fictional characters could get away with outrageous behavior? But an innocent little cat, just because she could speak, had to watch herself every waking minute?

It was later that night that Kit, at home with Lucinda and Pedric, left her warm nest on the bed between her two companions and trotted off, alone, to her tree house. As the older couple slept, Kit pushed out through the dining room window and onto the oak limb, and padded along the branch among the shadows to curl down in her cozy lair among her cushions, looking out at the starstuck sky.

The tree house had belonged to the children of the previous owners. It was, in fact, one of their main incentives in choosing this particular house. Now it was Kit's own, a secluded aerie in which to dream and to become a part of the night. She lay listening to the little sounds from the garden, to the rustle of a mouse far below scurrying among the dry leaves, to the shrill voice of a brown bat high above, banking and diving to catch his supper. She thought about Tansy and Sage, up in the hills among the clowder. She thought that last night when they had all attacked that man together, that something had changed in Sage. Afterward, the look in his eyes was different. As if he had learned, suddenly, what it meant to take decisive action and stand up for himself. She thought Tansy had looked at Sage differently, too. Maybe, Kit thought, all would be well with them now. The two seemed stronger now, as if their indignant response to that man's brutality had strengthened them and brought them closer together.

Smiling, Kit rolled over on her back, looking up from her tree house at the sky. The stars gleamed at her, the cool air rippled her fur, and for that one perfect moment, all was right with the world.

Up in the hills among the Pamillon ruins, Tansy knew that life was different. In the shadow of a broken wall, the pale cream female sat close to Sage, watching him devour the rabbit he'd caught. He'd caught two, and he'd given her the first one. Now as he greedily ate his own supper, Tansy smiled and purred. The decisive way he'd hunted, and the way he tore into the rabbit, told her that he was strong again and that the pain was gone—certainly he'd been stronger last night when they attacked the killer, when Sage clung to that man, kicking and ripping his face. Something had awakened in Sage last night. The cold cruelty of that human had stirred alive something new in him, something fine and bold, had awakened a keen and indignant ferocity within the tomcat's soul. She looked around them at the fallen buildings and crumbled walls of the old estate, at the dense cover of overgrown bushes, at the tumbled trees hiding tunnels deep beneath their fallen trunks. This was a fine world for cats, here were a hundred places to hunt, a hundred more where a cat could hide from danger. Here, the cruelest predator of all seldom ventured—there were no twisted humans here to bedevil them. This world, abandoned by humans was, Tansy thought, a finer world than she, as a kitten, had ever imagined. Certainly it was a fine world in which to raise a family.

It was two weeks later that the crime scene tape was removed from the remodel, allowing Ryan to pour new gravel and cement and finish up the work on that house. Later, while Fernando was shoveling dirt back into the pit, he stopped suddenly, looking down at a small plastic container lying in the freshly turned earth. He called to Ryan, and she picked it up with a tissue, wrapping it carefully. When she gave the inhaler to Dallas, it was duly bagged and booked in as evidence. The department found Ed Becker's prints on it, though it would probably never be needed in a court of law.

Ryan and Clyde bought an old cottage in a crowded, hilly neighborhood not far from Lucinda and Pedric's home, an ugly little place that anyone else would call a teardown but which they meant to give new life. And they weren't done shopping yet, they were looking at a ranch up near the Harpers' and who knew what else? Gently amused, Joe Grey put aside his misgivings about the project and turned his attention to other matters, leaving the newlyweds to their folly.

Kit didn't see Tansy or Sage for a long time, though she looked for Tansy whenever she and Pedric and Lucinda went up in the hills to walk. Indeed, she didn't see the two ferals again until the end of August, when the days were long and the weather had turned dry and hot. As Kit stood high on the hill above her resting housemates, looking up toward the ruins, she could see looking back at her a small pale smudge atop a jagged wall. Now Tansy seemed very far away, and they did not approach any closer. That was another world up there, so very different from Kit's world, she realized. But still they were friends, they would always be friends, she thought, smiling.

But then suddenly, in what seemed a vision or a dream, Kit saw the tiniest speck leap up onto the wall beside Tansy, and then another, both little smudges as pale as moonlight. Then a third, and the three went frolicking along the wall, chasing one another. Then Sage was there, strutting a little and gamboling with his babies, and Kit laughed out loud. Tansy had made her choice, between an exciting life among humans and that frolicking family. And if still, deep inside Tansy, there burned a touch of longing for the wonders of a larger world, maybe she'd give those dreams to her babies. Maybe they'd grow up yearning, too.

And who knew where that would take them?

As for herself, Kit knew that somewhere in the world there was a tomcat filled with her own kind of dreams. That was the mate she wanted, a cat who was all fire and muscle and challenge, who had soaring dreams and the steady spirit to follow them. A tomcat with fire in his eyes, but with a steady gentleness and a joyful laugh. One day there would be such a cat. She could almost see him, maybe a great golden or red tabby cat with curving stripes, with eyes the color of moonlight and claws as sharp as sabers.

Kit thought about Joe and Dulcie, so happy in their love and in the work they had chosen. She thought about Christmas, soon to come, with all its ceremonies and pleasures. She thought about how wonderful and exciting the world was, and suddenly she was so filled with joy that she raced down the hill straight for Lucinda and Pedric, leaped on the wall beside them and raced along it and down again, running in circles, jumping over bushes and over nothing at all, racing like a wild thing—knowing, down deep in her own cat soul, that somewhere out in the world, that tomcat was waiting, and he was looking for her.

HARPER LUXE

THE NEW LUXURY IN READING

We hope you enjoyed reading
our new, comfortable print size and found it
an experience you would like to repeat.

Well – you're in luck!

HarperLuxe offers the finest in fiction and
nonfiction books in this same larger print size and
paperback format. Light and easy to read, HarperLuxe
paperbacks are for book lovers who want to see
what they are reading without the strain.

For a full listing of titles and
new releases to come, please visit our website:

www.HarperLuxe.com